THESE ARE NOT THE STONES YOU'RE LOOKING FOR

JEFFREY POOLE

Jeffrey Poole's Epic Fantasy Books
Bakkian Chronicles:
The Prophecy
Insurrection
Amulet of Aria
Disneyland Debacle (short story)
Winter Wonderland (short story)

Tales of Lentari
Lost City
Something Wyverian This Way Comes
A Portal for Your Thoughts
Thoughts for a Portal
Wizard in the Woods
Close Encounters of the Magical Kind
The Hunt for Red Oskorlisk (short story)
May the Fang be With You (Pirates trilogy #1)
The Hammer is Strong with This One (Pirates #2)
These are Not the Stones You're Looking For (Pirates #3)
Blast from the Past

Dragons of Andela
Harness the Fire
Strike the Spark
Clear the Water

Mysteries by J.M. Poole
The Corgi Case Files Series
19 delightful cozy mystery novels featuring corgi
sleuths, Sherlock and Watson

These Are Not the Stones You're Looking For

Tales of Lentari, Book 9

Jeffrey Poole

Secret Staircase Books

These Are Not the Stones You're Looking For
Published by Secret Staircase Books, an imprint of
Columbine Publishing Group, LLC
PO Box 416, Angel Fire, NM 87710

Book layout and design by Secret Staircase Books
First Secret Staircase paperback edition: April, 2024
First Secret Staircase e-book edition: April, 2024

* * *

Publisher's Cataloging-in-Publication Data

Poole, Jeffrey
These Are Not the Stones You're Looking For / by Jeffrey Poole.
p. cm.
ISBN 978-1649141774 (paperback)
ISBN 978-1649141781 (e-book)

1. Lentari (Fictitious location)—Fiction. 2. Epic fantasy fiction
3. Dragons and mythical creatures—Fiction. 4. Time travel—Fiction.
I. Title

Tales of Lentari : Book 9.
These Are Not the Stones You're Looking For
Poole, Jeffrey, Tales of Lentari epic fantasy series.

BISAC : FICTION / Fantasy/Epic.

813/.54

For Giliane —

Insert supremely heartfelt dedication here. :)

J.

Acknowledgments

Thank you to my wonderful wife of 20 years, Giliane. She has demonstrated over and over that I am the luckiest man on the Earth to be able to have her by my side. Thank you for all you do, babe. Always & forever!

Thank you, all Posse members, who helped me out with this book. If it wasn't for you guys & gals, then I would most definitely look—and sound—like an author. Jason H., Wendy E., Louise "Weezie" C., Carol M., Caryl N., Elizabeth D., Michelle "Mefe" E., Sharon R., and Diane "mom". Also, Secret Staircase Books beta readers: Sandra Anderson, Susan Gross, and Paula Webb—you guys are the best! I'd also like to thank one of the fans, Rick P., for suggesting a name for me to use: Calibran. Thanks, Rick!

Finally, thanks have to be given to you, the reader. By purchasing this book, you have helped support an author, and that means the world to me!

Okay, without further ado, let's find out what those pirates have been doing!

J.

Table of Contents

Chapter 1 – On Your Marks…

"What was he like?" a powerful female voice asked, disrupting the silence that the two of them had been enjoying for nearly an hour. "You *must* tell me!"

"I *have* already told you," an exasperated male voice answered. "Several times. Yes, I met him. Yes, I talked to him, and yes, I've spent a little time with him, but it's not like we're best buds or anything. I really don't know that much about him."

"You've been to his sacred isle, haven't you?" the female voice accused. "Admit it!"

"You know I have, Pryllan. I really didn't have much of a say about it. One minute we were on the ground, and one snap of the fingers later, we were thousands of feet up in the air."

"What was it like?" Pryllan softly asked. "Many of us have dreamed of visiting Astral."

Steve Miller, resident of Coeur d'Alene, Idaho, glanced

up at the distant head of his wyverian friend and smiled. Pryllan, an enormous emerald-green dragon, and mate to Kahvel, ruler of all dragons, had to be his closest friend in Lentari.

"Are you sure you shouldn't be back in your nest?" Steve hesitantly asked. "Don't get me wrong, I *am* grateful you're here. However, you're a new mother, and…"

Steve trailed off as Pryllan's long, reptilian neck bent completely around until she was regarding him with a stern look.

"As I have previously said," the green dragon calmly began, "Pylaria's welfare is now in the capable hands of her guardian. You need not fear for her safety."

"The female zweigelan," Steve recalled, remembering how the two-headed dragon had volunteered to watch over the dragonlet not that long ago.

Pryllan nodded. "Precisely. I do not believe either Lamira or Yamira will admit it, but they have grown quite fond of little Pylaria."

"That's definitely good to hear."

"How much longer do you wish to search?" the dragon inquired.

"As long as it takes," Steve vowed. "That temple is out there. We just have to find it."

"We have been flying over this area for close to three hours now," Pryllan reminded him. "We are no closer to finding it than when we started."

Steve shook his head. "True. However, we can't give up. I saw the map. That diamond key we found purposely moved to a spot up here, in the forest. That means it knows the location of the temple. We're in the right area, Pryllan. We *have* to be!"

"Then why aren't we seeing it?" Pryllan countered. "I can understand why you might have missed the temple, with your inferior vision, but my…"

"My inferior vision?" Steve interrupted, with a laugh. "Thanks, pal. My visual abilities might not be as sharp, or as pronounced as yours, but I still scored a 20/20 on my last eye exam, thank you very much."

"I do not know what that means," Pryllan admitted, as she dipped her left wing. Once they were flying in the opposite direction, dragon and rider leveled off and dropped even lower. "I assume it means your eyesight is considered adequate among other humans of your advanced age?"

"Age jokes," Steve groaned. "Not you, too. Have you been talking to Sarah?"

Pryllan chuckled, but remained silent. Steve gazed down at the passing treetops and sighed. From this height, Anakash Forest resembled nothing more than a rolling sea of green, endlessly stretching away in all directions. It was no wonder they hadn't found the temple yet, even though the key had indicated it was in the area.

"Why are you feeling so depressed?" his wyverian friend asked, as they reached their unspoken boundary and had turned for another pass. "You haven't given up hope, have you?"

"What do you think?" Steve grumbled. "It seems clear to me that we're not going to spot this temple from the air. For all we know, the pirates have found it first."

"You don't even know if Captain Windbag knows of the location," Pryllan soothingly told him.

Steve snorted with laughter. It didn't matter how many times he heard it. If someone else referred to Captain Flinn of the pirate ship *Emberbrand* by any other name, and *especially* if they used Captain Windbag, Steve would indubitably end up snickering like a schoolboy.

"We are getting nowhere," Pryllan reported, as they passed over a section of forest that was identical to the dozens of other areas they had already checked. "Perhaps we have drifted away from our course? Could you refresh my memory and indicate where we should be?"

Steve craned his neck to look up at Pryllan's distant head. "Prithee, how shall I accomplish that task, my scaly friend? It's not like I have instant recall and can bring up an image of that map again."

A series of images began flipping through Steve's mind, causing him to gasp out loud. The images were appearing and disappearing in his mind, like a slideshow going way too fast.

Suddenly, an image of the map and the griffin key appeared and remained in place, a memory from nearly three hours ago after the discovery of the temple key.

The image expanded and focused on the griffin marker the moment Sarah had placed it on the map. The scene shifted, allowing the diamond griffin to remain centered in the image. As soon as the marker stopped, the image zoomed out to show the entire map of Lentari.

"We are in the correct place," Pryllan announced. "It should…"

"Would you mind giving me a warning before you do something like that?" Steve grumped. "It's freakin' weird how you can manipulate my own thoughts and memories like that."

"Were you not aware we were sharing senses?" Pryllan asked, confused.

"Well, yeah, but…"

"Have you not previously asked me to search your senses when we are seeking a specific memory?"

"Well, when you put it like that…"

"And did we not just obtain the information we needed?"

"Well yeah, but…"

"Then why are you complaining?" Pryllan inquired, matter-of-factly.

Steve waved a hand dismissively. "All right. Forget about that for now. You saw the memory of me looking at the map. We're in the right area? Well, what do we do? Can't your spectacularly superior eyesight penetrate that canopy to see what's on the ground below?"

"It can, but in order to be of any help, our velocity must be much slower," the dragon reported.

"Fine. So we'll go slower."

"May I propose another solution?"

"I'm all ears, Pryllan."

"That's a strange expression," the dragon admitted, as she gave the approximation of a shrug. "Can you imagine what a human comprised of nothing but ears would look like?"

Steve groaned. "It's only an expression. It means…"

"I know what it means," Pryllan interrupted, good-naturedly. "What I was going to suggest is that we abandon our efforts to locate the temple from the air and, instead, approach from the ground."

Steve leaned out over Pryllan's side and gazed down. "Ground? What ground? How can you even think about landing on the ground when we can't even see it? Maybe if we… what are you doing? Pryllan, don't even think it! There's no way you can … holy crap! Watch out!!"

Pryllan had tucked her wings and dropped like a rock, propelling them toward the ground at a frightening rate. Steve cringed and crossed his arms over his face in a feeble attempt to avoid injury. There was a brief moment where branches and tree limbs scratched at his arms, drawing a few choice expletives. Almost immediately, they came to an abrupt stop, so abrupt, in fact, that Steve flew off Pryllan's back. A huge, scaled hand plucked him from the air.

Steve rolled onto his back and grinned up at his benefactor. "Nice catch. Man alive, that would've hurt."

"My apologies. I hadn't realized the extent to which you had fallen out of practice. With regard to riding a dragon, that is."

Steve's grin melted into a frown. "I don't get a lot of practice back home, all right? It's not like there's a steady supply of dragons living nearby. Okay, we're on the ground. Look around, Pryllan. How are you going to be able to navigate through this forest? You're much too big."

Pryllan leaned forward and dropped to all fours. Belying her massive size, the emerald dragon gracefully threaded her way, reminiscent of a lizard slithering through the jungle. He should have taken her flexibility into consideration.

"Yes, you should have."

"Would you stop that? We're not flying anymore, so there's no need for you to be in my head."

Pryllan chuckled again and moved off. Bemused, and still shaking his head, Steve followed.

"That's impressive," Steve commented. "It almost reminds me of how the creeg dig their tunnels."

Pryllan paused to work her way around a clump of trees growing too close together. "Oh? How so, if you don't mind me asking?"

"They moved like snakes when they were digging," Steve replied, stepping up beside his wyverian friend. "Somehow, their physiology allows them to move forward without using their legs."

"It's called rectilinear locomotion," Pryllan informed him, as she returned her attention to what lay before her. "Or, more specifically, it's a variant of it."

"Okay, would you care to explain just what that is?" Steve asked, as he began following her once more. "Pretend I don't have a clue what recto…"

"Rectilinear," Pryllan corrected. "It's a type of locomotion that… you are familiar with 'locomotion'?"

Steve's face colored slightly. "Yes."

"Excellent. Rectilinear locomotion is one of the slowest methods of locomotion. It…"

"Beg to differ," Steve cut in. "If you're talking about those creeg, then I've seen those guys dig. First hand. They can tunnel through solid rock faster than any creature can move."

"You didn't let me finish," Pryllan scolded. "I said it's one of the slowest forms of locomotion, but the creeg developed a variant of it which allows them to move at extreme velocity."

"That's cool," Steve decided.

"Would you like me to expand on its definition?"

"Is it that obvious that I still don't know what it is?"

Pryllan lifted herself a little higher off the ground, pointed at a series of larger scales along her belly, and turned to Steve. "Do you see these scales? Do you see how they're larger than the others? There is a row of them here and another here."

Steve stepped close and stared at Pryllan's abdomen. "Okay. I can see some scales which look a little bigger than the others."

Pryllan nodded. "Good. Now, if I so choose, I can use these as a means of locomotion. Each of these scales are alternately lifted slightly from the ground, and then pulled forward. Those scales are then pulled downward and then backward. Since the scales stick to the ground, my body is actually pulled over them. Once I've moved far enough forward to stretch the scales, the cycle repeats."

Impressed, Steve nodded. "Really? I had no idea you dragons had that much control over your individual scales. I… hey, wait a moment. Are you telling me you can also move along the ground like the creeg?"

Pryllan shrugged. "If you're asking whether or not we're limited to our legs or wings, then the answer is no. We're not."

"You dragons are cool as hell," Steve murmured. "You learn something new each day."

Pryllan chuckled. "I don't. We dragons know everything we need to at an early age. For those rare occasions that we need help, we rely on the Collective."

"We're getting nowhere down here," Steve complained. "Could you ask your Collective and see if anyone has ever spotted something that resembles a temple in this area?"

Pryllan was silent for a few moments.

"An intriguing notion. I will inquire."

"It'd be my luck that someone will know where it is," Steve grumbled softly to himself. "I can hear them now: 'What do you mean you can't find it? You're blind as a bat. It's right in front of you. Why didn't you ask me earlier?' I'll never live this down, Pryllan."

"In our defense," the dragon smoothly began, "none of my brethren have ever searched for this temple. Besides, we would never belittle a human because of their inferior eyesight."

"Oh, the belittling would be coming from Sarah, not you guys," Steve wryly corrected.

"Ah. I… Very well. I thought as much."

"What?" Steve asked. "What's going on?"

"I have received a reply from the Collective. No one has encountered this temple before. The precise location remains unknown."

"Well, that makes me feel better," Steve admitted. "A little. Listen, is there any way you can telepathically link Sarah's mind to mine right now?"

"You know I can. I've done it before."

Steve took several calming breaths. "Sorry. Poor choice of words. Will you? Will you join us together so I can talk to her?"

"Of course. One moment, please."

Just like that, Sarah's voice could be heard in his head.

There's no way Steve is going to go along with this, Sarah was thinking.

There's no way I'm going to go along with what? Anyway, is there any way you could join us? I'm pretty sure Pryllan and I are just going around in circles. I'm hoping you might be able to work your magic and see if you can find this place any easier than us.

What is it you think I'll be able to do?

Steve laughed, but forgot that Sarah wouldn't be able to hear him, *Oh, please. You're always telling me that your eyesight is better than mine.*

You have a point.

Snot. I was kidding.

But I'm not. Very well. Let me make sure Emily is okay and… wait. How am I supposed to find you?

Get Gareth to help you. He was able to land on Pryllan's back when she was airborne, so I figure locating an immobile dragon should be a lot easier.

Okay, I'll be there as soon as I can.

"She's on her way," Steve told the dragon. "You can disconnect us now."

"Done," Pryllan reported. "How long before she'll be able to…"

Gareth and Sarah appeared on Pryllan's back, in the exact same place the young wizard had appeared several days prior. Steve waved to her from the ground and waited for Sarah and Gareth to join him. Once they were standing beside him, Steve gave his wife a hug.

"It's good to see you," Steve told her. "I'm hoping you can help us out. Gareth, thanks for bringing her."

The acolyte wizard nodded. "You're welcome. Are you sure you don't want to try taking Deez to your world? I'm sure your little griffin could use a playmate."

"Emerion has a playmate," Steve replied. "And we call her 'Peanut'. Thanks, but no thanks. You're not pawning your problems off on us, amigo. Besides, Deez wouldn't want to be separated from you. Like it or not, you're stuck with him."

Gareth sullenly nodded. "You're probably right. Can I

help? I might be able to…"

Sarah was already shaking her head. "Oh, no you don't. Remember what you promised me. You're looking after Emily, remember? She's a visitor to this land and we cannot let anything happen to her. Besides, Deez will be missing you."

Gareth smiled sheepishly, shrugged. and vanished.

"What I wouldn't give to have that kind of power at my disposal," Steve quietly whispered.

"No, you wouldn't," Sarah contradicted. "With that much power comes a whole heap of responsibility, and let's face it, that's the last thing you need right now."

Surprised, Steve turned to his wife. "Are you saying I wouldn't be able to handle the responsibility of being a wizard?"

Sarah smiled and raised an eyebrow.

Steve sighed. "Okay, fine. Maybe you're right. So, do you think you might be able to help us out and find this damn temple? Pryllan and I are pretty certain we've been flying in circles."

"What would you like me to do?" Sarah asked. "You've been doing the searching. What will I be able to do that you two haven't?"

"We wonder whether your jhorun might be able to locate the temple faster than we can search."

"My jhorun? I've never been to this temple before."

"True," Steve acknowledged, nodding, "but you might be able to wiggle your nose and find it for us."

Sarah put her hands on her hips and frowned. "For the last time, I *don't* wiggle my nose. But, I suppose it couldn't hurt to try to see if I can get a vision. Just don't get your hopes up, okay?"

Steve and Pryllan anxiously watched Sarah close her eyes. Steve shared a look with the dragon and grinned. If anyone could do the impossible, it'd be Sarah. Hadn't she been able to visualize locations without having stepped foot on them before? Steve could only hope his wife would be able to do the same once more. However, after only a few seconds, Sarah's eyes opened and she frowned.

"Hmm."

"What's the matter?" Steve asked, as he hurried to her side. "Everything okay? Do you see anything?"

"Nothing. Let me try that again."

Sarah's eyes closed, but less than three seconds later, they opened. Her frown quickly escalated into a full-fledged scowl.

"Okay, what's wrong?" Steve asked. "Clearly, something isn't going the way you'd like."

"Every time I close my eyes, and ask my jhorun for a picture of this temple, my eyes open. It's like I'm not allowed to see the image. Why would that be?"

Steve shrugged helplessly. "I should've known there'd be enchantments on it, which would prevent its location from being revealed."

"This time," Pryllan grunted.

"What?" Steve asked.

"I have a theory."

Sarah gratefully smiled. "Good. Let's hear it."

Pryllan took a few steps forward, stretched a scaly foreleg out in front of her, and pointed. "The reason Sarah is unable to get a vision is that there is no need to. I do believe it is less than a hundred feet from our present location."

Steve's eyes shot open. "What? Seriously? I don't see anything."

"I don't either," Sarah admitted.

Steve grinned victoriously. "I *knew* we were in the right area."

"No, you didn't," Sarah said.

"No, you didn't," Pryllan echoed.

"So, where is it?" Steve anxiously asked.

"Just at the top of that ridge."

"I still don't see anything."

Pryllan sighed and nimbly navigated her way through a clump of trees. They followed. Pryllan turned to point straight ahead. Steve looked in every direction.

"Okay, so, I'm clearly blind as a bat. Where is it?"

Sarah was silent as she studied the hill directly in their path. "Oh! I see it now! It's right over there. Do you see the hill?"

"The one directly in front of us? You're telling me that's the temple? No way."

What lay before the three of them resembled nothing more than a pyramid-shaped hill that had been reclaimed by the forest. With broken slabs of stone here and there, it didn't come close to what Steve had imagined. No wonder they hadn't found it. There was nothing left!

"It's a mess! There's nothing there that resembles a temple."

"You aren't looking past the obvious," the dragon accused. "Look beyond the vegetation. Look beyond the neglect and disrepair of the structure. What do you see?"

"A big green hill with a few broken rocks," Steve reported. "I don't think that's it, Pryllan."

"It's there," Sarah exclaimed. "That's why my eyes kept opening after I tried to get a vision. My jhorun was telling me that the temple was in front of my face the entire time! Granted, I will admit it doesn't look like much. Clearly the reason this place hasn't been found is because it's been completely neglected."

Pryllan strode forward until she was standing before the base of the hill. Then, she leaned forward and sank one of her talons deep into the turf, bringing up an enormous chunk of earth, complete with shrubs, grass, and roots. She made a second swipe, this time coming up with an even bigger chunk of earth. Visible beneath the thick layer of vegetative material were portions of a stacked stone wall.

It was the temple, the place the map had shown where the second of the Alchos Stones awaited!

"I never would have found it," Steve quietly admitted. "I never knew plants and trees could completely grow over a building like that."

"Maybe an Ancient had something to do with its disguise," Sarah guessed. "You're right. Do you see how thick those roots are? If Pryllan wasn't here, we'd be spending the better part of a day just to see this much."

"No wonder no one has found it," Steve mused.

"You two look for a door," Sarah instructed. "I'm going to fetch the gang."

Steve nodded. "We'll do our best."

By the time Sarah had returned with Breslin, Athos, Gareth, Deez, and Emily, Pryllan and Steve had managed to clear a section nearly forty feet long and at least half that high. The architecture of the building was definitely appearing pyramidal in shape, but thus far, no entrance had been found.

"Would you look at that?" Emily excitedly exclaimed, as soon as she pulled her hand off of Sarah's. "It looks Mayan!"

"How can you tell?" Steve asked, perplexed. He gestured at the torn strip of earth. "Look at this. All we see are stones."

The paleontologist walked over and pointed at the closest one. "Look at this. Do you see how large it is? Just as with the pyramids of Egypt, each consecutive layer sits back nearly two feet and rises by at least four. But, I will say that this temple appears smaller than what the Mayans built. Oh. Wait a moment. Umm, Pryllan, could you remove this section next?"

Emily was pointing at the ground under her feet.

"The ground levels off there," Steve pointed out. "What are you looking for?"

"I just want to test a hypothesis," Emily answered. She hastily moved out of the way as Pryllan sank her talons. "If I'm right, then that means…"

Pryllan tore away the ground, pulling up a chunk of dirt that had to weigh at least five hundred pounds. The dragon tossed the mass of dirt and roots away, as easily as Steve would have discarded a wad of paper. Everyone crowded around the hole.

"There!" Emily exclaimed, as she knelt in the dirt and used her hand to brush away the loose soil. "Do you see this? It's more stone! Do you know what that means?"

"It means we're gonna be digging here until the end of time," Steve groaned.

Sarah smacked his shoulder. "Hush. No, what that means is that part of the temple is underground!"

Emily beamed brightly at Sarah. "Yes! Exactly. We really have no idea how large this temple is, unless we choose to properly excavate the entire hillside."

"Could we not simply look for a door?" Athos asked.

Breslin nodded. "My thoughts exactly. We shouldn't need to do any additional digging once we find the entrance."

Everyone turned to Emily, who sat back on her haunches and studied the temple. "Well, Mayan history is not my specialty, but I have taken quite a few archaeology classes. Let me think. If this temple was modeled after what the Mayans built on my world…"

"And why would they?" Gareth suddenly interrupted. "That doesn't make any sense."

"Don't you remember what Eion told us?" Sarah asked as she turned to the young wizard. "He specifically mentioned that he had been to Idaho, our home, several times. Clearly he's familiar with our world, so why would the other Ancients be any different? You never know. The Ancients might have influenced the Mayans and Egyptians from my world."

"That's a bizarre thought," Steve decided. He shook his head. "And it's one I'd just as soon not think about right now. It'll give me a headache. Okay, Doc. Assume this temple is similar to what you know about the Mayan temples. Where would we find the door?"

Emily pointed. "There. Up at the top will be a sanctuary. Or, there *could* be one. I can't say for certain. Anyway, the sanctuaries were usually heightened by a crest, or some type of roof comb. Now, based on the overall shape of this hill, I'd have to say this temple doesn't have a crest, but that's where I'd start looking."

Steve, Breslin, and Athos silently gazed upward. About ready to ask Pryllan if she'd have any problem climbing to the top of the temple, Sarah opened her mouth, but rapidly closed it. She had just spotted Gareth, who was kneeling beside Deez.

"Do you think you can do it?" Gareth was saying to the guur. "I mean, I know you can dig through rock, but what about something softer, like dirt?"

MEDIUM INCONSEQUENTIAL. COMPOSITION MATTERS NOT.

Gareth looked at Sarah and shrugged helplessly. "Does

that mean he can or he can't?"

Sarah squatted next to the strange pair and smiled at the two of them. "It means Deez can more than likely dig through practically any substance."

"Oh. I was starting to think that he was telling me he couldn't."

"Perfect," Steve added. He gave Deez a friendly pat on the head. "What do you say, pal? Will you start digging at the top of this hill? We're looking for an entrance."

Deez's armored head turned toward the hill and then angled up.

DESIRE ENTRY INTO HILLSIDE?

Steve nodded. "Exactly, pal."

Emily suddenly appeared and placed a hand on Steve's shoulder at the same time she placed a hand on Deez's head. "Wait a moment. We need to find the *entrance*. We don't want to possibly destabilize the structure by just tunneling our way through."

DESIRE TO LOCATE CONCEALED ENTRY INTO HILLSIDE?

Gareth's face lit up with pleasure. "Aye! Find that concealed opening. It should be near the top."

Deez promptly scuttled up the side of the hill, as easily as on a flat surface. The guur stopped after climbing near the upper quarter of the hill. Deez picked a spot at random and began digging. Specks of green and vegetation flew into the air and fell onto the hillside below.

STONE DETECTED.

Gareth cupped his hands to his mouth. "If you hit stone, you're digging in the wrong place. Try again!"

Deez abandoned the hole and, instead of climbing higher, moved to the right. As before, the guur efficiently dug his way through the vegetation covering the temple.

STONE DETECTED.

"I feel terrible," Emily said, after instructing Deez to try other places. "I thought for certain the entrance should be at the top. Granted, Mayan temples aren't my specialty, but that's how it is in our world."

"You aren't in our world any more, Doc," Steve reminded her, good-naturedly. "What if there isn't an entrance anywhere? What then?"

"We'll have to decide where to put the entrance," Emily answered. "From what I've seen, Deez is capable of creating us one. Hopefully, it won't come to that."

Twenty minutes of tireless digging, and no entrance appeared. Everyone felt discouraged until Breslin finally heard a new message.

NO STONE DETECTED. INGRESS DISCOVERED.

"That's it!" Emily exclaimed.

"An entrance," Sarah said. "How wonderful!"

"Where are you, Deez?" Gareth called out. "We can't see you!"

Everyone spread out to determine where the guur might be digging.

"I found a hole," Breslin's voice reported. The dwarf was standing on the opposite side of the temple, pointing at the ground. "Looks like this entrance must have been buried."

"Or overtaken by the vegetation," Athos added.

Two long, segmented legs suddenly sprouted out of the hole, followed almost immediately by a second pair, and then a third. In moments, the guur was standing before them, covered with dirt and tufts of plants, and chittering excitedly.

Steve peered anxiously into the dark recess of the hole. "Now we're talking. Okay, guys. I'd say it's time to make like Indiana Jones! Who's with me?"

A sea of confused faces stared blankly back at him.

Chapter 2 — Tables Have Turned

What happens if we don' make it there first, Cap'n? What happens if they find that temple before we do? What are we suppos'd to do?"

Captain Flinn glanced at the questioner. His gut reaction would have been to chastise Puck, or threaten the fool with a sword thrust through his gullet. However, he was the third crewman in the last hour who had asked the same question. While Flinn had never considered failure as an option, this time he was close.

There was a loud grunt and Flinn jolted forward on his mount. Cursing heavily, the captain glanced down at the straggly beast. Whatever this creature was, this species didn't exist in the *Seven Kingdoms*. It was shorter than a horse, but larger than a pony. The long, narrow head loosely resembled that of a horse, but larger. Each of the creatures sported a shaggy gray mottled coat and a set of spiraled horns, which curved out and back from where the ears should be.

The animal lurched again, nearly dislodging Flinn from

his saddle. From the sounds of the cursing coming behind him, his steed wasn't the only one that had just stumbled. Damn the Maker and all he stood for. What the blazes was he doing, astride a mangy beast the men were calling a "goofy donkey"?

Flinn silently fumed as the creatures continued to gallop north. He had been assured by his stone that the strange beasts would know where to go. How was that possible? Then again, he wasn't going to press his luck. The animals had practically appeared out of nowhere, just when he and his men needed them most.

"Where do you think we can get some normal horses, Captain?" Rusty's voice angrily called out from somewhere behind. "I think I can speak for the men when I say…"

"Ye will say nothin', Q," the captain dangerously replied, dropping his voice so that it could be barely heard over the thundering of the beasts' cloven hooves. "Do ye see any horses around here? Do ye want to take the time to look for a horse when we clearly need to find that temple before the blasted Fire Thrower? No? I thought not. Now, button yer lip, Q, and suck it up. No one be having the time o' their lives, myself included."

"Damn that Fire Thrower," Flinn heard someone say. It sounded like Puck. "He ain't mortal!"

"He is so," another voice argued. Was that Von?

"No, he ain't!" the first voice insisted. "You saw it happen with your own two eyes, right? The whole blessed roof collapsed on him. He should've been crushed flat, yet he continues to make a pest of himself. How can that be possible?"

"Puck, stop complaining," Rusty ordered. "I saw it with my own two eyes, too, yet I can see he's clearly the same as you or me."

Puck angrily faced the quartermaster. "You're tellin' me that, if a whole mess of stones happened to fall on you, then you'd be fine? Is that it?"

"You'd be dead," Jino sniggered, from somewhere on the left.

"Yet the Fire Thrower still lives," Puck grumbled. "Why

is that?"

"I'd like to know *how* that was possible," Grenden miserably grumbled, from his own mount.

Flinn risked a glance back at the *Emberbrand's* doctor. Being the oldest crewman aboard, Grenden had the most experience on horseback, yet he also struggled.

Almost as soon as he thought about bringing their ungainly steeds to a stop, the stone nestled inside his coat pocket suddenly grew warm. And then, for the first time ever, Flinn heard a voice besides his own in his head.

You must make haste.

Flinn grew angry. *Really? Do ye have any idea how many times I had to find a secluded place to consult with ye, ye blasted rock? Now, ye be tellin' me that ye can speak to me, inside my own head?*

Your adversaries have located the first temple, and are closing in on the entrance. Should they be allowed to explore unchecked, the probability of your defeat increases.

"Blast," Flinn softly growled. "How do I…" Realizing he had almost asked the stone a question out loud, the captain scowled and promptly snapped his mouth closed.

The Fire Thrower. He be with the Lentarians?

Aye.

How do we slow them down? Can ye do anything?

Before the stone could answer, a loud commotion erupted from somewhere behind him. Captain Flinn turned angrily on his mount's back and noticed yet another fight had broken out. This time, it would appear that Jino was preparing to take on Casimir and Rusty, at the same time.

"Jino! Put that sword away. That be an order! So help me, if ye don' stop messin' around, then I will personally clap ye in irons. Be that understood?"

"They said we have already lost!" Jino angrily replied as he pointed an accusatory finger at the two men. "They want to give up! If that's the collective decision of the crew, then so be it. I quit. I'll do it alone if I must. I will personally wipe the smile from the Fire Thrower's ugly face."

"If ye threaten me with mutiny, lad," Captain Flinn calmly began, as he reined his mount to a stop, "I will also string ye up to the closest tree and leave ye there. Be that understood?"

Jino gave a dangerous growl as he swung his leg over his steed's back and jumped to the ground. He took a few menacing steps toward the captain. The rest of the crew gasped with alarm. Jino's cutlass appeared in his hand and, unfortunately, he looked as though he was preparing to use it.

Flinn's eyes narrowed to slits and his hands clenched into fists. Before anyone could realize what was happening, jets of condensed air appeared out of nowhere and slammed into Jino, launching him into the air, as though he had been rammed by a galloping horse. Just before Jino was due to slam into the ground, the pirate was struck a second time by yet another blast. Finally, a third jet of air caught the crewman and held him firm.

His face showed stunned silence, then fear. The air jet holding the pirate in place then changed direction. Within moments, Jino found himself pinned to a giant pine tree by a blast of air. The pirate whimpered as Flinn slowly strode toward him.

"Never, in all my years of piracy, have I had a man contemplate mutiny," Flinn growled. "Do ye know what I do with mutineers, Jino? Would ye care to take a guess?"

Jino's gaze fell and he refused to look the captain in the eye. Flinn contemplated the motionless man a few moments longer before he pulled his cutlass free of its scabbard. Flinn held the blade straight up, as if challenging Jino to a duel.

"I'm… I'm sorry, Captain," Jino whispered. "Please forgive me. I was frustrated. We all are."

"Are ye now?" Flinn demanded, as he spun in place to face the rest of the crew. "Who among ye think they can do a better job than the likes of me? Who has the tenacity to challenge my authority?"

It was so still that Flinn could hear every man's labored breathing. When it became apparent no one could look him in the eye, he returned his cutlass to its scabbard. The hiss of metal sliding on metal made everyone jump.

Flinn pointed at the mangy beasts that were huddled together, grazing. "Back on yer mounts, lads. There be no time for this. Jino, ye had better impress me, or else I will finish what ye started. Be that clear?"

"Perfectly, Captain."

Once the pirates had spurred their mounts back into a gallop, Flinn turned to Rusty. Perhaps it was time to address the crew's concerns. They would soon face the wretched Fire Thrower.

"Are ye scared?" Flinn called out, in a loud voice.

"No!" the men thundered.

"Are ye scared o' the Fire Thrower?" Flinn asked, guiding his mount around a fallen tree.

"Er, no?" one voice tremulously said.

Flinn's confident smirk melted from his face, to be replaced by a frown. A hesitant 'no' was not what he wanted to hear. So, it was the Fire Thrower that the men feared? Over him? Well, this nonsense had to be put to rest once and for all.

The men grumbled about the power of the Fire Thrower, but Flinn's attention went to the flash of heat near his chest.

Let them bellow, like useless cattle.

The stone's voice sounded like a bitter drunk.

"All I'm tellin' you," Casimir was saying, "was we've never faced a foe like this Fire Thrower before. How are we supposed to fight someone like that? It can't be done."

"The thing to remember," Rusty patiently told the crewman, "is that the Fire Thrower couldn't beat the captain, either."

"How does that help us?" a new voice added. Captain Flinn quickly glanced backward. It was Von. "We were told that there'd be no one to worry about over here."

"True," Rusty was forced to admit, "but look how far we've come! We won the hammer and we won the fang!"

"And yet, they found the location of the temple first!" Puck's voice whined miserably.

"Leave the Lentarians to me," Flinn growled. "That Fire Thrower will be…"

Seek ye not the Protector's wrath.

"What's the matter, Captain?" Rusty asked. "Why have you fallen silent? Are you well?"

"I be collectin' my thoughts, Q," Captain Flinn answered, thinking quickly.

You've said that before, Flinn communicated to the stone. *Explain yerself. What does that mean?*

Seek ye not the Protector's wrath.

The Protector be the Fire Thrower, Flinn guessed. *The two of us be fairly evenly matched, but I* will *defeat him. Er, I can defeat him, right?*

The Fire Thrower can be defeated by you, aye, but only if you possess a second Alchos Stone. Forget about him for now. Focus on the second stone. You must make haste.

I will get that second stone and defeat yer precious Protector once and for all.

He is one of the Protectors, the stone suddenly clarified. *The other Protector is the one you cannot defeat.*

Flinn's eyes widened with disbelief. *The woman? Am I to understand ye are warning me about the woman? Pah. The woman be inconsequential. It be the Fire Thrower I be concerned about. I…*

Listen carefully, imbecile. It's the woman you must be concerned about. She has powers that even she doesn't realize she possesses.

Did ye just call me…?

I most certainly did. Enough with this charade. Do as I say and there will be a chance you and your men will emerge victorious. Defy me and your failure is all but guaranteed. Do we understand one another?

Captain Flinn was silent as he digested this alarming bit of news. His Alchos Stone no longer sounded like an omniscient seer. Was the stone possessed? Could there be some type of evil spirit residing within the stone, trying to lead him astray?

Flinn shook his head. That couldn't be the case. If it had been, the stone could have done so the moment he acquired it all those years ago.

Of course I could have, you dolt.

If anyone will be using names, it'll be me, ye blasted lump of rock. Since when do I take orders from the likes of ye? What do I have to fear from ye?

Mutiny, should your beloved crew discover you've been carrying around a jewel the size of your fist. Aren't you the one who thrives on convincing others that you are always fair with your men? How do you think they'd feel if they knew you've been holding out on them?

Flinn was silent as the ramifications of the stone's threat became clear. The crew was already on the brink of mutiny.

The revelation of the stone's existence would push every single one of them over, especially Jino. His jhorun was formidable, aye, but he wasn't sure how he'd fare if he had to face all of his men at the same time.

You'd lose, that's what would happen. Now that I have your full attention, let's get a few things straight.

Who are ye? Flinn interrupted, before the stone could continue. *Methinks ye be not some sentient jewel.*

Who I am is of no importance to you. What is of importance is your complete obedience. Follow my orders and you and your men will become rich beyond your wildest dreams.

I be already there, mate, Flinn mentally argued.

Your alleged wealth is nothing but a drop of water in the sea. Do as I say. Perz will be the Eighth Kingdom, and become the mightiest of them all.

Flinn sighed as he contemplated the offer. Clearly there was something amiss with his stone. Logic dictated he should get rid of the cursed object before falling even further under its influence, and he certainly didn't need the gold, but the comment about Perz started him thinking. Perhaps he could play along with the ornery stone. It would be worth it just to see Perz recognized as its own kingdom, with he alone sole ruler.

Wise choice. Now, listen carefully. You must avoid the Teleporter at all costs, and here's why.

For the next fifteen minutes Flinn galloped in silence as he listened to the stone give orders. While still reluctant to follow anyone's lead other than his own, he did have to hand it to the cantankerous stone. There was still a chance they could prevail. After all, he did still possess the fang, as well as the special hammer. All he had to do was simply make it to the temple before the Lentarians and the Fire Thrower had a chance to unlock its secrets.

The warning about the woman teleporter unnerved him, however. What was she capable of? Why would the stone claim the woman had powers even she wasn't aware of? Regardless, the stone—aside from developing a grumpy personality—hadn't led them astray yet. If the woman was as dangerous as the stone suggested, then he would give her a wide berth. All without her or the Fire Thrower knowing that's what he was doing, of course.

Their galloping mounts finally broke through the trees and into a large clearing. Flinn cringed as he regarded the open sky. Loss of their overhead cover was a concern. A quick scan of the surrounding countryside confirmed there was nothing he could do about it. A large ridge of rocks stood to the west, and an almost impassable wall of trees to the east. He and his men would have to risk the clearing.

Flinn guided his mount out into the open sunlight. At this speed, they could cover the open ground in less than ten minutes, avoiding someone, or *something* that could report their presence to the Lentarians. However, the voice in his head kept urging him on. The more he dallied, the stronger the possibility that the Lentarians would take what they wanted at the temple and be on their way.

"Come, lads. Be quick about it. I like this not, but we have no choice. Make for the trees to the north. Hurry!"

The instant all the pirates emerged into the clearing, the skies were filled with madly flapping wings, piercing squawks, and large tawny bodies zipping through the air.

Griffins. He knew at once although he'd never seen one.

They were wickedly fast, and squawking something fierce. Men clapped their hands over their ears, while scanning the skies, looking for the source of the confusion.

A large slab of stone suddenly fell out of the sky, barely missing Flinn and his steed. The animal reared and almost dislodged the captain. Flinn generated a large jet of air and flung it upward at the noisy monsters.

Several griffins squawked with surprise as the blast of wind knocked them head over wing. More stones fell from the sky, coming closer still to him and his steed.

"Watch yerselves, men! The damn beasties are dropping stones! Keep moving. Don't make yerself a target!"

The stone's voice appeared in his head once more. *They dare attack me? Me?? Of all the insolent, foolish, idiotic —*

Flinn's eyes widened with surprise as he listened to the ranting voice. The thing was surely possessed.

Then he noticed more griffins, coming perilously close

to his crew. He generated ferocious blasts of wind, creating a shield. The griffins lost significant amounts of feathers every time they ventured too close. Safe once more, Flinn tuned back in to the voice in his head, which hadn't stopped ranting from the moment the winged beasts had arrived.

This is how they repay me? After sharing my own private sanctuary, they have the gall to defy me? Why, just as soon as I… what? Speak your mind, pirate captain.

Who are ye, mate? I know ye certainly be no simple stone.

Who I be, er, who I am, is of no concern to you. What I say is. Now, do not concern yourself with the griffins. I will deal with them.

How? Flinn demanded.

Show them the stone.

Flinn automatically frowned.

Reveal the stone, the voice commanded again.

Anything but that, mate. Now be not the time to divulge its existence.

You've lost enough time already. Stop your arguing and do as I say.

Anger and defiance coursed through the captain's veins. He took orders from no one!

So, how badly did he want that second stone? Enough to put up with the incessant insults and demands made by this one? Sure, Flinn had enough treasure back on his private island in the Perz Archipelago to last several lifetimes, but the desire to see what additional powers a second stone had sorely tempted him.

I told you before, if you want these griffins to cease their attack, you must reveal the existence of the stone.

The griffins renewed their attack. *Blast. Fine. Ye had better know what yer doing.*

Flinn reached inside his jacket, grasped the Alchos Stone, and pulled it out. He hastily unwrapped the large sapphire and held it aloft. Amazingly, the griffins screeched with surprise and immediately veered away, madly flapping their wings.

Call them back, the stone instructed.

What the blazes for? I thought we wanted them to leave us be!

They fear the stone, as they should. Now, call them back. The griffins insulted me, and it's time for restitution.

Still holding the stone aloft, Flinn cleared his throat. "Oy!

This is addressed to all ye griffins! Get back here, on the double."

For some inexplicable reason, nearly two dozen griffins reluctantly headed back his way.

Order them to land.

Flinn pointed at the ground. "On the ground. Now. Be quick about it."

In a matter of moments, every avian was on the ground, its head lowered, as if the creatures were bowing to him. Flinn eyed the glittering jewel. Were they? Bowing?

"How are you doin' that, Cap'n?" Von asked, amazed. "If you could control those monsters, then why didn't you call them off the moment they attacked?"

"That's what you're asking about?" Jino asked, appalled. The pirate pointed at the captain's hand. "Look what he's holding! That is the biggest jewel I have ever seen! Have you been hiding that from us, Captain?"

Flinn nodded. "Aye, I have."

The men fell silent as they stared at the jewel in the Captain's outstretched hand.

"I knew it," Rusty was saying. "I knew you were carrying something inside your pocket, only I had no idea it was a massive jewel. Captain, how much is that thing worth?"

"More than all the gold we have ever won," Flinn admitted.

"You should have told us," a hard voice snapped.

"Button yer lip," Flinn snapped back. "Ye want to know why I didn't reveal this? This stone has magical powers. How do ye think we've managed to escape capture? How do ye think I was able to make the *Emberbrand* disappear?"

"You said you had a spell," Jino accused. "You've been lying to us?"

"This be not the time to get into this. Should I have told the lot of ye about this stone? Aye. Should —"

"What *else* haven't you told us about?" Jino angrily asked. "How are we supposed to trust you now, Captain?"

Flinn grunted and waggled the Alchos Stone. "Because of this, mate. This be called an Alchos Stone. Four, and only four, exist in this world."

Jino's eyes widened with surprise. "Is that what we're doing here, Captain? Is there another of these stones in this wretched kingdom?"

Flinn nodded. "Aye. And if ye want to reap the rewards of what possessing a second stone will bring, then ye need to bite yer tongue and follow my orders. The longer we stall, the closer the damn Fire Thrower be to finding the temple."

"Is this temple where we'll find the stone?" Grenden tremulously asked.

Flinn started to speak when he realized he didn't know the answer.

Will we? Find the stone at the temple?

You will find a stone at the temple, aye. However, not this temple. You will visit three temples. The location to the second can only be found in the first. And the location to the third?

Found in the second? Flinn guessed.

Correct.

"The stone be in a temple, aye," Flinn began. "Jus' not this one. We be on the way to the first." He explained what the stone had revealed to him.

Movement attracted Flinn's attention. A quick check confirmed his suspicions. Jino was slowly advancing toward him. A look of determination had appeared on the pirate's face, and the fool even had the tenacity of drawing his cutlass.

"Unless ye plan on using that, Jino," Flinn nonchalantly began, "I would suggest ye put it away. Before someone gets hurt."

"The only person that'll be hurt will be... oooof!"

Jino's comment came to an abrupt end as a jet of air bodily picked up the crewman and slammed him against the nearest tree, pinning him in place. Flinn casually walked over to the tree and regarded the man pinned by his air jets.

"Jino, I be tired of this. Should I have informed the crew about the stone? Aye, I should have. Why didn't I? Think about it, lad. This stone be powerful. Even I have not yet unlocked all its powers. However, it has gotten us this far, has it not? Look at those strange monsters. They are all sitting on the ground, awaiting my command. I could simply instruct them to take ye far from here and have ye for supper, but will

I? No. Why? 'Cause ye are my best fighter, mate."

The winds lessened somewhat, but continued to hold Jino against the tree.

"Now, listen carefully. There will be no more challenges to my authority, Jino. Not from anyone, be that understood? Most of ye have followed me for years. Have I ever cheated any of ye? Not once. This stone will allow us to procure a second stone. Think of what we can do with two of 'em, lads. Two!"

Flinn waved a dismissive hand. The blasts of air disappeared and Jino collapsed to his knees. Within seconds, the pirate was back on his feet. He made no more moves to pull his weapons out.

"Ye have a choice, mate," Captain Flinn continued. "Ye have already cost us precious time, and now, I will waste no more. Ye are free to go, Jino. If ye think ye can find the temples better on yer own, then so be it. However, no one here will follow ye. The only people here are Lentarians, and they are out for blood, including the Fire Thrower and his mate, the Teleporter. Refresh my memory. How many times have ye gone up against the Teleporter and not been tossed about like a piece o' trash? None."

Jino was silent. The pirate's gaze dropped to the ground and stayed there.

"Ye are still welcome to be a member o' my crew, but I will promise ye something. Should I hear a single peep out of ye, or if ye give any indication ye be still considering mutiny, then I will personally hand ye over to the Fire Thrower. Are we clear?"

Jino sullenly nodded. "Aye, Captain."

"Choose yer path."

"I go with you, Captain."

Flinn nodded. "Good. I be glad ye choose to fight by my side. Just be warned, mate. One step in the wrong direction, and ye will wish ye had gills. Do ye catch my meaning?"

Jino hurriedly nodded.

"Good. Now, about these winged beasties, we should…"

Griffins.

Eh? What was that?

They're called griffins. Instruct them to lead you to the Temple. Once there, instruct half the griffins to attack the Lentarians. The rest will assist you in clearing the Temple's obstacles.

Flinn blinked with surprise. *Obstacles? What obstacles? Why is this the first time ye have brought up this?*

Dolt, why do you think I told you about the fang? Or the hammer? They are essential if you plan on completing the obstacles successfully. And you had best hurry. The longer you stall, the closer they get to discovering how to enter the temple.

Flinn quickly relayed instructions to the griffins. The winged monsters immediately took to the air and, once they were certain Flinn and his men were following, they angled to the north and flew off.

You had better hurry. Your time has run out. They have entered the temple.

Flinn swore loudly and spurred his mount.

Chapter 3 — Temple Trial

It's awfully dark down there," Sarah observed, as she knelt next to the hole to get a closer look. "Do we have any idea what's waiting for us at the bottom?"

Steve shook his head. "No, but does it really matter? We've got to go, regardless of what we may find."

"I will go first, Lady Sarah," Breslin declared.

"No you won't," Athos argued. "I will."

"Neither of you will," Steve decided. "I…"

Breslin whipped his axe off his back, and before anyone could protest, jumped into the hole. He was swallowed up by the darkness almost immediately. Afraid he wouldn't be allowed to follow, Athos hurriedly pulled his own weapons free and, in the blink of an eye, followed his companion down the hole.

"Dwarves," Steve scowled. He peered anxiously into the hole, hoping he might be able to see where it led. A look of disgust appeared on his face and he snapped his fingers. A large chaser appeared in his hand, which he then proceeded to drop into the hole.

"Watch where you put that thing!" an angry voice bellowed up from below. It was Breslin. "You damn near burned my beard off!"

Steve cringed. "Sorry! I just wanted to see how deep the hole is. Is it far?"

"Not far," Breslin called from the darkness. "It drops maybe ten feet, and then curves to the right. Get down here. You need to see this, Sir Steve."

"Did he say it was a ten-foot drop?" Sarah dubiously asked. "That's a good way to sprain an ankle, or break a leg. We need to find a safer way down."

Emily nodded. "Agreed. Maybe we could find something to use as a rope?"

Deez chittered loudly and scurried into the hole. Gareth looked at his fellow humans and shrugged.

"Well, he did dig the thing. It doesn't surprise me that he's not afraid of what's down there."

"For the record, I'm not afraid of what's down there, either," Steve clarified. "Now, if you want to talk about broken bones, then I'll say *that* is what has my attention. What we need is… wait. Sarah? Could you safely lower us to the bottom?"

Sarah was silent as she considered. However, before she could respond, everyone was gently lifted off the ground and positioned over the hole. Emily let out a mild scream of surprise. Everyone turned at once to Gareth, who — naturally — was chanting.

"Are we all ready?" the young wizard inquired, as if the phenomenon was an everyday occurrence.

"How about a little warning first?" Steve scolded.

"He's old," Sarah said, smiling at Gareth. "He scares easily."

Steve's eyes narrowed to slits as he stared at his wife. Detecting a soft snort coming from his left, he turned to see Emily trying desperately not to laugh. The paleontologist also kept her eyes on the ground.

"Don't even think about taking her side," Steve warned, waggling a finger.

Emily slid a couple of fingers across her sealed lips, mimicking a zipper.

"Are you ready?" Gareth asked. "Expendable people first."

Steve's eyes shot open. "What was that?"

"Oh, did I say that out loud? I'm sorry. I mean, Fire Thrower first."

"Right. You're a barrel of laughs, kid."

"Be sure to light the way, will you?" Sarah asked, as he began to descend into the uncomfortably narrow hole.

"It's on the top of my To Do list," Steve assured her. Just like that, he was gone, only now they could see a comforting warm light emanating from the hole.

"Me next," Sarah declared.

Once everyone had been lowered, and Gareth was standing beside them, Steve turned to lead them away from the entrance. Deez, as was the norm with him, was pacing alongside them, only from the ceiling. What the friendly guur had against running along the ground, Steve didn't know.

"I've changed my mind again," Emily quietly murmured to Sarah. "I think your jhorun is better than Steve's."

Sarah stifled a giggle and turned to her new friend. "You mean, there was a time when you thought *his* was better? For shame!"

Emily laughed out loud, which caused Steve to glance backward. Catching sight of the two women laughing conspiratorially amongst themselves, he shook his head.

The tunnel was in surprisingly good shape. The floor was level and unbroken. The walls were even and unmarred. And aside from the small divots Deez was leaving the ceiling was also in pristine shape. Steve was confused. Wasn't this temple supposed to be in ruins? If he didn't know any better, he'd say someone had been taking care of it. Steve stooped to run a finger along the ground. No dust. Make that, someone was taking *extremely* good care of it.

"What is it?" Sarah asked, as she knelt next to him.

Steve held out his finger, as if the answer was painfully obvious.

Sarah frowned. "I'm not pulling it, if that's what you think."

Steve heard Emily give a slight giggle.

"No, look here. Do you see any dust? What about cobwebs? Granted, this is the first temple I've ever been in, but doesn't it strike you as odd that this one is super clean? Check out the floor, the walls, and even the ceiling. This temple looks brand new!"

"He's got a point," Emily agreed. "Take it from someone who's done a lot of archaeological digs. Ruins never look this nice."

This is no ruin.

Why do you say that, Pryllan?

I have continued to clear vegetation as I wait. I am convinced this temple is not abandoned. There is no evidence of damage to the structure, and it seems newly constructed. Based on what I've overheard you say, it would appear you agree with my observation.

He relayed her thoughts to the others.

"Then why does this place resemble a hill?" Gareth asked. "That tells me no one has bothered with it for years."

"It's a ruse," Breslin added, as he appeared from around the corner. "Someone didn't want the temple to be found. I have no more answers than you, young wizard, but I would most certainly be in agreement with Pryllan. Something is amiss here. This isn't what it seems."

Emily wandered over to the nearest wall and felt the stones. She leaned forward for a closer inspection before she grunted and leaned back. Catching Sarah's questioning eyes, the paleontologist cleared her throat.

"It's diorite," Emily offered, by way of explanation. When she was met with blank stares, she continued. "Do you see how it looks like part of the surface is reflecting light? That's quartz."

"What's diorite?" Steve reminded her.

Emily nodded. "Diorite is an intrusive igneous rock which is phaneritic in nature. In fact, these specimens appear to be porphyritic."

"English, Doc," Steve complained.

Emily sighed. "I'm sorry. I minored in geology. Umm, where'd I lose you? Igneous?"

"I know that means volcanic," Steve told her.

"When is the last time there's been any volcanic activity around here?" Emily asked, as she turned to Gareth.

"Centuries," Breslin answered, as he stepped around Steve and looked up at Emily. "Many centuries. The last eruption happened when my father was close to my age, I believe."

Sarah was nodding. "That means this temple is old. Very old."

Emily smiled and gave her a thumbs up. "Exactly. This temple is anything but new."

"So, does that mean someone has been taking care of it?" Steve asked.

Sarah shrugged. "Or there are spells in place to keep it clean. You never know when magic is involved."

"You'll want to see this," Athos' voice suddenly announced from somewhere up ahead.

"What is it?" Steve asked, as he hurried down the tunnel and around a corner.

The tunnel angled downward. Athos kept calling them forward. Just around the sharp bend, the sight brought them all to an abrupt halt.

They were standing in an open chamber, illuminated by three torches on each wall. The torches were able to cast enough light so that they could easily see there was a large—sealed—stone door directly in front of them. Sitting on either side of the door, sentry-like, were life-sized statues of griffins, glaring at the intruders. There were also carvings, symbols, and figurines carved into every square inch of the exposed walls, with the exception of the ceiling.

"Holy cow," Steve said, whistling with amazement. "Get a load of this. I wouldn't have expected to find this down here."

There was an audible clang. Emily and Sarah jumped. Steve turned to see Breslin angrily confronting Athos. He was pointing at the torches.

"First, you wander off, and then you take it upon yourself to light the torches? We have no idea what chain of events this might have set off. You have to be more careful than this!"

Athos righted his helmet, which Breslin had knocked sideways, and shook his head. "I didn't light those. I saw the light and I investigated."

Overhearing, husband and wife approached the two dwarves.

"You guys didn't light these?" Sarah nervously asked as she eyed the blazing torches. "Honey, did you?"

Steve shook his head. "It wasn't me. I have a rule against setting things I can't see on fire."

"Does that mean we were expected?" Gareth cautiously asked. He was gripping a small figurine in each hand and was eyeing the dancing shadows in the far corners of the room.

Emily cleared her throat. "I think this could be a pylon."

"A what?" several people echoed.

"In an ancient Egyptian temple, a pylon was the main gate to the temple itself. There were usually obelisks and statues on either side of the gate. In this case, there are statues, but no obelisks."

Steve walked up to the imposing stone door and knocked his knuckles against a large stone set in the center.

"How are we supposed to get in?" Steve wondered out loud. "There's gotta be a way."

"Deez ought to be able to dig through it," Gareth suggested, as he joined Steve at the door.

Athos and Breslin appeared and started inspecting the door. After a few moments, both dwarves sadly shook their heads and stepped away. If there was a secret way to open the door, it had escaped them.

Steve suddenly looked around. "Hey, where *is* Deez? Has anyone seen him lately?"

In unison, everyone slowly looked up at the ceiling. Deez was there, slowly picking his way across the vaulted roof of the chamber.

Gareth cupped his hands around his mouth. "Deez? What are you doing? Why are you moving so slowly?"

STONE IS NOT STONE.

"Huh?" Steve asked, turning to his wife. "What's that

supposed to mean?"

Sarah looked up and spotted the guur overhead. The large ten-legged insect had now come to a stop and was using his two front legs to cautiously tap the ceiling directly in front of him.

PROGRESS IMPEDED. STONE IS NOT STONE.

"I really don't know what to make of that," Steve admitted, turning to Gareth. "Do you?"

"No, I don't," the young wizard admitted. "Deez? What's the problem? Is there something wrong with the stone up there?"

"Of course!" Emily suddenly exclaimed. "It's the diorite, I'm sure of it. I'm willing to bet Deez has never had to dig through igneous rock."

"Rock is rock," Gareth defiantly argued. He caught the frown on Emily's face and his confidence faded. "Isn't it?"

"Not even close," Emily told the boy. "Deez? Perhaps you should come down from there?"

Sarah nodded. "Good idea. Come on down, Deez. It'll be safer if you stick close to us."

COMPLIANCE.

Deez reversed course and retraced his steps. Within moments, the large insect was standing beside Gareth, who was skimming a hand over the sealed door. The friendly guur watched for a few moments before he approached the door and raised his two enlarged front legs. Gareth looked up just as Deez started to dig.

"No! Don't touch the door! I think we need to... what's going on? You can't dig through it?"

STONE IS NOT STONE.

"Regardless of the stone's composition," Steve began, "I would think Deez should still be able to dig through it. It shouldn't matter if it's igneous, or sedimentary, or metamorphic."

Emily was nodding. "You know your rocks. I'm impressed."

"That's because he oftentimes has rocks for brains," Sarah quipped.

Steve's smile melted into a frown. "Couldn't give me this moment, could you?"

Sarah blew him a kiss. "It's what I'm here for, honey."

Steve wandered over to the closest wall and studied the symbols and pictures covering the surface. He idly traced an image of a shield, and then of a griffin, but then he hesitated. He was looking at an unknown rune, a triangle with a line through it. Before he could ask any questions, he was startled to discover Emily standing beside him. Steve pointed at the strange symbol.

"You're the doc, Doc. What do you think that means?"

Emily studied the symbol and nodded. "Do you know what? I saw this symbol up on the surface. In several places. I'm not sure. It could be…"

"Before I say, would you all do me a favor? Spread out. See if there are any more marks like this one."

Sarah wandered over. "What are you looking for? That pyramid with the line through it? I just saw the same thing a little while ago, only it was just the triangle and no line."

Emily immediately perked up. "Where? Can you show me?"

Sarah led the paleontologist back into the tunnel. She only took a few steps inside the tunnel when she stopped and pointed at a section of the wall.

"Steve, could you give us some light? It's hard to see anything over here."

"How'd you see that the first time?" Steve asked, pumping more jhorun into his hands and illuminating all four walls of the rectangular tunnel.

"I was walking beside you," Sarah answered. "You had both your hands lit. That's when I noticed it."

Emily looked up at Steve and inclined her head at the wall. "Do you see this? This is the same image as the other, only it has been flipped vertically."

"And you have a theory why that is?" Steve slowly asked.

Emily nodded. "I do. I just want to see if —"

"I found one," Athos' gruff voice announced. He was facing the left-hand wall, nearly a dozen feet from the closed door.

Everyone hurried over to the dwarf, who was holding his axe by the blade and tapping the handle against the symbol. Emily hurried over and peered anxiously at the mark.

"It's a match for the first one," Emily announced.

"Excellent. Are there any others?"

Athos started to shrug, but almost lost his grip on his axe. As he grabbed for it, the handle bumped the wall. Everyone heard a loud, audible *click*.

"What was that?" Sarah asked.

Athos and Breslin wordlessly pointed up at the wall, at the point where the handle hit the stone. The symbol was now recessed.

Steve stretched upward and felt along the two-inch square. "Okay, so, it pushes in, like a button. Do the others behave the same way?"

Emily returned to the first symbol, the one Steve had found, which was on the wall opposite from the temple's entrance. She gingerly pushed it. Sure enough, there was a loud click, and the symbol sunk into the stone, just like the other. Eager to see whether all the symbols were buttons, Sarah moved back to the mouth of the tunnel and pushed the symbol she had found.

Nothing happened.

"That must mean something," Gareth softly murmured.

"That's what I think, too," Sarah quietly confided. "But what that is, I haven't the foggiest idea."

"I think I see another one over here," Breslin called, from the opposite side of the chamber.

"Push it," Steve instructed.

"I am unable to reach it."

Sarah hurried over to assist.

There was a loud click, and now three of the pylon's walls had sunken symbols on their surfaces.

"Does anyone else see the pattern here?" Steve quietly asked. "Left, front, and back. What do you want to bet there's another of these symbols on the wall to the right?"

"Spread out," Sarah ordered. "Let's find it."

A few moments later, Deez climbed a dozen feet up the wall and inadvertently pressed on the fourth symbol. There was a loud clacking noise, and the pylon trembled. Steve watched for a hidden trapdoor but nothing happened. Everyone let out a collective sigh of relief.

"What was that?" Steve wanted to know. He turned expectantly to Emily.

The paleontologist laughed. "I study dinosaurs, not rocks. I haven't a clue what happened. It could have just been a minor earthquake."

Sarah wandered over to the closest symbol and let out an exclamation of surprise. She pointed at the wall, which had reverted back to its normal state, not indented.

Emily was smiling. "Hah! I knew it!"

"Knew what?" Steve asked, confused.

"These symbols need to be pressed in the correct order," Sarah guessed.

"Let's each stand beside one of the buttons, and we'll try them again."

"What order do you want to try?" Sarah asked, as she held her hand over the picture of the upside-down pyramid. "How many attempts do you think we have?"

Emily's eyes widened. "Ooo, good point. I was planning on just entering in all the combinations until we get the right one, but you bring up a very valid point. What happens if we're only allowed a few guesses? What's to prevent this place from protecting itself?"

"Okay, well, how do we find the right order?" Steve wanted to know.

Emily swept an arm around the pylon. "The answer has

got to be here somewhere. Spread out. Look for clues."

"What are we looking for?" Steve heard Athos quietly ask Breslin.

"I'm not too sure, lad," Breslin admitted. "Perhaps some kind of diagram?"

Athos shrugged. "I don't know. There are symbols and carvings on every surface."

Steve turned to Gareth. "What do you say, sport? Do you think you can figure out the correct order?"

Gareth shrugged. "You never know until you try. I'll see what I can do."

Once again, Deez came to their rescue. The guur had silently watched his human companions spread out around the room, and — wanting to be included in the hive's activities — climbed the closest wall, intent on inspecting the stone he had detected earlier. Quickly traversing the ceiling, he found the small patch of strange stone that resisted his efforts at digging.

STONE IS NOT STONE.

Steve, Sarah, and Gareth paused in their search and, in unison, angled their heads up at the guur perched upside down on the ceiling.

"What are you doing?" Gareth demanded. "Get back down here, Deez!"

STONE IS NOT STONE.

Sarah held up a hand once she saw Gareth take an angry breath.

"Just a moment. Deez, is it all the stone?" Emily curiously asked. "Or just the patch in front of you?"

In response, Deez tapped the stone in front of him with his front legs.

"Do you think he's found something?" Steve asked, as he turned to Sarah.

Sarah smiled. "Emily and I will go take a look."

Emily's eyes widened. "We will? And, um, how are we

supposed to do that?"

Sarah slipped her arm through the short blonde woman's and instructed her jhorun to gently lift the two of them into the air. Keeping their progress slow, Sarah gently maneuvered the two of them until they were only a few inches from the ceiling. Less than a foot away, Deez cocked his head and curiously stared at them.

"What's the matter, Deez?" Sarah teased. "Not used to seeing humans on the roof?"

BIPEDS DO NOT FLOAT.

Sarah nodded. "Don't worry, I can keep us in the air long enough to get the job done."

Emily tilted her head sideways to look at the guur. "So, what's wrong with the stone up here?"

Deez tapped the spot and Emily gasped, noticing the small patch of stone Deez had singled out.

"What is it?" Sarah asked.

Emily pointed at the roof. "Look! Do you see this? This stone isn't diorite, like the rest of the pylon. How did I not notice this before? It almost looks like it could be limestone."

Sarah shrugged. "Okay. Diorite. Limestone. What does that tell us?"

"Have Steve check out those symbols and see if the stone is different."

Sarah called out the instruction, and within a minute, the others had verified that the buttons were a slightly different color than their surroundings.

"We should have caught that earlier," Breslin mused. "*I* should have caught that. I'm grateful my father wasn't here to witness my mistake. I'd never hear the end of it."

"Let's make certain no one tells him," Steve snickered, drawing dark looks from both dwarves. "Don't worry. My lips are sealed."

Breslin harrumphed and resumed studying the symbol.

Steve looked up at the two women floating high above his head. "What now? How does that help us?"

"There are a series of lines on this tile," Emily reported.

"From left to right, there's four lines, then three, then one, and then two."

"How do we know which one is which? For that matter, how do we know it shouldn't be read from right to left?"

"Because we're not in Egypt," Emily patiently told him. "And these aren't hieroglyphics."

"So, which wall is which?" Steve asked.

"We don't know," Sarah told him. "There's no other markings on that tile, just the lines."

"Wouldn't we be running the same risk as before?" Steve persisted. "We can't just keep punching in combinations. Something tells me it'd be a bad idea."

Emily suddenly turned to Sarah and smiled. "What if… what if the location of the symbols doesn't matter?"

"Of course it would," Sarah argued. "How would it not?"

"Perhaps this number refers to the order in which the symbols were discovered?" Emily wryly suggested.

Sarah's mouth opened, and then closed with an audible snap. "That's one way of looking at it. It's an impressive guess, coming from someone who woke up several days ago believing magic didn't exist."

"I've seen you and your husband at work," Emily informed her. "I've encountered creatures that aren't supposed to exist. And, I'm currently floating off the ground, while the biggest bug I've ever seen is less than five feet away. Why wouldn't magic play a part in this?"

Sarah nodded. "It's worth a shot."

"What's worth a shot?" Steve called up.

"We think the sequence might be the order in which they were discovered," Sarah told him. "Everyone, take your places next to the symbol you discovered."

"Could we watch what happens from the ground?" Emily asked.

Sarah grinned. "Sure. Spoilsport."

Once the two ladies were on the ground, Sarah looked straight up at Deez — clinging upside-down on the ceiling — and gave the signal. The guur stepped forward and pushed his symbol in. There was a soft click as the button locked in the 'down' position. "We need to get the right order. After

Deez should be Breslin."

Breslin tapped the handle on the symbol. A soft click.

"Next!" Breslin announced.

"That'd be me," Steve said, as he pressed the symbol near him. "Athos, you're last, pal."

Athos grunted and reached for his axe. It took the dwarf a few tries, since the symbol was over his head, but eventually, the axe handle made contact. Athos expertly flipped his axe in the air and caught it with his left hand. One of his throwing weapons, an orix, appeared in his right.

Time slowed to a crawl. The large stone door slowly lifted, with a loud grating noise as it slid up into the wall. Simultaneously, a second door opened above the entrance, releasing large rocks and boulders that threatened to flatten everything below. Suddenly, the falling rocks inexplicably slowed until they appeared to be gently spinning in place.

Steve pulled everyone out of harm's way and turned to Sarah. "Whew! Quick thinking. That would have definitely left a mark."

"Is everyone clear?" Sarah asked. "I'd really like to let go of these things now."

"All clear," Breslin called out.

The stones suddenly dropped to the ground in a loud crash.

"Booby traps," Steve grumbled, as he approached the rock pile. "What would we have done if you hadn't been with us?"

Sarah shrugged. "I have no idea. I'd rather not think about it. Well? The door is now open. Let's see what goodies are waiting for us, shall we?"

Steve nodded. "After you, milady. I… wait. Scratch that. I'll go first."

He ignited his hands and peered anxiously through the open door. His vision of a great big treasure chest vanished. What he saw was a tunnel, and it sloped steeply downhill.

"Damn," Steve swore. "I'm thinking there's more than one challenge to overcome."

Chapter 4 – Pain in the Temple

Steve raised a hand and stepped through the door. Two torches on the walls emitted small puffs of smoke and sprang to life. Steve took another couple of steps and the next set of torches ignited. He turned to his wife, but she was already pushing past him to hurry down the tunnel.

"Hey! What are you doing? There could be booby traps around every corner! You don't want to set anything else off!"

Emily passed him next, followed immediately by Gareth and Deez. Bringing up the rear were the two dwarves, who both had smirks on their faces. Breslin gave Steve a wry grin and disappeared down the tunnel.

"Where did I lose control of this situation?" Steve grumped, as he turned to follow.

Several minutes later, they found themselves in a much smaller, simpler chamber with no symbols, no runes, and no markings anywhere. The floor was tightly packed dirt, and the walls appeared to be made of small beige stones no larger than cinder blocks. And, there wasn't a door to be found anywhere. It looked as though the tunnel had dead-ended in this small chamber.

Only one item in the room convinced him they were still on the right path: a life-sized metallic statue of a man. The metal figure had his arms extended, as though he should be holding something. The statue wore some type of protective armor and a hood, which had been pulled over his head, concealing his facial features.

"I wonder who this is supposed to depict," Steve mused. "Can't really see his face, can you?"

"What about his hands?" Sarah asked.

Steve turned to his wife. "What about them?"

Sarah pointed at the statue. "He doesn't have any."

Emily, Gareth, and the two dwarfs crowded close as they inspected the large metal figurine. Deez promptly climbed up the closest wall and perched in the direct center of the ceiling. The guur chittered softly as he watched the members of the Hive converse among themselves.

"She's right," Emily observed. "There are no hands, yet both arms are extended. Why?"

Steve felt the smooth ends of the statue's arms, where the hands were supposed to be and shrugged. "What if his hands were under his clothes? Like, maybe his sleeves were too long and… yeah, okay. It was just a stupid theory. Sorry. Will everyone stop staring at me like I'm two sandwiches short of a picnic?"

"I don't know what that means," Gareth said, turning to Sarah. "Do you?"

"No one does," Sarah decided. "But that's okay. I have to put up with him on a daily basis, for years on end. I've become immune to his ramblings."

Steve chuckled as he looked over at his wife. Meeting his eyes, Sarah blew him a kiss.

"As I was saying," Steve continued, "maybe his hands are there, but we just can't see them. What do you think?"

"Looks as though he was expectin' something, doesn't it?" Athos decided, as he turned to Breslin, who nodded agreement.

Emily suddenly laughed out loud. "Of course! It makes

perfect sense! Good job, Athos!"

Confused, Athos sidled up next to Steve and tugged on his sleeve.

"What makes perfect sense?"

Steve shook his head. "Haven't a clue pal."

"Don't you get it?" Emily walked up to the statue and inspected the arms. "We're in a temple. Usually sacrifices are made in temples. We need to make an offering."

"Of what?" Steve and Gareth echoed.

Emily shrugged. "That's the million-dollar question. Ordinarily, I'd say some type of animal, or maybe offerings of crops would do the trick. However, we're in a magical land. Who could say?"

"Let's not forget the absence of a door," Steve reminded everyone. "For the sake of argument, let's say we put something in this dude's arms. Then what? What's the purpose? There's no door here for us to open."

"Perhaps the door is concealed?" Sarah suggested.

Steve pointed at the wall opposite the tunnel. "I say we have Deez make an opening."

Overhearing, Deez tapped his front legs excitedly.

"We can't risk violating the rules," Emily announced. "This temple has placed some very specific puzzles before us. It's up to us to solve them."

Steve groaned. "Fine. Where do you want to start? It's not like there's a lot of choices around here."

Emily looked at Sarah and her face became somber. "What do you think? Couldn't you teleport whatever we need?"

"Let's go with some of your ideas," Sarah began. "What are some examples of typical offerings? And don't tell me a dead person."

Emily snorted with laughter. "No, that was predominantly the Mayans. Thank goodness I haven't seen anything that was Mayan in nature."

"Give me something to fetch," Sarah urged.

Their paleontologist friend crossed her arms over her chest and was silent for a few moments.

"Animals," Emily finally decided.

Sarah was horrified. "I am *not* going to sacrifice some helpless animal just because we're trying to defeat some damn obstacle. I won't do it."

"What kind of animal?" Steve finally asked. He looked over at Sarah and gently took her hand. "I don't plan on sacrificing any animals, either, but there may be ways around it."

Emily shrugged. "Goats, pigs, and the like."

"That shouldn't be too hard to accomplish," Steve decided, as he shared a look with his wife.

A look of comprehension appeared on Sarah's face. "Oh, you mean like a slab of pork?"

"I know we have several packages of bacon in the big freezer back home," Steve announced.

Sarah stifled a giggle. "You think if we put a frozen package of bacon in that statue's arms, then something is going to happen?"

Steve shrugged. "It's worth a shot, right?"

Sarah finally nodded, closed her eyes, and held out her hands. Moments later, the frozen package of breakfast meat appeared.

"You teleported that all the way from your home in Idaho?" Emily asked, incredulous. "I definitely think I like your jhorun better. Umm, no offense, Steve."

"None taken," Steve assured her. "Personally, I'm in total agreement. Okay, who wants to do the honors?"

Emily took the frozen package of bacon. "I'll do it. Okay, let's see what happens."

She balanced the frozen meat on one of the statue's arms and stepped back. After a few moments, when nothing discernible happened, she moved it to the other arm. Again, nothing.

"Perhaps we need to think larger? Something that would sit on both arms?"

"I don't have a whole pig in my freezer," Sarah pointed out. "Where am I supposed to find something bigger than that?"

Breslin stepped forward. "Perhaps I can be of assistance? No one roasts meat better than the dwarves. We have plenty of meat stockpiled. If you'll wait a moment, I will write out a message and you can deliver it to my father. We'll have everything we need in no time."

Sarah nodded gratefully. "That's perfect, Breslin. Thanks."

The bacon vanished from Emily's hand, sent back to their freezer in Coeur d'Alene, Idaho.

Breslin handed a slip of paper to Sarah, who closed her eyes and brought up a mental picture of Maelnar's private desk.

"Are you sure he's there?"

Breslin held up a second piece of paper. "If he isn't, I have another, which you can send to the Council Chamber. He'll be at one of the two."

The paper vanished.

"How long should I give him?" Sarah asked Breslin.

"He shouldn't take any longer than a few minutes, lass," Breslin answered. "If he's in his office, he'll be summoning his staff right about now. He'll inform the cook to locate the largest uncooked piece of boar they can find and return with it to his office."

They waited the requisite time and Sarah asked the two dwarves to be ready to receive the bounty. Athos and Breslin both stepped forward. They stood side-by-side and wordlessly held out their arms.

"Thank you. Now, are you ready?"

Both dwarves nodded. A few seconds later, a large, dark brown carcass appeared, draped across both dwarves' arms. Breslin let out a grunt of surprise and stumbled forward. Deez rushed to Breslin's side. The friendly guur raised his large front legs and locked them over his head. Then he scuttled under the carcass and lifted.

"You have my thanks, Deez," Breslin told the guur, giving him a friendly pat on the head. "Consider this my father's revenge. This must be the largest swine to be found anywhere in the clan."

"Well, don't drop it," Sarah ordered. She waved a hand in front of her nose and pointed at the statue. "Phew, that stinks. Just place it there and let's see what happens."

The carcass of the dead animal was draped across the

statue's two arms. The group waited with bated breath to see if anything would happen. Nothing did.

"Scratch that idea," Sarah decided. "Ugh. The smell from that thing is nauseating. Where can I put it to get rid of it?"

Right here will do nicely.

Steve's head jerked up.

Pryllan? You've been eavesdropping again?

It's Pravara. Isn't my mother with you?

Wow. Maybe Sarah is right and my memory is shot to hell.

I'm not sure I know what that means.

Don't worry about it, Pravara. What were you saying?

Yamira and Lamira had to leave, so I am here, in my mother's nest, watching Pylaria. It's boring.

Are you hungry?

I could eat.

"Breslin? Would you mind if Sarah sends the carcass to Pryllan's nest? Pravara is there and said she'll be more than happy to take it off your hands."

Breslin bowed. "I would be honored. I assume she is listening? Enjoy the meat, friend Pravara. Consider it a gift."

You have my thanks, friend Breslin.

"She says thanks," Steve relayed.

Only too eager to be rid of the ripe, smelly carcass, Sarah sent the meat straight to Pryllan's nest.

"Did she get it?"

Indeed, she did, the dragon confirmed. **The dwarves have excellent taste. This meat is very flavorful.**

Well, you two can compare recipes later. Right now, we need to figure out what to give this blasted statue.

If you need my help, then please don't hesitate to ask.

I will. Thanks, Pravara.

Steve looked at Breslin and grinned. "You definitely made her day. She has been taking care of her baby sister and was bored. And hungry. You just gave her a tasty snack. She appreciated it."

"Delighted to be of help," Breslin said.

"Back to this statue," Sarah announced, as she wrapped her knuckles on the closest outstretched arm. "Should we…"

She trailed off as she looked over at Gareth, who had been sitting cross-legged on the floor with his eyes closed. Deez was standing beside him, appearing very much like he was standing guard. "Gareth? Do you have any suggestions?"

"Treasure," the wizard answered, without opening his eyes.

Sarah shrugged and then turned to Breslin. "That's not a bad idea. I've read of ancient civilizations who gave gifts of gold and jewelry to their deities. That might work here. Any suggestions on what we could use?"

Breslin was already scribbling out another message. He folded the paper and held it out to Sarah. A split second later, the paper vanished.

"What did you ask for?" Sarah wanted to know.

"Well, we need something large enough to set on both of these arms," Breslin began, as he tapped each arm with his axe handle. "I asked for a chest, filled with an assortment of jewels, coins, ingots, and so on. Hopefully, something inside the chest will trigger the next step."

"What *is* the next step?" Steve asked, as he looked around the room. "Does anyone know?"

Emily cleared her throat. "If I were to venture an educated guess, I'd suggest, perhaps, the appearance of a door?"

A short while later, Breslin indicated Sarah should teleport the chest so they could see if they were on the right track. Once the treasure-laden chest was sitting at their feet, Athos and Breslin both lifted the chest and slid it onto the arms of the outstretched statue.

Nothing happened.

"It still doesn't like us," Steve mused.

"It just means we haven't gotten the right offering yet," Sarah corrected.

"I don't even think we're on the right page," Steve complained, as soon as Sarah sent the chest back to Maelnar's office. "What else could we use?"

Emily had wandered over to the statue and was studying it intently. She felt the unusual handless arms, and then scrutinized the face hidden beneath the hood. Slowly, she straightened and started nodding her head.

"Have you figured something out, Lady Emily?" Breslin anxiously asked.

"I think so. I think... I think we need to figure out who this statue is supposed to depict. Maybe then we could determine what offering we should place in its arms."

Husband and wife wandered over to the statue and gazed helplessly at the strange character.

"I've never seen anyone like that before," Steve began. He looked at Sarah. "You?"

"No. Perhaps if we... wait. What about Pryllan? Do you think she could help?"

I am here.

"She's here," Steve relayed. "Are you still up there, by the temple?"

Aye.

"Pryllan, we need to identify who this is supposed to be," Sarah said, as she pointed at the statue. "I think we're supposed to make an offering, but we don't know what that should be."

I'm asking the Collective.

"What about you, Gareth?" Sarah prompted, looking over at the young wizard. "You're unusually quiet over there. Is there anything you can do to identify who this is?"

Gareth sadly shook his head. "I've tried at least twenty different spells. I cannot make any of them work in here."

Steve snorted. "That's not too surprising, kid. This *is* an Alchos Temple, isn't it? They probably have a spell in place to prevent people from using their jhorun."

Gareth pointed an accusing finger at Sarah. "But *she* was able to use her jhorun! She teleported the dead animal and the chest. What about you? Can you light anything on fire?"

Steve glanced down at his right hand and ignited it. He generated a large chaser, instructed it to fly around the room, and then return to his hand. Moments later, the fireball poofed out.

"Mine's working just fine," Steve reported.

Gareth scowled. "So, I'm the only one who can't use his jhorun? That's not fair!"

The image depicted on the statue has been seen

before, but in different poses than this. It's one of the Ancients.

"Which Ancient?" Breslin wanted to know, when Steve repeated the message.

Do you know who that's supposed to be?

"I wonder which one it is," Gareth quietly wondered. "Earth? I mean, could that be Usol?"

Air. That's the likeness for the Master of the Winds— Eion.

Emily suddenly snapped her fingers and shook her head in amazement. "Of course! It's Air! That's the elemental symbol we keep seeing. That pyramid with the line through it? It's an ancient alchemical symbol for the air element."

"We've all met Eion," Sarah reminded everyone. "And he didn't look like that."

"True," Steve agreed, nodding, "but I do recall hearing him say that his natural form wasn't human. I can't even begin to imagine how many forms he's taken over the years. But, then again, does it really matter? Now that we know who it is, how does that help us?"

"Because now we know what the offering should be," Emily answered. "Air."

"Air?" Breslin repeated, confused. "How the ruddy hell are we supposed to gift air to a statue?"

Athos shrugged. "Blow on it?"

Sarah was nodding. "Athos has a good idea. I can use my jhorun to move air around, essentially creating a breeze. I've done it before. If I were to angle it so that it hits the statue, then maybe something will finally happen."

Steve held out a hand in an open invitation. "Be our guest. Do your…"

"If you tell me to wiggle my nose," Sarah interrupted, "then you're giving me a thirty-minute back massage tonight *while* covered in glitter."

Steve mimicked zipping his lips closed.

A mild breeze circled about the small room a few times before flowing toward the statue. A few seconds later, the statue's arms lowered, and the stone blocks comprising the rear wall crumbled away, leaving a large, gaping hole. However, before anyone could take a step, mammoth bouts of flame flared through the makeshift door, as though a dragon was on the other side.

Steve threw himself in front of Emily and Sarah and managed to get both hands up, just as the flames hit.

The fires roared and swirled around him. Steve gave the order to his jhorun to absorb every last ounce of the flames. He couldn't risk hurting anyone else.

His jhorun began tingling like mad, which meant large, damaging explosions weren't far behind. Now, his entire body had become engulfed in flames. Steve grunted. As long as it meant the others were safe, so be it.

It felt like an eternity although no more than ten seconds, before the flames tapered off and eventually poofed out. With his body still burning merrily away, Steve turned to make sure Sarah was safe. She and the others had retreated to the farthest wall, to escape the jets of fire. She cracked open an eye, glanced around the chamber, and sighed with relief. Then she caught sight of him and her brow furrowed.

"Steve? Are you okay? Tell me you're allowing yourself to burn like that on purpose."

"I'm all right," Steve assured her. "Fairly sure I am. I've given the order to extinguish the flames, only something is wrong. No matter how hard I try, I can't seem to do it. I think my jhorun is ignoring me."

Your jhorun has become saturated with excess power. You must decrease your jhorun before you can absorb any more.

"Pryllan says I need to blast some energy off," Steve relayed. "I don't think that's possible down here, so all of you should steer clear of me. Gareth? Is Deez okay? I know the guur don't particularly care for fire."

Gareth automatically looked up for his insectoid friend. Deez wasn't there. A quick check of the surroundings didn't reveal the friendly guur anywhere. Then, just before he could start working on a spell to locate his new friend, Gareth took a few steps backward and bumped into a low boulder, which turned out to be Deez, curled into a safe little ball.

The guur chittered a greeting as he rose to his full height.

"I didn't know he could do that," Gareth admitted.

"Who would've known they could make like a rock to protect themselves," Steve admitted. "Whatever. I'm glad he's okay."

"What's through there?" Sarah asked, pointing at the dark opening in the wall.

Steve shrugged and lifted an arm, intent on lighting the way. A blast of superheated flames shot out of his arm and blasted down the tunnel. A few moments later, the flames impacted something; the floor trembled.

Surprised — and horrified — that a bout of jhorun escaped without his consent, Steve dropped his arm and jammed both hands in his pockets. However, since he was still engulfed in flames, no one saw his sheepish grin.

"All right," Sarah announced, raising her voice. "I have an important safety tip. No one asks Steve to do anything. No pointers, no chasers, and certainly no lighting *anything* on fire. It's just too risky."

Steve sighed and he nodded. "Agreed. Sorry, guys."

"Don't be, Sir Steve," Breslin told him. "Between you and Lady Sarah, you have saved us from certain death."

"How would those pirates have survived that?" Steve asked, perplexed. "I mean, what if they'd made it here first?"

Ah. I see now. That's why they needed the fang. For protection.

"Amazing. Pryllan suggested that was why the pirates stole the fang. Since the fang offers protection against physical threats, it would have deflected the falling stones and shielded them from the flames. That's why they needed it."

"And my hammer?" Breslin gruffly inquired. "How does that play into this scenario?"

"The Narian power hammer cannot protect against flames, can it?" Gareth asked.

Breslin shook his head. "No."

"Perhaps it'll be needed for another temple?" Sarah suggested. "Or for some obstacle we haven't encountered yet?"

"It'll be our luck that we're going to need it and not have it," Steve grumbled.

"We'll cross that bridge when we come to it," Sarah assured him.

"We're wasting time," Breslin announced. "Come. Let's see where this tunnel leads us."

Walking single-file through the darkened tunnel, with Steve leading the procession and Athos bringing up the rear, they traveled in silence for nearly fifteen minutes before the tunnel leveled off and deposited them into a third, even smaller, chamber.

This chamber, the smallest so far, resembled the first, with symbols and carvings over every square inch of the irregular surface, including the walls, ceiling, and floor. Steve immediately spotted an irregularity. A large gray button, near the base of one wall. A quick glance around confirmed there were more of these buttons on the other walls, floor, and even the ceiling. Circular in shape, some were larger than others, with the largest around ten to twelve inches diameter. The smallest, from what Steve could see, was only a few inches around.

Some of the walls had more than one, while as far as he could tell, the ceiling and the floor only had one button apiece. The one on the floor was less than two feet away from where he was presently standing. In fact, had he taken a few more steps to the left, he would have inadvertently stepped on it.

"Now what's this place gonna do to us?" Steve asked. He glanced down at his still-flaming torso. "What are the odds that, if I step on this, I'd get doused with enough water to put this out?"

Sarah was nodding. "That'd make for a great facial."

Emily giggled and Sarah winked. "She gets it."

"What do you think we need to do here?" Steve asked. He pointed at the button on the floor and took a few steps toward it. "It's a button. Think I should push it?"

"Absolutely not," Sarah snapped. "Until we know what to expect in here, no one touches anything. And that goes for you, too, Deez."

COMPLIANCE.

"At least this room has a door," Breslin observed, as he turned to face the large rectangular slab of rock directly in front of them. He wandered over to the door and ran his hands along the surface. "Basalt, all the way through. This door must be incredibly heavy."

Steve grinned. "Hey, as long as there's some contraption that'll open it, I don't care how big it is."

"So, what do we do?" Sarah asked. "Should we follow Steve's suggestion and see what one of these buttons does? Look around. They're on every surface, and every wall. That must mean they have relevance, right? Emily? What do you think?"

The paleontologist knelt next to the button Steve had located and was silent as she studied it. After a few seconds, she straightened, and let out a sigh.

"I really don't want to recommend we do anything that could put any of our lives in danger," Emily slowly said, "but it's clear to me that these buttons must play a role. We've faced two other obstacles…"

"Both of which tried to kill us," Sarah interjected.

"…which required us to solve puzzles. That's what this has to be. Some type of puzzle."

Steve raised a flaming arm.

"Let's try this. All of you get back in the tunnel. I'll try pressing this one on the floor. Let's see what'll happen."

"That's a terrible idea," Sarah said, as a frown formed on her face. "However, I really don't see what choice we have. Very well. Okay, everyone, let's head back to the tunnel. Steve, if something starts to happen, I'll teleport all of us back to the castle, only I'll probably dump you in the moat."

Steve nodded. "That's fine by me. Is everyone clear? Good. Here we go."

Steve looked down at the button, closed his eyes, and stomped his foot down. Almost immediately, he heard the button emit a soft click. Just as he opened his eyes and moved his foot out of the way, the recessed button rotated open, like a mechanical iris. It was followed immediately by a loud blast of air, which knocked him squarely on his butt. A low rumbling note, sounding like a tuba, echoed noisily throughout the chamber.

Steve rose painfully to his knees just in time to see the button, which had sunk into the floor, spin closed and pop back up, as if it was eager to be pressed again. A quick check of the room confirmed that nothing else had happened. No hidden panels had opened, and there were certainly no falling rocks or spitting fire to contend with. He pointed at the button and turned to see if anyone else had seen.

"Tell me someone saw that besides me. Anyone?"

"What's the matter?" Sarah asked. She started to approach but had to veer off due to the intensity of Steve's flames. He also noticed his wife was jiggling a finger in her ear. "That sure was loud. It felt as though my bones were rattling."

"That's what I thought, too," Emily agreed. "That must've been the strongest bass note I have ever heard."

"A bass note," Sarah glanced around the chamber at the various buttons. "I wonder, do all of them make sounds?"

Gareth, standing next to the left wall, opposite the door, noticed a medium button situated on the wall, at waist-height. Without asking, he pushed it. They all heard the click, and just as before, the button sunk into the wall and spun open. A powerful jet of air blasted out of the tiny opening, hit Emily in the face and blew the ponytail right out of her hair. Then everyone heard it: a loud, resonating note. It was neither high, nor low, but comfortably midrange, somewhat like the chime of a church bell.

It was Steve's turn to jab a finger in his ear. He turned to look at the young wizard and saw that everyone was staring at Gareth. The teenager smiled sheepishly and scuffed a foot on the ground.

"I'm sorry. I guess I probably shouldn't have done that without letting you guys know first, huh?"

Sarah nodded. "There was no harm done this time. Just don't do that again, all right?"

"Nice look there, Doc," Steve murmured, as he turned to their paleontologist friend.

Emily ran her hands through her hair, which looked as though she had just finished a ten-hour high-speed motorcycle ride. She started gathering her hair together in an effort to smooth it down.

"Has anyone seen the band that holds my hair in place?"

"If it pleases you, milady, you may use this strip of leather. I keep a spare in case my beard comes loose."

Emily took the proffered leather strap and smiled appreciatively. "Thank you, Athos. I can honestly say I've never used leather in such a way before."

Steve snickered, which earned him a punch from both Emily and his wife.

Sarah walked over to Gareth and peered at the button. Then, she pivoted in place so that she could see the button Steve had pressed earlier. Then her eyes played across the surfaces in the room. A smile appeared on her face and her eyes sparkled with pleasure.

"I think I have it. These buttons play notes, like a piano. Breslin? Hit that one near your right hand."

The dwarf slapped a hand on the button and a split second later, a third note echoed noisily throughout the chamber. Having witnessed the power of the accompanying blasts of air, Breslin had wisely stepped out of the way. Once the note died off, he looked at Sarah and bowed.

"An excellent theory, Lady Sarah. Do you think we must play the notes in a certain order to open the door?"

Sarah nodded. "That's *exactly* what I'm thinking. However, that brings up the million-dollar question: what's the order? Is there anything in here that indicates what order the notes should be played?"

"The first one sounded like a low A," Steve murmured quietly. "Gareth's note sounded like a C, or maybe a D."

"And Breslin's?" Sarah asked. "Come on, dear. You've told me many times how much you liked your band class in high school. You should know this."

Steve sighed. "And do you know how long ago that was?"

"Fifty years?" Sarah innocently asked.

"Walked right into that one," Steve grumped. "Fine. Breslin, hit your button again."

The third note rang out, loud and clear. Steve closed his eyes and hummed softly to himself. After a few moments, his eyes opened and he smiled.

"That was an E. I'm sure of it."

"We should label all the notes," Sarah decided. "It's obvious we're going to have to play them in a specific order."

The seven companions spread out, including Deez, who once again climbed up to the ceiling where he positioned himself next to the smallest button and settled down to wait. Once Gareth noticed Steve was listening, he signaled to Deez to go ahead.

"That's the highest one yet," Steve observed. "G, I think. Coincidence, with it being on the ceiling?"

Sarah pointed at the button on the floor. "That one has been the lowest thus far. How many buttons are there?"

"Six, I think," Breslin said.

Athos tapped Breslin on the arm and indicated another button to the right of the door, slightly above his helmet.

"Seven," Breslin corrected. "I count seven buttons, Lady Sarah. Is that important?"

Sarah nodded eagerly. "There are seven different whole notes. A through G. That can't be a coincidence, since there are seven of us."

"Okay, we're back to playing these notes," Steve noted. "What order? Are we playing a song? Hopefully we won't need to hit a sharp or a flat note."

"Spread out," Emily instructed. "We need to find the order we need to play. There were instructions in the previous chamber that told us which symbols to press, in which order. I'm guessing there should be something like that here."

They searched for almost fifteen minutes. Gareth and Steve inspected the walls, Breslin and Athos took the floor, and Deez and Sarah - using her jhorun - inspected the ceiling. They found all kinds of interesting marks and symbols, but nothing to indicate what order the notes should be.

Damn, Steve mentally swore. *We're so close. There must be something here.*

Do you require assistance?

We found buttons, which play musical notes. We figure we're going to have to play them in a specific order.

In order to continue your quest?

Yes. We've scoured this chamber, and haven't found any clues as to what that order should be. There's a door here, which is sealed shut. Apparently, the seven of us need to form a band in order to make it through that door.

Perhaps what you seek cannot be found in that chamber.

What? Would you run that by me again?

Perhaps you already know the correct order, therefore the adventurer does not need to be reminded of the order.

How would we already know the order?

I am suggesting that one, or all of you, may have already been exposed to the solution to your dilemma.

"Pryllan thinks we probably already know what order these notes need to be played," Steve relayed.

"We do?" Emily repeated, confused.

Sarah was silent as she considered. "What an interesting notion. Let me think about that."

Gareth turned to Steve and helplessly held up his hands, in an 'I don't know' gesture.

Which notes can you play?

I can play all of them. I can play the piano, and the French horn, and the...

My apologies. I meant, which notes can be heard in that chamber?

Oh. All the whole notes. A, B, C, D, E, F, G.

Logic would suggest a melody should be played.

That's what we're thinking.

Or...

Or? What do you mean 'or'?

Perhaps you should use those letters to spell out a word?

Using those letters, the choices would be limited.

Then it would have to be a word with meaning.

I'm all ears, Pryllan.

"What's going on?" Sarah quietly asked. "What's Pryllan saying?"

"She agrees we should be playing some type of melody."

Sarah smiled victoriously. "I knew it!"

"Or, perhaps, spell out a specific word."

His wife sobered instantly and a look of surprise appeared on her face. "Ooooo, how interesting! I wonder what word it should be."

"She suggested a word with meaning."

I do have a suggestion, if you're interested.

Beautiful. Let's hear it.

Kahvel and I were discussing it. He believes the name of the Ancient whose temple you're in would be a wise choice.

This temple? This one is Air, which is 'Eion'. We can't play that with the notes. The only letter we'd be able to play is the 'E'.

Eion? I'm not familiar with that name. We wyverians have always called the Ancients by their true names. 'Air' is known to us as 'Bacaed'.

"What is it?" Sarah asked. "You're smiling. Do you know what we should do?"

"I think so," Steve answered. "Pryllan suggested we use the name of the Ancient, called Bacaed."

I am to remind you that it was Kahvel's suggestion. He wants full credit.

"That word wouldn't use all of the notes," Breslin pointed out. "I thought all had to be pressed?"

"That was just a guess," Sarah clarified. "There's nothing that says every one of them must be used."

It took several attempts, especially with Athos pressing his A notes in the wrong order, but they finally managed to tap out the correct spelling. As soon as they did, the stone slab of the door slowly lowered, like a castle's drawbridge. Through the door was the smallest room yet, and the only thing in the room was a stone dais. Even from a distance, they could see a flash of gold coming from within the darkened chamber.

Sarah pointed at Steve. "Would you do the honors?"

"Can't you do your…" He trailed off as he realized he was about to liken his wife's jhorun to a certain nose-wiggling television witch and thought better of it. "Er, umm, that is to say, can't you use your jhorun to make that thing come to us?"

Sarah nodded. "That's right. Let's do that. It's safer. But, just in case, everyone be on the alert. We don't know what'll happen when that gold object is moved."

"And I thought I've seen *Raiders of the Lost Ark* too many times," Steve chortled.

Sarah ignored his comment, held out a hand, and directed her jhorun to bring her the object. Almost immediately, the golden object flickered as it suddenly careened through the makeshift drawbridge and into Sarah's outstretched hand. Steve peered down at the object and frowned.

"This? This is what we're here for? That has got to be the gaudiest, ugliest looking trinket I have ever seen."

Chapter 5 — Trouble in Paradise

"A re we there yet, Cap'n?" Casimir's nasally voice asked. "When can we finally be rid of these accursed beasts? I swear, mine has tried to bite me three different times!"

"Quiet," Rusty ordered. "We're here when the captain says so. And your madger wouldn't try to bite you if you were nice to it."

"This ain't no madger," Casimir whined. "Madgers are nowhere near this ill-tempered. Or ugly."

"Close enough," Rusty snapped. "Do you think any of us are enjoying ourselves? Be silent, Casimir, or I'll have Jino throw you off your beast. Do you want to be left behind and fall into the Lentarians' clutches? No?"

Casimir's face darkened, and his brow furrowed. However, after the pirate noticed the look of loathing on Jino's face, Casimir wisely wiped the frown from his own. Satisfied that no more derisive comments were forthcoming, Rusty turned to look back at the captain, who was spurring his own animal to run even faster.

Rusty turned to eye the crew, all seven of them. He was still unsure how, exactly, a herd of these smelly beasts had appeared when they needed them most. Perhaps the captain had more tricks up his sleeves? Once Captain Flinn had returned from his reconnaissance mission to the Lentarian castle and announced that he had overheard where the temple was located, the crew had snuck back to the safety of the forest, only to find a herd of these *imitation* madgers waiting for them. Thinking that luck was still on their side, they had immediately departed, heading northwest.

Captain Flinn's mount stopped abruptly, almost causing Rusty's animal to rear end him.

"We be here, lads. Dismount."

"What about your mount?" Rusty inquired, puzzled.

"I said *dis-mount*, ye blatherin' imbecile. As in, get off yer animal. Find something to secure 'em with and… eh? What's that?"

"What was *what*, Captain?" Rusty wanted to know. "Who are you talking to?"

"Er, no one, Q. I be talkin' to myself. Let the beasts go. They've done their duty."

"You want us to let them go?" Casimir incredulously asked. "How are we expected to continue eluding the Lentarians? On foot?"

"Do as I say, mate," Captain Flinn growled.

The captain swung his leg over his mount and walked away. The animal turned tail and ran off in the opposite direction as fast as it could go, and the rest of them followed it.

Jino appeared at the captain's side and allowed his gaze to roam over the unkempt structure that was still partially hidden beneath several layers of vegetation. In fact, judging by the clumps of greenery lying nearby, someone had obviously peeled off the jungle's overgrowth, but who? Wouldn't that suggest they weren't the first?

"This? This is what we've been searching for? It doesn't look like much, if you ask me."

"I wasn't," Flinn idly remarked.

"Are we the first ones here?" Grenden hopefully asked.

"Did we beat the Lentarians?"

Before Jino could respond, Flinn stepped over to a large clump of vegetation and kicked it with his boot. He slowly scanned the clumps of dirt and bits of roots.

A scowl formed on Flinn's face. "Apparently not."

"How in the ruddy hell did they beat us here?" someone snapped.

Captain Flinn suspiciously stared at his men. Who had spoken? The voice sounded different, as though it hadn't been one of his crew.

"Who spoke?"

Fingers began pointing. Flinn growled. Disrespect was one thing the captain refused to tolerate. If a member of the crew lost respect for his captain, then that crew member became useless.

Rusty tapped Flinn on his shoulder and pointed east. There, situated at the base of the temple, the two men could see a dark, foreboding hole which angled steeply down.

"Captain, look! That looks like an entrance, does it not?"

"It does, aye."

"Then why aren't we headed inside?"

Flinn pointed at the hole. "How do we know them Lentarians aren't already down there? We should be discreet, lads. Jino!"

"I'm here, Captain," Jino said.

"Would ye do the honors, mate? Slip down there and see what's what, will ye?"

Jino pulled a dagger from his belt, slipped it between his teeth, and took several deep breaths. He nodded once to the captain, gave Rusty an inscrutable look, and disappeared into the hole. After a few moments, they could hear the pirate moving about.

"The coast is clear, Captain. I found a door, and it's sealed. It doesn't look like they've been here."

Flinn ordered several ropes to be tied off on nearby trees. Once his crew had all entered the temple, the captain let himself down using his jhorun's strong wind. Wiping bits of dirt and debris from his clothing, Flinn joined his men at the end of the tunnel.

"What do you make of this, Captain?" Rusty asked, as he idly traced a few of the carvings on the sealed door with his finger. "Do you think we need to … look out!"

Rusty jumped out of the way just as Flinn swung the special dwarf hammer at the door. Enormous chunks of rock and masonry went flying in all directions. Flinn swung again, and was rewarded with a loud series of cracks. The massive door trembled for a few moments as large, jagged cracks snaked their way across the surface, before finally collapsing in on itself. At the same time, however, a hidden panel above their heads slid open and the pirates gasped with alarm as monstrous boulders tumbled out.

"Gather round!" Flinn practically screamed. "Hurry, lads!"

The pirates sprinted toward the captain and leapt forward, knocking some heads together. Luckily, they made it before the first stones could make contact. The heavy stones bounced harmlessly away, as though the boulders were made of rubber. Once he was certain the falling rocks had come to a stop, Flinn pushed his way past his men. He looked up at the ceiling just in time to see the panel slide closed. Flinn pulled the oskorlisk fang from within his coat pocket, kissed it once, and slipped it back in.

"Wh- what was that all about, Captain?" Rusty hesitantly asked. "Why did those rocks fall on us?"

"Incentive," Flinn answered.

"Incentive for what?" Rusty wanted to know.

"To leave this place. I… now what's this?"

A strong breeze had picked up inside the temple and was swirling angrily around the chamber. As one, the pirates looked at their captain, who surprisingly, appeared just as confused as the rest of them. Flinn shook his head.

"I be not responsible for this, mates. I did just break through the door. Perhaps the wind be coming from somewhere within?"

Rusty promptly walked over to the large hole where the door formerly stood, licked a finger, and held it out. The rest of the crew fell silent as they watched. After a few moments, the quartermaster looked back at Flinn and shrugged.

"I feel air blowing out, aye, but I also feel air blowing in. I cannot explain it, Captain."

Flinn waved a dismissive hand. "Forget about it, lads. It be harmless. Let's go take a look, shall we?"

You are wasting my time. Head back to the surface.

Flinn hesitated and his eyes widened. He surreptitiously slipped a hand inside his jacket pocket and cupped the large sapphire nestled within.

Eh? Listen, mate. We didn't ride all this way just to leave now. We look and we plunder. It's who we be: pirates.

Flinn felt the stone grow warm in his hand.

You pig-headed idiot! You are wasting time! I told you…

Be silent, Flinn angrily thought at the stone. *We rode those blasted beasts for hours. Let the crew have their fun. We'll be checkin' out this Temple, so kindly be silent, or else I just might drop ye down the first bottomless hole I find, yes?*

Flinn felt the anger emanating from the jewel. Clearly, the stone wasn't pleased. Then again, neither was the captain. He had done everything it had asked, and what were the rewards?

"So, what do we have through here?" Flinn asked, as he poked his head through the broken door.

Jino appeared by his side and gazed into the darkness. The pirate looked over at Flinn, who nodded his permission. With a dagger clutched tightly in either hand, Jino slipped through the opening and disappeared.

"It's another tunnel, captain," Jino's voice called out. "It ends in another room, only this one is smaller. Much smaller."

Without waiting to see if his men were following, Flinn stepped through the hole and hurried toward Jino's voice. Upon reaching the end of the tunnel, Flinn drew up short. Jino's assessment had been correct. This chamber was much smaller. There were no carvings, no symbols, and—unfortunately—no door. The walls were made of some type of manufactured beige stone—an assumption made by Grenden, who observed all the stones were uniform in size and color—and the floor looked to be hard-packed earth.

There simply wasn't anything in the chamber of note, with the exception of a strange metallic life-sized statue of a man, holding his arms out in front of him.

"That thing gives me the creeps," a voice suddenly said from behind him. Flinn whirled around to see Puck glaring at the statue. "That be ugly as sin, Captain. Let me destroy it. I think I can push it over."

Flinn hooked a thumb back in the direction of the previous chamber.

"Ye saw what happened in there, did ye not? Rocks fell from the ceiling. That tells me this place be tryin' to kill us. Nay, ye must do and touch nothing without direct permission from me, agreed?"

Puck scowled, but didn't say anything. Flinn's hand dropped to rest on the hilt of his cutlass.

"Do ye think I said that for my own health? Agree to it, mate, or yer journey stops here."

Puck sighed. "Agreed, Cap'n. I won' touch nuthin'."

Flinn approached the wall opposite the tunnel and stared at the doorless surface. The other walls were as featureless as this one. Coincidence? Could he use his hammer to bash his way through again? If so, which wall should he try first?

Flinn hadn't taken two steps when the nagging winds from before appeared in this chamber, too. Bits of debris stung his skin. Surprised, and a little annoyed, Flinn turned to look back down the tunnel from which they came. What was the source of the wind?

Leave this foolishness be. Return to the surface. There is nothing for you here. Your adversaries have beaten you, and if you don't hurry, they will most certainly find the second temple before you.

I told ye, Flinn angrily thought at the stone, *we will not be leavin' here until we get what we came for.*

They have *what you came for*, the stone angrily insisted.

If ye want us to leave so badly, then help us figure this out. Where be the blasted door? How do we make it open?

Go stand near the statue. Then gather your followers close.

Flinn blinked with surprise and cast a speculative look at the statue.

Why? What will happen?

Just do it, you ignorant, idiotic, imbecilic, moronic...

Scowling irritably, Flinn walked over to the statue as the stone continued to spew insults. His crew watched. The wind swirled. Just as he stepped in front of the statue, the winds immediately died off, as though someone had flipped a switch.

Flinn glanced at the metallic figure and saw that the statue's arms were slowly lowering in place.

"What's it doin', Cap'n?" Puck nervously whispered.

"That can't be good," Rusty murmured, at the same time.

How did ye know that would happen? Flinn asked the stone.

You didn't listen to me before, so why should I answer you now?

The instant the statue's arms had lowered to its sides, they all heard a loud rumbling. The far wall, the one without a door, fell backward and crumpled apart, as though its supports had been yanked away. Huge flames rushed through the hole and straight toward them. The pirates closed the distance to Flinn in a flash. All but Jino. The *Emberbrand's* best fighter stifled a curse, and made it to Flinn's side one second before the flames struck.

The onslaught tapered off after ten seconds, leaving the far wall illuminated and red hot. Stunned, the band of pirates finally broke their huddle.

"I don't like this place," Casimir decided.

"I'll second that," Grenden added. "How I yearn to be back on the open sea."

"We'll be back there soon enough," Flinn promised. "Now do ye see why we stole the fang?"

"The fang protected us?" Rusty asked.

"Why do ye think them boulders bounced off of us earlier?" Flinn challenged. "For the same reason that fire be ineffective."

"It's too bad we're the first ones here," Flinn overheard Rusty say. "It would have been nice to have someone else set off all these ruddy traps and not us."

"I think they be here before us," Flinn said, raising his voice.

Oh? Now you believe me?

"What makes you say that, Captain?" Rusty asked.

"It's a hunch, lads."

Then head back to the surface, you dim-witted buffoon!

All in good time, mate. All in good time.

As one, the pirates peered through the opening. Flinn, not wasting any time, immediately stepped through the doorway and headed off. His crew reluctantly followed.

"Do we have any idea what we're doing?" Flinn heard one crew member ask another.

"No," another gruffly responded. "Then again, I ain't paid to think. The captain is."

Flinn nodded, pleased. Grenden just earned himself a few extra pieces of gold.

Your insistence on focusing on the inane continues to astound me.

Flinn automatically scowled. *What was that?*

You're wasting time, and you want to reward one of your men for giving you a compliment?

I reward loyalty in my crew. Nothing be more valuable than that.

Nothing except, perhaps, unlimited piles of gold? Jewels so big that it takes two people to carry them?

Is that what's waiting for us at the end of this blasted temple?

The stone grew warm again. He stifled a chuckle. It was getting far too easy to rile it up.

There is nothing waiting for you at the completion of this temple. The obstacles have all been overcome. You. Are. Wasting. Time.

Flinn turned to check that his crew was following, which they were.

"Double-time it, lads. I think we be getting close to the end of this accursed place."

Now you speed up?

Ignoring the sarcasm emanating from the stone, Flinn hurried forward, intent on reaching the next obstacle. The tunnel dead-ended a few minutes later, bringing him to an immediate stop. He was in a chamber much like the first, with strange symbols and markings everywhere, including the ceiling.

"Captain!"

Rusty hurried toward him. "The wall became whole again! As soon as the last man stepped through, the stones jumped back into the wall and sealed itself up. I think we're trapped down here."

No, you're not, the stone contradicted.

"No, we be safe," the captain assured his quartermaster. "Fear not."

I'm telling you, there's nothing for you here.
If ye want me to hurry, tell me how to open this blasted door.
Use the hammer.
Be there not an easier way?
Not unless you have an ear for music. Use the blasted hammer.

Five minutes later, Flinn stepped over the rubble of the smashed door and inspected the inside of the tiny chamber. There, in the middle of the small room, a stone dais stood empty.

* * *

You wasted my time, Flinn accused.

I wasted your time? the ethereal voice hissed back. *I told you it was now useless.*

So, the Lentarians beat us here. They must now know where to go next, am I right?

The Lentarians have returned to their castle. They have not yet discovered the location of the next temple.

Flinn recalled the stone telling him there were three temples. *Where be the next?*

On the coast.

Pleased, Flinn nodded. *Excellent. This will give us time to…*

On the opposite *coast,* the stone interrupted.

What? We have to go to the west coast? Blast. Ye best have something faster than those nasty beasts for us to ride. How do ye expect us to make it to the western coast first when they can cover that distance in the blink o' an eye?

You leave the Teleporter to me. You only need to follow my instructions without argument, is that clear?

Perhaps ye ought to be more forthcoming with yer information, mate.

I warned you a long time ago, the stone insisted.

Ye warned me when we arrived at these blasted ruins. Why didn't ye warn us sooner?

The stone fell silent.

Ye didn't know, did ye?

Do you want to spend the rest of your days in a dungeon?

What? Of course not. Why?

Should the Lentarians claim the second Alchos Stone as their own, that is precisely what will happen to you and your crew. Never again will you see your beloved Emberbrand. Never again will you ever sail the seas. The infamous Captain Flinn will disappear from the history books, forever lost in a foreign dungeon. Is that what you want?

Captain Flinn scowled and shook his head.

Return Topside. We must be off. And this time, we must make haste. The Lentarians have already started deciphering the prize.

What was the prize? Can ye tell me?

A gold idol.

"Blast. Sounds like it'd fetch a princely sum. Very well. We head Topside. Ye had better be ready."

I already am. Once again, I'm waiting on you.

Flinn snatched up the jewel, wrapped several layers of fabric securely around it, and stowed it back inside his pocket. He grabbed his hat, which he had placed next to him, and hurried back to his crew.

"On yer feet, ye disgraceful excuse for a crew. We return Topside. Make haste!"

"I'd still like to know how the Lentarians beat us here," Jino grumbled.

"That makes two of us," Flinn quietly added, under his breath.

Brandishing his pilfered dwarf hammer, Flinn eagerly strode back the way they had come, pausing only long enough to clear any obstacles that appeared in their path.

After the last crewman had shimmied up the rope at the Temple entrance, Flinn used his jhorun to lift himself up through the hole. Outside, he breathed a sigh of relief. He had never been fond of going underground, not even when they had to steal the hammer. However, before he could return the hammer to the loop on his belt, his gaze fell upon what was waiting for them less than twenty feet away.

"What are they, Cap'n?" Alquin quietly asked. "Why are they there?"

Flinn scowled. "They be griffins, mate. Half lion, half eagle."

"What are they doing here?" Grenden whispered.

Flinn groaned as he realized that the stone expected them ride these creatures all the way to the western coast!

"Oh, *hell* no."

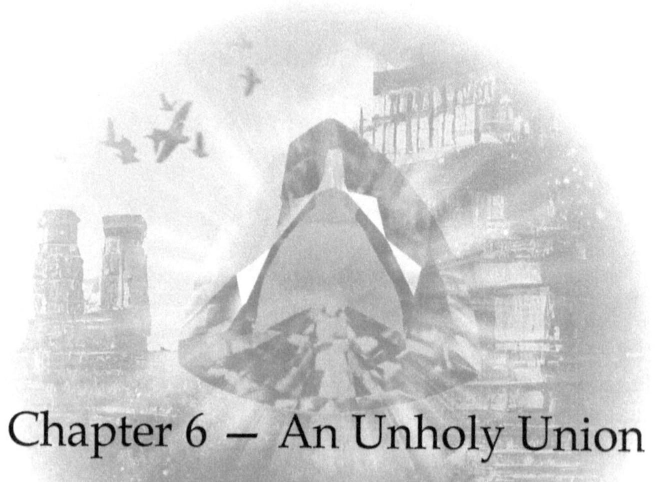

Chapter 6 — An Unholy Union

I have to admit, I'm really getting tired of this library. No, don't look at me like that. I know you're not fond of this place, either. And from the look on Gareth's face, he would concur."

Sarah playfully swatted his arm. "Stop your complaining. Even you will have to admit that Ms. Alwyn is getting better."

Steve gazed impassively at the stacks and stacks of books before them. He tilted his head to look up at the second floor, which housed even more meaningless tomes and stacks of papers. He sighed and gave Sarah a *what-can-you-do* shrug.

"Back again, I see," a curt voice said from behind.

All seven of their group, including Deez, whirled around to see Miss Andra Alwyn regarding them from behind her precariously perched spectacles. She absentmindedly pushed them up the bridge of her nose and waited, expectantly. Sarah was the first to offer the records keeper a smile.

"Hello, Miss Alwyn. Yes, we're back, and believe it or not, you're just the person we wanted to see. We could really use your help again."

Andra harrumphed, but promptly pulled out a chair and sat at the closest table, which prompted the rest of the group to do the same. Deez was content to go into his rock mode and watch quietly. Sarah encouraged Steve to extend his hand.

"You hold it. The darn thing is too heavy, if you ask me."

Steve shrugged again and held out his right hand, palm facing up. A few moments later, a short, chubby golden idol appeared. It was sitting, cross-legged, and was wearing nothing but a loin cloth made of a plethora of tiny sparkling gemstones.

Steve plunked the heavy statue down on the table and started to push it toward Andra, only to halt when it made gouges on the surface. Steve groaned, sighed, and offered the archivist a smile.

"Sorry about that."

"What's this?" Andra asked, ignoring the damaged table. The tiny woman only had eyes for the golden piece.

"We were hoping you could tell us," Sarah answered. "We found it in the first temple, and supposedly, this will tell us where to find the second."

A look of surprise washed over the octogenarian's face. "So, you found the temple after all, did you?"

The entire group nodded.

The surprise on Andra's face turned to wonder. "What was it like?" she softly asked.

Sarah tapped the statue on the table. "I'll make a deal with you. Help us identify this and I will personally give you a tour of the first temple."

Andra's mouth closed with an audible snap. Intrigued, she reached out a bony hand and pulled the piece closer.

"Well, this appears to be solid gold. And these jewels? I'd say they are diamonds. The style, I'm sorry to say, is not one I am familiar with." The Archivist pushed away from the table and slowly stood. "Let me fetch a few reference books. I'll be right back."

Once the cantankerous old woman was gone, Steve leaned forward to rest his elbows on the table. "Wow, you sure have a way of getting her to cooperate. That was a smart move, inviting her to take a tour of the temple. She seemed to take the bait."

Sarah swept an arm around the Archives, indicating the many stacks and columns of books. "Well, what did you think was going to happen? That woman loves knowledge. We have the chance to show her a few new things. Getting her to cooperate was the easy part."

"You make it sound like there's a hard part," Steve said.

Sarah nodded. "There is. Did you see her face when she saw the idol? She had no idea what it is, or who made it. I think she was seeing that statue for the first time."

"That's because I was," Andra coolly informed them, as she returned to the table with—surprisingly—only two books.

Steve eyed the two paperback-sized books and raised an eyebrow. Andra, catching Steve's look, sighed.

"I don't know what this piece is, or who it's supposed to depict. Since I don't, identifying it will be a problem. I've selected two books, which delve into Lentari's brief, but illustrious, history of art, but I'm almost certain neither will be of help to us. I think I should start by… hmm. You, Fire Thrower. You take this one and your wife can take the other. I'll deal with this."

"You'll deal with *what?*" Steve asked, confused.

The Archivist pushed away from the table and hurried over to a large crowd of people, which was steadily growing larger.

"There's nothing to see here," Andra began. "There will be no disruptions in here, so please disperse. Thank you."

"It's nice to not be on the receiving end of that," Steve quietly commented, which drew a snort from Gareth.

Sarah smiled and took his hand. "I keep telling you, if you want her to respect you, then you have to give her respect, too."

"You found her as annoying as I did," Steve reminded her, waggling a finger. "Remember?"

"That was before Lissa showed me how to get through to her," Sarah said. "A little kindness goes a long way. I'm glad we didn't have to ask Mikal and Lissa to intervene. I didn't even know we were drawing a crowd."

"You two always seem to draw a crowd," Andra mildly informed her, as she returned to her seat. "Now, let's see if we can figure out where this came from."

"Are we interrupting?" a new voice suddenly asked.

Husband and wife looked up to see the pro tem king and his lovely wife standing before them. They were holding hands and smiling down at them.

"Is there anything we can do to help?" Lissa inquired.

Andra was already shaking her head. "Not unless you can identify who made this ghastly statue."

Lissa frowned as she caught sight of the idol. She looked over at Mikal, who shrugged helplessly. After scrutinizing the bizarre golden idol for a few moments, Lissa sadly shook her head.

"I've never seen the like before, I'm afraid."

"I don't think anyone has," Andra added. A scowl formed on her face. "I don't like acknowledging there's something I don't know. This? This garish hunk of gold? I'm not sure it's even Lentarian."

Sarah eyed the two books on the table and then looked over at Andra.

"Are those the only two books you have on Lentarian art styles?"

For the first time ever, both Steve and Sarah noticed a flush of color wash over the cantankerous records keeper's face. Sharing a quick look with his wife, Steve looked back at Andra and offered what he hoped was a plausible smile.

"I think I discovered something I have in common with you, Miss Alwyn."

A thin smile formed on Andra's face.

"And what's that?"

"I'm willing to wager you like art about as much as I do."

Andra's demeanor cracked and she offered him a sheepish smile. "Aye. I am ashamed to admit this, but the Archives has a severe lack of anything that deals with this particular subject."

Sarah was nodding. "When it comes to handcrafted items, we thought of the dwarves. We already had Breslin and Athos examine it, and they are confident no dwarf made it, mainly because of the gemstones and the way they are mounted. Breslin estimates it is no more than one-hundred-fifty years old."

Breslin nodded in agreement with what Sarah had told the library archivist.

"Is there anyone else who might know?" Emily asked.

Steve looked over at Sarah, who shrugged. "I don't know of any others, sorry."

Indeed? Not even one?

Steve groaned aloud, drawing concerned looks from the rest of his companions. He held up a finger, signaling they should wait. Then he saw Sarah staring at him. The same finger then tapped the side of his head. A look of comprehension appeared and Sarah eagerly nodded.

I'm sorry, my friend. I didn't even think about asking you.

Your transgression is forgiven. Now, would you please look at this mysterious idol? Surely, we wyverians will recognize this piece of treasure when all others have not.

Steve strode purposefully over to the table, leaned over, and stared at the idol. When Pryllan failed to speak after a few minutes had passed, Steve tapped the side of his head again.

Hey! Still with me? Pryllan, you've gone silent. Are you consulting the others?

I am.

Good. What's the word? What is it? Do you know who made it?

Your answers, in the order the questions were given, are… waiting, unknown, and no.

Didn't you just say that the dragons would undoubtedly be able to identify it?

I did, aye. Perhaps I was a bit too brash when…

If you're pausing for dramatic effect, I should tell you that you chose a bad place to do it. What you should have done is…

Steve? A moment, if you please. Kahvel has additional information. I… I'm sorry. I must break the connection. I will be right back.

No problem. We're not going anywhere. At least, not yet.

"Was she able to help?" Sarah asked, as soon as he looked up.

"Not yet, I'm afraid. But, she just cut contact. Kahvel was telling her something, and I can only hope it was relevant to what we're doing."

"Kahvel?" Andra repeated, surprised. "As in, Kahvel the Dragon Lord?"

Steve nodded. "That's the one."

"You were speaking with the Dragon Lord?" Andra incredulously asked.

Steve shook his head. "No, not Kahvel, but his mate, Pryllan. She's a loyal, trusted friend. Well, both of them are."

"Amazing," Andra breathed. "I had heard this rumor, but I did not believe it."

Steve waved a dismissive hand. "We've known him for a number of years now. And, we can even say we were friends with the previous Dragon Lord, Rinbok Intherer, although he didn't tolerate nearly as much as Kahvel does."

Somewhere in the distance, they heard a door clang noisily open.

"Where's my Lovey Bear?"

The nine people crowded around the table—and one guur—slowly turned to the sounds of approaching footsteps.

"There you are, my one true love! I've been searching high and low for you!"

Castle R'Tal's resident wizard, Shardwyn, appeared resplendent in bright yellow robes. He was tall, skinny as a rail, and had thin gray hair. Belying his frail appearance, Shardwyn was holding a bouquet of flowers so large that he could barely see where he was going. The wizard crashed into Andra's desk, bumped half a dozen people with the large vase, and collided with a table, which scraped the floor with a sound like fingernails on a chalkboard.

Miss Andra Alwyn, Sourpuss Extraordinaire, actually blushed like a school girl. The elderly records keeper smiled and hastily pushed her spectacles up the bridge of her nose and held out a hand, as though she was royalty.

Shardwyn didn't miss a beat. He firmly took Andra's hand, brought it to his lips, and placed a delicate kiss on her wrinkled fingers. Then, without waiting for permission, Shardwyn set down the giant vase, threw his arms around her, tipped her backward, and planted a kiss directly on her mouth.

"I told you before, not when I'm working," Andra scolded.

Shardwyn shrugged. "I couldn't help it. You make me feel like a boy again. I… oh! Hello, Sir Steve! Lady Sarah! I see you have some new acquaintances."

"This is Doc … er, this is Emily Benz. She's from my world."

"Am I supposed to curtsy?" Emily whispered to Sarah.

"No," Sarah said. "That isn't necessary."

Shardwyn kissed Emily's outstretched hand, which elicited a frown from Andra.

"Delighted to make your acquaintance, my dear."

Emily offered the wizard her best smile. "Thank you. I'm very much enjoying your beautiful country."

Eager to introduce the final member of their party, Steve tapped Shardwyn on the shoulder, side-stepped to the left and rested his right hand on Deez's head.

"And this sprightly fellow is Deez. He's been an invaluable companion to us. Deez, this is Shardwyn."

ANCIENT HUMAN IS MATE TO MANIACAL FEMALE?

Steve snorted with laughter, but managed to disguise it as a cough.

"The two of them are, umm, well, I guess they could be considered a couple. I mean … hoo boy."

"It's a guur!" Shardwyn delightedly exclaimed. "I never thought I'd encounter a live specimen. Can you hear me, dear creature? Can you understand me?"

Deez's armored head turned until it was staring at Gareth.

DOES ANCIENT HUMAN OFFER INSULT?

Gareth was shaking his head. "No, Deez. He's fine. He's a friend."

Deez returned his attention to Shardwyn and warily eyed

the wizard. Steve patted the guur on the head a few times, calming the creature.

"It's okay, Deez. I've got your back. You're safe here."

Puzzled, Shardwyn eyed the two of them. "Safe from what, dear boy? There's nothing to fear here."

Sensing an opportunity to change the subject, Sarah tapped her fingers on the golden idol, drawing Shardwyn's attention.

"Do you think you might be able to help us out? We're trying to learn more about this object. What it is, who it's supposed to depict, and who made it. Can you shed any light on the subject?"

"This is why I called you," Andra quietly whispered, once the wizard was seated at the table. "I must confess that I am unable to discover anything about it."

Shardwyn merrily chuckled. "Ah, woman. I will make an art lover out of you yet. Don't you recognize a wonderful piece when you see it?"

As one, everyone looked down at the gold idol sitting on the table.

"There's nothing pretty about that thing," Steve argued.

"Have you seen anything like this before?" Sarah asked.

Shardwyn stared at the idol for a few moments before he slid it across the table for a closer look. Now, with three matching sets of gouges on the wood table, wizard and archivist began chatting amongst themselves, oblivious to everyone else.

Shardwyn was tapping a section of the bejeweled clothing. "Do you see this, my dear? There's a gemstone missing. If I'm not mistaken, that was indicative of the Jawu Reckoning."

"If you don't know," Andra was saying, "then it's perfectly acceptable to say so. You know just as well as I do that there is no such thing. Really. The Jawu Reckoning?"

Shardwyn nodded so vigorously that he almost dislodged his tall, conical hat.

"You're very much mistaken, my dear. It's okay if you don't remember, seeing how you've admitted your knowledge of art is subpar."

Andra's eyes widened with surprise, then narrowed to slits.

"You're saying my knowledge is 'subpar'?"

Steve recognized the warning signs of an irritated female, and knocked his knuckles on the counter.

"Guys? Er, and gals? Perhaps we can table your art discussion for another time. Is it safe to say that neither of you can figure this one out?"

Andra took a deep breath and sighed. "I am unable to help you. I cannot identify your idol."

The argumentative archivist etched herself a few notches higher in Steve's eyes.

"Shardwyn? How about you? Don't make anything up. If you don't know what it is, just say so, all right?"

Fully aware that all sets of eyes were upon him, Shardwyn also sighed. "I am sorry, Sir Steve. I thought I recognized the style, but upon closer examination, I must concur with my Lovey, er, Miss Alwyn here. I simply do not know what to make of it."

The scratching of quills could be heard. Husband and wife turned to see both Athos and Breslin furiously scribbling on twin pieces of parchment. In fact, if Steve didn't know any better, he'd say their two dwarf companions were in a race to see who could complete their message first.

It was Athos. The Kla Chanu dwarf hastily folded his parchment into a tiny square and thrust it at Sarah.

"Lady Sarah, would you please send this message to my nephew, Lukas, who happens to be in Borahgg? He's likely in the Council Chambers, with Master Maelnar. So, if you…"

"Oh, no you don't," Breslin scolded, as he batted Athos' hand out of the way and presented his own wadded-up message. "You will give my message to my father, and none other. If any clan will be able to identify this trinket, then it'll be the Kla Guur."

Breslin's message was placed in front of Sarah, who regarded Breslin with a neutral look. The dwarf immediately began to backpedal.

"Where are my manners? My most profound apologies, Lady Sarah. If it pleases you, I would have you deliver that message to the Council in Foronlir. I believe *that* is where you'll find my father."

Sarah held out a hand and waited for Athos to give her his message. It vanished in her hand. Then she glanced down at Breslin's message, which disappeared a split second later. Sarah then returned her attention to Breslin.

"Athos asked first. Politely, I might add. But, you suggested an alternate location. So, I figured I'd cover all the bases and send both. No one likes being ordered around."

Breslin bowed low. "Once again, my apologies."

Steve nudged the dwarf in his ribs. "Been there, done that, amigo."

The dwarves will be unable to assist.

Pryllan? There you are. I was beginning to wonder what happened to you.

There have been some interesting developments. We are sending Pravara to you.

What? Why? Is there a problem?

Kahvel insists that you will need wyverian assistance.

Steve relayed the message to the group.

"Who is Pravara?" Emily hesitantly asked. "Is this another dragon?"

Steve quickly explained the dragon relationships, wondering, in the back of his mind if they should be concerned about the impending visit.

He turned to Sarah, but she merely shrugged. "Until we know more, we shouldn't worry. Would you care to go for a walk? It's nice outside and I think I'd like some fresh air."

It seemed everyone else was on board with that idea, except Athos and Breslin, who couldn't stop bickering about who of their clans would come up with the answer about the golden idol first.

Leaving the two dwarves to their argument, the rest of the group quietly left the main floor of the Archives and headed outside. Andra stopped at her desk and started rifling through the papers that were there. Shardwyn, acting like a love-struck teenager, remained by her side.

"Was anyone else grossed out by that?" Steve asked, once they were out of earshot.

Gareth raised a hand. "I sure was. They were acting like, like, well, like they were kids! Adults shouldn't behave like that. It's not right!"

Emily giggled and shook her head. "I thought it was rather sweet. To see two old people find love at that age is a remarkable thing to witness."

"I agree," Lissa added.

"I do not," Mikal grumbled. "I'm with Steve. Maybe I've known those two for too long?"

Outside, the sky was a brilliant shade of azure blue, with small fluffy white clouds visible as far as the eye could see. The sun had just reached the apex of its daily journey across the sky, and many of the street vendors were hurriedly setting up shop in anticipation of a thriving lunch crowd.

"It sure smells good out here," Emily decided. She breathed deeply and slowly exhaled. She suddenly turned to Sarah and threw her arms around her in a hug.

Surprised, it took Sarah a few moments to return the hug. "What was that for?"

"For bringing me here," the paleontologist answered. "In my wildest dreams, I never would have imagined such a place existed. I never want to leave."

"You'll be tired of it soon enough," Steve promised. "You can only handle so many dragons, or griffins, or creeg, before you start pining for your mundane existence back home."

"Please," Emily scoffed. "This place is so much better than our world, and you know it."

"Well, of course I do," Steve returned, with mock exasperation. "Who wouldn't love to have a magical ability? Who wouldn't want to live where dragons roam? Who wouldn't want to call a flock of griffins their friends?"

Emily paused for a few moments as she studied both husband and wife.

Sarah hooked her arm through their new friend's and led her toward the open drawbridge.

"Trust me, once all this is over with, we'll give you the grand tour of the place."

"But, won't I be forced to go back home?" Emily asked, confused. "I mean, I don't live here. I'm not even supposed to be here."

Mikal approached and smiled at the short, blonde woman.

"I'll hereby grant you permission to visit whenever you'd like. In fact, based on how much you've helped Steve and Sarah, I'd be willing to wager my parents will offer you permanent citizenship, if you so desire."

"Oh, don't tempt me," Emily moaned.

Steve paused at the edge of the drawbridge and looked down into the murky depths of the moat. His hands ignited as several ripples formed on the surface of the water. Sarah and Emily edged away from the water.

"What is it?" Emily whispered. "Don't tell me there's a monster in there."

"There is," Mikal confirmed. "Bredo. He's a large sea serpent."

"Friendly?" the paleontologist hopefully asked.

"Hardly," Steve scoffed.

Thankfully, moat guardian slithered away, undoubtedly searching for some hapless prey who might have wandered into his domain. Steve extinguished his hands and turned to find Gareth standing beside him. Deez had wandered over to the edge of the water and looked as though he was ready to extend a leg down to the surface. "Deez? Come away from there. Umm, there's danger in the water."

THE HIVE WILL PROTECT ME.

Surprised, Steve shared a look with the young wizard and then hurried over to Deez's side. He politely tapped the top of the guur's head.

"Hey, consider this your hive stepping in to protect you. Don't mess with the water."

COMPLIANCE.

"Do you think Usol knows the location of the second temple?" Gareth quietly asked.

Steve shrugged. "I'm really not sure. I hope not."

"What if he knows and has already told those pirates where to find it?"

"Then we had best step up our efforts in figuring out

what to do with that idol," Steve said.

A brisk wind appeared from the north. It rustled noisily through the nearby trees, picking up leaves and pine needles. Steve and Gareth watched with amusement as the wind created a veritable mini-dust storm in the sky.

"That one looks like a dragon," Gareth decided, pointing at the cloud. "Now it looks just like Shardwyn. Look, do you see the tall pointed hat?"

Steve stared, amused and then alarmed, as the cloud's gyrations created a very recognizable shape. It was a Y, followed immediately by an E, and then an S. He turned to the others.

"There? Do you see that?" Steve pointed up at the sky. "Gareth had asked me if Usol knows where the second temple is located. Then the breeze appeared and spelled out 'yes'. Sarah, that *has* to be Eion's doing!"

The letters disappeared and then the cloud began spelling out another word.

O...B...V...I...O...U...S...L...Y.

Sarah was frowning. She pointed up at the sky. "This is not good. Eion confirmed Usol knows where the second temple can be found. That must mean the pirates are already on their way. Our only hope now is to find out where we have to go and teleport there before they arrive."

"But we don't know where to go!" Steve protested. "No one knows what clue the idol is supposed to give us. Eion, come on, man. Help us out. What are we supposed to do?"

The cloud swirled again. More letters started appearing.

G...A...R...E...T...H.

Steve, Sarah, Emily, Mikal, and Lissa turned incredulously to the teenage wizard. Even Deez turned his head to stare at his human friend. Gareth, for his part, was slowly backing away. He helplessly raised his hands.

"Hey, don't look at me. I've never seen that thing before. I don't care what he says. It's not me."

"But Eion spelled out your name!" Sarah reminded him. "Clearly that must mean something. Think, Gareth. You obviously know the answer."

"But I don't!" Gareth insisted.

At once, a look of comprehension appeared on Steve's face. A grin slowly appeared. He looked up at the cloud, gave it a thumbs up, and turned excitedly to his wife. At the same time, the wind disappeared without a trace. All the swirling leaves and bits of debris fluttered to the ground.

"What is it?" Sarah asked. "What have you figured out?"

Steve simply pointed at Gareth and grinned victoriously. "I think Eion means the *other* Gareth."

Chapter 7 — Shealk Surprise

"My father?" Gareth repeated, confused. "What about my father? You think he knows something about that idol? That couldn't possibly be right."

"Didn't Gareth senior, I mean Balthor, tell us that he was hundreds of years old?" Mikal asked. "Back when you transformed us all to shealk and met him for the first time, he said that he was going on nine hundred years old. Do you remember that?"

Gareth was slowly nodding. "Come to think of it, I *do* remember something about that. Maybe he can help us. Hang on, I'll ask him."

The acolyte wizard leaned over the edge of the drawbridge, looked down at his reflection in the water, and cleared his throat.

"Father."

The surface of the water immediately shimmered. Gareth's reflection was replaced by that of a vision that would have typically inspired terror in just about anyone. As it was, everyone knew that Gareth's father, Balthor, was a water dragon, otherwise known as a shealk. Everyone except for Emily, that is.

"Omigod! What's that?"

Sarah leaned over and smiled at the image. What she was looking at was a long, serpentine form which had tiny vestigial legs, no wings, and somewhat curved horns that angled straight out from its skull. The water dragon was several shades of blue, with the top half of his body a deep dark blue, which gradually brightened as it approached the lower half. The image of the shealk blinked a few times before shimmering again. This time, a middle-aged human male was staring back at them. His hair was graying at the temples, he had intense, piercing blue eyes, and his nose was slightly crooked, suggesting he might have broken it at some time. Those blue eyes softened once they focused on Gareth.

"Son. Are you well?"

"I am, aye. I'm sorry to contact you like this, Father, but I was hoping you'd be able to help me out. Well, help *us* out, actually."

"What is the nature of your emergency?" Balthor sternly inquired.

Steve stepped forward and clapped a friendly hand on Gareth's back. He leaned over to look in the water. The shealk wizard's eyes flicked over to his.

"Hey there, Balthor. We're in a bit of a pickle. We need to find a second Temple of Alchos and haven't the foggiest idea where to look."

"Greetings, Fire Thrower. I know not of any such place."

Steve shrugged. "Fair enough. But, do you know anything about gold idols?"

Balthor's reflection cocked his head and he blinked a few times.

"A gold idol? I am afraid not. Why would you think that?"

"Because Eion mentioned your name when dropping hints about what we should do next," Steve answered, with a smile.

As predicted, that got the shealk's attention.

"Eion mentioned me? By name?"

Gareth held up a hand. "Yes, we're fairly certain. Could you join us here? I'd like you to take a look at this item."

"Is this important to you?" Balthor asked, as his intense eyes locked onto his son's once more.

Gareth nodded. "Incredibly so. We have to beat the pirates there, and if we don't hurry up, we run the risk of them showing up first."

"Very well."

A series of bubbles suddenly broke the surface of the moat, growing in intensity until towering watery spheres rose off the surface of the water. One such bubble, larger than the others, remained intact as it floated up toward the drawbridge, growing in size as it did. Once it touched down on the ground, it popped, and there was Balthor, standing straight as a board and appearing uninterested in the magical means in which he had appeared.

"Son. It is agreeable to see you again."

"Hi, Dad. Umm, do you know everyone here?"

Balthor's head turned as he studied those who were present. Before he could say anything, though, a large serpentine head rose out from the depths of the moat and hissed angrily at the newcomer. Gareth's father raised an eyebrow and turned to see that Bredo the sea serpent was preparing to strike.

"Unwise, my friend," Balthor coolly stated.

Bredo lunged forward, his jaws opening wide. But, before he could make contact, the large snake's mouth snapped closed. Then, before anyone could say anything, the monstrous serpent was flung out of the water. Bredo's coils flopped helplessly in the air as the large snake tried valiantly to return to the safety of the moat.

Balthor didn't say a word as he coldly stared at the distant cousin of the oskorlisk. After a few minutes of thrashing about, Bredo became perfectly still. The giant serpent's head finally lowered and remained there.

"That's better," Balthor whispered. "You will do well to mind your manners."

The shealk wizard snapped his humanoid form's fingers, and Bredo splashed back into the moat. In the blink of an eye, the large serpent disappeared from sight, leaving a trail of bubbles as the only evidence he had ever been there.

Steve whistled. "Wow. That's impressive. I've had to back him down a few times with my fire, but I like your way better."

"Tell me more about this idol," Balthor instructed. "Where was it found? Who made it?"

"We found it in the first Temple of the Alchos," Sarah answered as they began walking back into the castle. "As for who made it, well, we were hoping you'd be able to tell us."

Inside the Archives, Balthor approached the table, looked down at the idol, and smiled, which wasn't lost on the group. Steve shared a quick smile with Sarah, before turning to Gareth and giving him a thumbs up.

"Epan," Balthor whispered. "I had a feeling it was you."

"Epan?" Steve repeated. "Is that a person?"

"Epan Terius was an artist," Balthor explained. "He favored the use of gold in all his creations, and since he was friends with the Kla Orikum, he had a steady supply of jewels. He used them for everything. Do you see here? These diamonds are supposed to be clothes."

"Yeah, we noticed," Steve confirmed.

"It's rather hideous, isn't it?" Balthor chortled. "I've never been fond of his work. I can only assume it's an acquired taste."

Steve nudged his wife. "See? Glad I'm not the only one."

"Hush," Sarah scolded.

Mikal and Lissa visibly relaxed as Gareth's father stared at the strange idol.

"Epan Terius, is it? I do not believe I'm familiar with his name."

"You wouldn't be, young Mikal. Er, my apologies. Your Majesty."

Mikal waved a dismissive hand. "It's all right, Balthor. You can call me Mikal, if you'd like. Now, let me ask you something. *Why* wouldn't I know this artist? Was he that obscure?"

Balthor shook his head. "He died nearly two hundred years ago."

"And you're certain about this?" Sarah solemnly asked.

"Of course. He was a friend of mine."

"Are you really over eight hundred years old?" Steve incredulously asked.

"I am. And you?"

"Nowhere close," Steve laughed.

"But getting up there," Sarah added, eliciting a giggle from Emily.

Steve grinned at his wife. "Snot. Balthor, ignore her. She's only hungry. She gets a little… whoa! I'm sorry! I'll behave! Put me down, woman!"

Steve had suddenly found himself outdoors again, floating in the air and tipped upside down, with only a few feet of empty space between his head and the surface of the moat.

"Next time you're going swimming, Paco."

Steve mimed zipping his lips closed.

"Ignore my husband," Sarah was saying, as she turned to Balthor and dumped her husband back inside the Archive room. "Please continue. What can you tell us about this artist?"

"Epan lived a life of solitude," Balthor explained. "He was quiet, had few friends, and enjoyed being outside. In fact, it was on one of his walks along the coast that I originally encountered him. I was in human form, of course."

"He never suspected you were a water dragon?" Mikal asked.

Balthor shook his head. "No. If he did, he never let on."

"So, you knew him," Steve said. "Okay, what was he like? What were his interests?"

"He was quiet and intelligent. Very creative. He was very gifted at sketching. I remember seeing him pick up a piece of charcoal to sketch portraits of the royal family, which he did in less than an hour. That was what he was known for, his gift of illustration."

Steve looked down at the idol. "And yet he tried his hand at making ugly little golden statues. Why?"

"I never really understood his fascination for jewels as clothing. I've seen a few other pieces of his that were similar. One was a horse, with a bejeweled saddle, and another was a kyte, with sapphire encrusted wings."

"I'll bet those are better looking than this thing," Steve decided.

Balthor shook his head. "You would think, but no. Now, what else would you like to know?"

"Where did he live?" Sarah asked.

"Capily, on the far western shore," Balthor answered.

Sarah turned excitedly to Steve. "That must be where the second temple is! In Capily! I can get us there in no time flat!"

"You won't find anything about Epan Terius in Capily," Balthor hastily informed them.

"Sure we will," Steve countered. "I've seen the constable's office. Fensham has tons of records there, and that which doesn't fit in the office is sent here, to be stored in the Archives. There's gotta be something there about this artist."

Balthor was nodding. "Perhaps I should have rephrased the answer. You won't find anything about Epan in *that* Capily."

Confused, Steve looked to Sarah for an explanation, but his wife was as surprised as he was. In *that* Capily?

"I can see from your eyes that you know the answer to my riddle, records keeper," Balthor announced, as he looked over at Andra. He offered her a smile. "I think it would be better if the explanation came from your mouth and not mine."

Andra pulled her hand free from Shardwyn's and nervously cleared her throat. "Very well. What our visitor suggests is true. There was once another Capily."

Mikal leaned forward in his chair, surprised. "How is it that I know nothing of this?"

Lissa smiled. "Because, as I'm sure you're aware, my love, your studies weren't something that you gave your full attention. I could answer Balthor's riddle, but I won't. Miss Alwyn, would you please continue?"

Andra nodded. "Of course, Kre'Lissa. The seaside village of Capily wasn't always located where it is today."

"Then, where was it?" Gareth asked.

Andra opened her mouth, but promptly closed it. She looked around her immaculate collection of material before her eyes settled on Steve. "Perhaps I could explain this better if I had a map. Fire Thrower. Do you see the wall directly behind you? The other side has our collection of maps. You'll find a long brown tube rolled up on the bottom shelf, all by itself. Would you fetch it for me?"

Steve turned to study the wall in question. Then he noticed Deez had reverted to his 'rock' form and was patiently waiting for them at the base of the same wall. Steve stomped on the floor a few times in order to get the guur's attention. Deez's head lifted from his body and he turned to look at Steve.

He repeated Andra's instructions.

COMPLIANCE.

The guur's ten legs neatly unfolded themselves from around his body, like a hermit crab emerging from its shell, and he rose to his full height. Steve could hear a soft chittering as Deez disappeared around the wall. A few moments later, he was back, and clutching the brown tube in his left front foreleg. Steve pointed at Andra.

"Would you give it to her? She's the one who needs it."

"Why did you do that?" Andra demanded. "That humongous bug frightens me. I don't want him anywhere near me."

"Deez is a member of our group," Steve calmly told the archivist. "He…"

"Hive," Sarah corrected.

"Right. We're his Hive. Deez enjoys helping. Look, he's holding the map out to you. I know he's a guur, and typically he's the stuff of nightmares, but not this one. He's harmless. Just take it and show us where the first Capily used to be, okay?"

Andra tapped the dot signifying Capily's present location.

"After the catastrophe," Andra began, "the survivors…"

"Hold up," Steve interrupted. "Catastrophe? Survivors? Am I the only one here who doesn't know anything about that?"

Lissa was the only one who admitted she'd paid attention in history classes.

Andra's face was threatening to break into a smile. She

composed herself and began speaking.

"Very well. It would appear I need to start a few hundred years ago. Now, as you can all see, Capily is currently situated here, almost directly in line with Donlari. However, it wasn't always there. Several hundred years ago, the village was here, on the southwestern tip of the kingdom."

"Near this river?" Sarah asked, as she traced the path the river took through the countryside.

Andra nodded. "Aye. This branch of Zylan River forks here, in the middle of the forest. Now, back then, the corner of Lentari here extended farther out into the sea as a peninsula, only… Drat. If only I had my census map, then I could properly show you. Oh, well."

"Where is this map now, love?" Shardwyn gently asked.

Andra pointed back and up.

"It's on the third floor, back near the census records. My joints have been acting up lately, and I do not wish to go after it at this time."

"Would you allow me to bring it here, my darling Lov… er, my darling Andra?"

The elderly records keeper fixed the wizard with a steely stare.

"Only if you can guarantee that's all you'll be summoning."

Shardwyn waved off her concerns. "But of course. Very well. A moment, if you please."

The resident wizard started rummaging through his robes. He pulled a few vials out, mixed several of them together, and then started going through some scraps of paper that had fallen out of one of his many pockets. Gareth immediately dropped to the ground and scurried under the table.

"What are you doing?" Sarah quietly asked, as she peered under the table.

Gareth beckoned her to join him. "Just taking precautions. There's plenty of room under here."

A loud rumbling began. The floor started to tremble; nearby books rattled off their shelves. A few moments later, a veritable tidal wave of papers, scrolls, and books crested over the handrail on the top floor and fell to the main floor below. Sarah and Emily both cried out in alarm and scooted under the table, joining Mikal and Lissa. Just before the onslaught of paper could touch them, Steve and Balthor side-stepped out of the way and watched the proceedings from behind a marble pillar.

Once the deluge of papers and books stopped, there was utter silence. There, standing just as she was, in the direct center of the mess, was Andra Alwyn. Standing next to her, wearing the biggest, most sheepish grin he could muster, was Shardwyn. Also of note was the lack of debris around Andra and Shardwyn.

"Good thinking, pal," Steve observed, as he waded his way through all the papers. "I'm glad you were able to cast some type of protection against that paper tsunami. Hoo, boy, what a mess! Sarah, Emily, are you guys okay? Gareth? Do you have Deez with you?"

An almost perfect circular dome of papers and notebooks, located where the table *was*, suddenly shifted, and then collapsed in on itself. Sarah and Emily emerged, pushing and shoving papers aside so they could be free of the mess. Once the two women had joined Steve, Sarah turned to survey the damage. Together, the three of them looked incredulously at Shardwyn.

"You're going to have your hands full for months, aren't you?" Steve quipped.

"Yes, he is," Andra dangerously replied, as she shot Shardwyn a dark look. "I don't care how long it takes, my dear, but you will return my Archives to the exact condition it was in before *this* happened. Are we clear?"

Unaffected by the sheer scope of the disaster, Shardwyn enthusiastically nodded. "Of course! Think of all the extra time I will be able to spend with you. I would be delighted."

Steve stooped to see under the table. The young wizard was not there!

"Where's Gareth? Wasn't he under there with you?"

Surprised, both women turned to look back under the table. Sure enough, the acolyte wizard was nowhere to be seen."

"Guys?" Gareth's voice called out. "I'm over here. Would you tell Deez it's safe to put me down?"

Perched halfway up the perimeter wall, was Deez, who was holding Gareth tight with his two front forelegs. The guur didn't appear to be struggling with the added weight, nor did he give any inclination that he was coming down. Plus, the guur was chittering angrily, no doubt directing his ire toward the wizard responsible for the mess.

CARELESS, RECKLESS, ANCIENT HUMAN PLACED HIVE IN DANGER. REPERCUSSIONS MUST BE ADMINISTERED.

"You can bring Gareth down now," Steve told the overly protective guur. "It's safe down here."

"For the time being," Mikal quietly muttered, as he crawled out from the other end of the table. He helped Lissa gain her feet and then turned angrily to Shardwyn. "Look at the mess you've created, Shardwyn. What were you thinking?"

Shardwyn removed his hat and humbly bowed. "I was only trying to help my Lovey Poo. I…"

"Shardwyn!" Andra hissed. "I told you *not* to call me that in public!"

"My apologies, Lovey P-, er, Andra. Fear not. I'll have everything back in order before this night is through."

Steve cleared his throat. "So, um, do you see that census map you were looking for in this clutter?"

Surprised, Andra looked down at the mess of papers that were nearly waist-high, grunted once, and carefully extricated a long, white paper tube. She turned to Shardwyn, whacked the end of the tube on Shardwyn's head—which flattened his hat—and then started wading through the papers and books, angling toward a table on the far side of the room. Once there, she unfurled the map as before, waited for the rest of the group to join her, and then tapped the southwestern tip of Lentari on the map. This time, a small peninsula could be seen, jutting westward into the Erudian Ocean. There, on the tip of the peninsula, was a dot with a tiny label: Capily.

Steve tapped the village and looked up at Balthor. "Did you say an earthquake caused the city to sink?"

"No, I said a terra tremor," Balthor corrected.

"Same thing," Steve explained. "Hey, if you don't mind me asking, how did you know it was a terra tremor? Were you actually there?"

Balthor shook his head. "I was not on dry land when the terra tremor struck, but I do remember feeling the effects in our own community. Lord Phaedren dispatched me to assess the threat level to the shealk. When I surfaced, and saw that the city was slowly submerging, I called for every available shealk. We managed to save many humans, even as their homes were filling with water and rapidly sinking, but there were those that we were unable to help. Or find."

"Epan was one of the unlucky ones, wasn't he?" Sarah quietly asked.

Balthor nodded. "He was. Nearly two hundred humans lost their lives that day."

"I'm surprised you didn't use your jhorun to try and stop Capily from sinking," Gareth said to his father.

Balthor regarded his son with a wisp of a smile. "I did. I tried shoring up the sinking land. I tried to absorb the excess energy from the terra tremor. I even tried a symbiotic spell. I tried to link a stable piece of land with that of the doomed peninsula's, hoping I could at least slow the progress of the sinking, but alas, I didn't have enough time. The human village of Capily was lost to the watery depths of the sea. I never saw Epan again."

Sarah, Emily, and Lissa quietly dabbed at the corners of their eyes. Andra smiled warmly at all three of them before catching sight of Shardwyn. The smile quickly morphed into a frown. She shook her head and returned her attention to the map.

"Continuing on," the records keeper began, "it was decided that Capily was too remote; it was too far away from the other villages, so the decision was made to move it farther north."

Mikal leaned over the table and studied the map and the tiny peninsula. He looked over at Andra and offered the octogenarian a smile.

"Miss Alwyn, do you have any maps that show more detail? We suspect the second Alchos Temple to be somewhere in the vicinity. Perhaps if we could study the terrain, we'd be able to determine its location?"

Andra nodded. and pushed away from the table. "A reasonable request. Let me…"

Andra trailed off as she turned around and came face-to-face with her brutal reality check —the extensive mess.

With a frown at Shardwyn, she pushed her way through the waist-deep mass of papers, en route to the far side of the ground floor, which happened to be debris-free.

Andra reached for a thick yellowing tome resting on the bottom shelf. She pulled the heavy book free, plopped it on the closest table, and then cracked the book open. After perusing the contents for a few moments, she made eye contact with Mikal and motioned for him to come over.

"What's this?" Mikal asked, as he joined the records keeper at the table. "Is this as old as it looks?"

"I just remembered about this book," Andra explained, as she carefully turned the yellowing pages. She flipped to the end of the book and clucked with approval. "There. Do you see? Maps. To answer your question, Kri'Mikal…"

Mikal briefly smiled as he recognized the proper title of 'king' applied to his name.

"…this is a collection of reports and testimonies taken from the survivors of Capily. As you can see, several maps have been included."

"I wonder why?" Steve softly mused.

"No doubt to chronicle the damage inflicted upon them by the terra tremor," Mikal guessed. "As Andra was flipping the pages, I saw several restitution claims made against the Crown. If you're going to petition the King for damages, then you had better provide proof to back it up."

Andra nodded. "Correct. Now, do you see the next dozen or so pages? They are all hand-drawn maps of various farms and settlements. Perhaps what you're looking for could be found somewhere within these pages?"

Sarah nodded thoughtfully and reached for the book, waiting for permission. Once the archivist gave it, Sarah slid the heavy book over and began to skim through the maps.

"Here, I'll help you," Emily said, as she sat down next to

Sarah. "You take the left page and I'll take the right page."

"Do you even know what we're looking for?" Sarah asked.

Emily shrugged. "I would imagine it would have to be an area devoid of houses or farms. If the temple was somewhere in the area, and it remained hidden, then logic would suggest that, the land should appear vacant."

Sarah was nodding. "Okay, let's see what we have here."

"May I make a suggestion?" Steve asked. He leaned over to look at the drawing Sarah was studying. "I think we can speed things along if we only search for the maps which depict sunken land."

Sarah began flipping through the pages of maps.

"No. Nope. Nada. Well, this farmer lost part of his land, but only a small piece, so it couldn't be there."

"What about this one?" Emily asked, as she tapped her page. "This plot belonged to a peasant by the name of 'Acton'. The last drawing I saw, on the previous page, showed what was to the east, which consequently, was flooded land. Acton's farm borders this farm on the west, but to the west of this one? Nothing, from what I can tell."

"And I'd say we have a winner!" Steve exclaimed. "Nicely done, Doc!"

Emily beamed. Sarah, on the other hand, continued searching through the restitution forms. Steve tapped his wife on her shoulder.

"What are you still looking for? We have one to check out. Isn't that good enough?"

Sarah shook her head. "And if it falls through? We'd have to come all the way back here and start over. No, we're already here. We should find at least three or four good possibilities before we start to search."

Emily nodded. "That's a good point. Redundancy is our friend here."

Once they had four different possibilities, Sarah slid the book back over to Andra and gave the Archivist the most welcoming smile she could muster.

"Thank you very much, Miss Alwyn. You've been a tremendous help. Is there any way we could leave this book out? I mean, in case none of our choices pans out?"

Andra nodded. "Of course. I'll see to it that no one bothers this book."

Sarah automatically held out a hand. "All right. All those heading to the southwestern tip of Lentari, climb on."

Steve frowned as he looked at the stack of hands, which were growing steadily larger.

"What about Athos and Breslin?"

"I've already sent for them," Mikal answered. "They should be on their way here."

"Can you even get us there?" Steve asked. "I don't recall you ever going that far south before."

Sarah nodded. "True, but I can get us as close as possible and then use line-of-sight jumps to get us there. It still beats us walking, right?"

"Absolutely," Steve agreed. "Just don't overdo it, okay? I don't want you depleting your jhorun."

Sarah batted her eyes and blew her husband a kiss. "Yes, dear."

Once the two dwarves arrived, and everyone was in physical contact with one another, Sarah took a deep breath and readied herself. She brought up a mental picture of the farthest southern point she could remember and ordered her jhorun to teleport the lot of them there. The familiar wrenching motion made a brief appearance, but thankfully, her days of becoming queasy after her teleportation jumps were long over. However, her luck usually didn't extend to those who were not used to her jumps. In this case, the dwarves.

Both Athos and Breslin looked ashen, their breathing ragged, and they couldn't take more than a few steps without stumbling. Steve warily eyed them.

"Are you two okay?" he asked, concerned.

"I've said it before," Breslin grumbled, "and I'll say it again: I'll never get used to Lady Sarah's jhorun."

"Dwarves were never meant to teleport," Athos weakly agreed.

"Well, brace yourselves," Sarah told them, as she pointed south. "We're not there yet. Now, I can only teleport as far as I can see. So, we still might have three or four jumps to go before we get there."

Both dwarves groaned.

As it turned out, it took *seven* jumps from Sarah's jhorun before they arrived at the original site of the seaport village of Capily. All that remained were a few jagged rocks along the water's edge, the only evidence that a massive chunk of land once jutted out into the water.

"There's nothing out here," Steve complained. "I don't think the second Alchos Temple is here. I mean, look at this place. There's no place for it to hide."

Sarah cautiously made her way to the edge of the rocks and looked down at the surface of the water, nearly thirty feet below. The others joined her and all fell silent as they studied the site. The two dwarves were the first to back away from the water's edge.

"Not again," Athos was saying. "We had better not have to climb down that. Dwarves were not meant for climbing, especially when that much water is as close as it is."

"Brings back memories, doesn't it?" Breslin added. "It feels like only yesterday we were trying to solve the puzzle on your nephew's back. I didn't care for the cliffs back then, and I sure don't care for them now."

Just then, Sarah let out an exclamation of surprise. She turned to Steve, threw her arms around him, and started dancing a jig. The look on her face, Steve noted, was priceless: she was glowing.

"All right, you clearly know something. Spill. What's going on?"

Sarah stopped dancing and pointed victoriously at the water. "Don't you get it? No wonder no one has found the temple after all these years. It must've sunk with the rest of the city. The temple is underwater!"

Chapter 8 — Fighting Fire with Fire

And how, exactly, is a temple submerged in water supposed to help us?" Athos demanded. The dwarf was appearing even paler than he had, moments ago. "You're not suggesting we have to wade into … into … *that*, are you?"

"Please say you're not," Breslin moaned miserably.

Sarah shook her head. "I'm not. Well, not yet. What I'm thinking is that…"

Steve looked back at his wife as her voice trailed off. He caught the look of alarm on her face and turned to see what had spooked her.

"Man your battle stations, guys!" Steve called out, igniting his hands. "We're gonna have some visitors! Gareth, you're with Sarah and Emily. Don't let anything happen to them!"

The teenager thrust a hand into a pocket and nodded. He sighted Sarah and Emily, standing nearly thirty feet away, and then closed his eyes. When he opened them a split second later, he was standing next to Emily.

"That is very impressive," Emily quietly remarked. "You people are so lucky."

Gareth grinned at her and quickly started casting protection spells.

Almost instantly, the sky filled with screeches, squawks, trills—and whoops—as griffins and pirates dropped down upon them. Steve briefly wondered whether Flinn was among them when a swirling blast of air appeared out of nowhere and tried to blow him off his feet. Yep, Flinn was here. Flinn's griffin barely touched down and Flinn had hopped off. If Steve didn't know any better, the ornery captain appeared to be a little green around the gills.

"Captain Windbag!" Steve called out, using his friendliest tone. "I was just thinking about you guys. Riding on the backs of griffins, huh? You guys must've really wanted to beat us here. Too bad you didn't. For the sake of all present, why don't we—"

Steve's unspoken suggestion of settling their differences man-to-man came to an abrupt halt as the swirling air formed a very recognizable fist and launched itself straight at him. Steve fired off a jet of flames, impacting the blast of air head on. Both attacks fizzled out as neither could overpower the other. Steve clucked his tongue and grinned at the pirate captain.

"Are we still doing this? Neither of us can defeat the other. We're too evenly matched. We both know this. Now, as I was trying to say earlier before I was so rudely interrupted, was that—"

A loud rumble started up and the very ground they were standing on began to shake. Cracks snaked through the rocky terrain, sending splinters of stone tumbling into the sea below. Louder and louder the rumbling became, until no one could hear anything else. Worried, Steve spotted Sarah, squatting low, next to Athos and Breslin. Before he could take a step in her direction, Steve noticed the sudden appearance of the wind, and not just one of Flinn's air jets. This felt like a raging hurricane.

He glanced over at the pirate captain and saw Flinn

crouching low to the ground, with an equally shocked look on his face. A shiver went down Steve's spine. As much as he didn't want to admit it, whoever—or whatever—was responsible for creating these quakes and raging wind was something no one had encountered yet.

The shaking ground let up for a moment. Then, a split-second later, the trembling increased ten-fold, throwing everyone except the pirates to the ground. Every one of the pirates had managed to stay on their feet and, if possible, now seemed to be even more certain of themselves.

Steve caught sight of Jino, who had a wicked, evil expression on his face. A dagger was clenched between the pirate's teeth, and he held additional daggers in each hand. Jino strode toward him confidently. At once, Steve felt strength surge through him, like a direct blast of dragon fire. The roar of the wind faded away. And just like that, he found he could nimbly walk over the shaking ground.

"What's going on?" Sarah shouted, surprising him.

To Steve, it felt as though he was sharing his senses with Pryllan again, and he was able to see and hear everything, even when she was flying at top speed.

Of course you can! I can feel the surge of energy throughout your body. Do you not know what has happened?

Should I, Pryllan?

Eion has augmented your physical attributes.

And the pirates? Why would Eion boost them, too?

He most certainly did not. Usol has no doubt augmented the pirates, just as Eion has augmented you. Most likely Usol acted first, prompting Eion to reciprocate.

The ground started shaking first, Steve recalled. *Then the wind.*

There's your answer. Get moving! Pirates are behind you.

You got it.

See to yourself first. Lady Sarah is more than able to take care of herself. In fact, the pirates are giving her a wide berth.

They're afraid of her? Why? I'm the one they should be afraid of.

Tell that to the pirates who are advancing on you.

If things become too dangerous, Sarah will teleport us out of here.

Acknowledged.

Steve turned to confront the pirates. They were more afraid of Sarah than him? Well, it was time to remind them who was more dangerous. Steve curled his flaming hands into fists and blasted a jet of flames directly at them, almost tipping himself backward with the velocity.

The pirates avoided his blasts of fire, but barely. Steve's flames poofed out on their own, leaving him stunned. The vegetation had been stripped away and even the rocks were blackened. In fact, several nearby rock formations were still glowing red. What? He'd only felt flames this strong during the battle against the evil sorceress, Celestia.

Again, your power has been augmented, by Bacaed—Eion, the Wind Master.

Steve spun to see that Jino was still advancing on him, along with a second pirate, twirling his cutlass through the air, as though he believed himself to be the world's greatest swordsmen. Steve readied his jhorun to heat the weapons, but a large misshapen boulder landed with a thud directly in front of him. Stunned, he watched as the boulder sprouted ten heavily armored legs, lifted itself off the ground, and chittered angrily at the pirates.

"Whoa, better back off there, Deez," Steve told the protective insect who had appeared at his side. "They've got swords, and…"

But the guur suddenly sped off, toward the pirates. Jino easily leapt over the large insect and thrust his sword straight down, expecting to impale the guur through its abdomen. However, Jino's smug smile vanished as his weapon actually shattered. Before the pirate could question, Deez lashed out with his front forelegs, catching him by surprise, launching him into the air like a baseball. The second pirate leapt back, tripping on an exposed piece of rock and falling to the ground, just as Deez's leg whizzed by above his head.

"Damn, Deez! I had no idea your carapace was that… wait. Did Eion get to you, too? Are you stronger than normal now?"

PRESENCE OF UNEXPECTED STRENGTH CONFIRMED.

"Sweet. All right, do me a favor. Have you ever wondered if you could rip a person in two?"

CLARIFICATION REQUESTED. YOU WISH MALODOROUS BIPED TO BE DISPATCHED?

Steve snorted with laughter. "Dispatched? Why not? These guys have been a pain in my butt for a while now. Feel free to go over there and have some fun with either of them."

Both Jino's and the second pirate's faces drained of color. Jino sheathed his dagger, picked up the second one, and darted away, followed by Grenden. Steve watched, finding it odd that the pirates were deliberately avoiding the water.

Steve stared. Weren't these guys pirates? Why were they suddenly afraid of getting their toes wet?

"What devilry is this?" Breslin demanded, appearing at Steve's side. "What have your ruddy pirates done to us?"

"You can feel it?" Steve glanced down at his own clenched fist and gave the order to extinguish, but his jhorun refused to comply. "I feel like we could take on the world. It's Eion. He's making sure everyone fights fair."

"I can get used to this," Athos said, as he slid a long flat piece of metal out of the scabbard across his chest. The dwarf flicked his wrist. The metal object tripled in size and Athos flung it away, like a Frisbee. "I've never been able to accurately throw one of my orixes this far."

The spinning weapon sliced through the air, and slammed into one of Flinn's men, an impact that should have knocked him out. However, the pirate picked up the orix and tossed it aside, as if a bug had landed on him.

"Damn," Athos breathed.

"Damn!" Steve agreed. "Nice shot!"

"It didn't do us any good. The man is still upright. My orix was ineffective."

"How far away would you say he is?" Steve wanted to know.

"At least four hundred feet, yet I hit him as easily as if the distance was a quarter of that."

"Why didn't he go down?" Breslin asked, frowning.

"I don't know," Athos admitted. "Usually, a strike from my orix is enough to render anyone unconscious."

"It's because the pirates have been ramped up, too," Steve reminded his dwarf companions. "Everything you can do, they can do it, too."

"Only better," Flinn growled, from somewhere nearby.

"I doubt that, amigo. Give it up, pal. You guys aren't the only ones who have an Ancient in your corner."

Confused, Flinn shook his head. "What be ye prattlin' on about, ye daft fool? Are ye callin' me ancient?"

"Seriously? You didn't know one of the Ancients was helping you? You obviously knew where to find Pryllan's fang. You were able to sneak into a dwarf city to steal that hammer there. Haven't you ever wondered how you were able to do it?"

Flinn was silent as he considered.

"Believe me, don't believe me, I don't care," Steve continued.

Steve quickly noted where the pirates were standing. He knelt and smacked the ground with his flaming right hand. Glowing lines of fire streaked across the ground, insinuating themselves between the pirates and his friends. A split second later, the fire lines erupted with towering flames, creating a twisting wall of fire nearly twenty feet high. The flames crackled and snapped, the writhing wall remaining mired in place.

"Aieee!" one pirate wailed, as he tried to push his way through the flames.

"Serves you right, Casimir," one pirate exclaimed. "Who in their right mind would poke a finger into a fire?"

"I thought we were indestructible!" the pirate whined.

"Far from it," the second pirate advised.

"Way far from it," Steve seconded. "Start running, boys."

The pirates screamed in terror as the flaming wall suddenly jumped forward, intent on encircling them. Enhanced as they were, the pirates avoided the flames, but it wasn't easy. Steve's firewall was everywhere, and whenever a pirate ventured too close, the wall seemed to come alive and attempt to ensnare them.

"Impressive, Fire Thrower," Flinn called. "But it not be impressive enough. Ye want to talk about power? Then ye will want to…"

"Oh, enough of this already!" Sarah shouted. She appeared next to Steve's side and scowled at the pirate captain. "You want to see what true power looks like? Let's see what you think about this. You! Jino, is it? You're first."

Steve watched as Flinn curiously turned to his best fighter, unsure of what Sarah had planned. Then, just like that, Jino vanished. Steve was nodding.

"Nicely done, my dear. Where'd you put him?"

"Nowhere," came Sarah's smug smile.

"Then where is he?" Steve asked, curious.

"He's safely out of the way. Hang on, I see another one."

There was the pirate who had burned his hand. In the blink of an eye he, too, had vanished. Steve looked over at Flinn who had an incredulous look on his face. The shock quickly turned to rage.

"What the devil did ye do to my men, ye blasted harlot?"

Steve's eyebrows shot up. Did Flinn call his wife a prostitute? Oh, lordy, that wasn't going to go over well. Sure enough, one look at his wife's face confirmed she was no longer smiling.

"Attack them, ye daft winged beasts!" Flinn shouted, before Sarah could retaliate. "Drive them away from here! Force them into the water, I care not! Just do somethin'!"

The half dozen griffins, which had been carefully circling over everyone's heads—safely out of range of Steve's fire jets—suddenly broke ranks and dove from the sky. Talons extended, beaks opened, the shrill battle cries of the mythical monsters became deafening. Steve sighed as he raised his hands. The griffins were allies, despite them falling victim to whatever enchantment had befallen them.

Sarah laid a restraining hand on his shoulder.

"Honey, I've got this. We don't want to hurt them, right?"

Steve nodded. "Right. What are you gonna do?"

"Watch and learn."

The screeching griffins continued their descent. Once they were less than a hundred feet away, a massive wave rose from the sea and flung itself into the path of the winged monsters. Utterly surprised, they scattered, some taking refuge on the ground. One ended up in the sea as it tried to veer away from the water, and the last two rose unsteadily back into the air. Those that had landed on the ground vigorously shook themselves, squawking angrily as they turned to face Sarah.

"I wouldn't press your luck," Sarah told the griffins. "I can do a lot worse than just get you wet."

"Where are we?" one of the griffins asked, in its customary high nasally pitch.

"You're at the southwestern tip of Lentari," Steve told the griffin, correctly assuming that the poor creature had no recollection of being the pirates' beasts of burden. "You attacked us, and my wife essentially splashed some water on you to wake you up."

One of their companions pulled itself from the sea and a few moments later, six angry griffins were standing before Steve and his friends.

"Don't look at us," Steve said, thankful his hands were still ignited. He turned to point at the pirates. "Blame them. They're the ones who ordered you here."

As one, six avian heads turned to regard the remaining pirates. Flinn's face turned stony, and he opened both of his clenched fists. Jets of air appeared then, shockingly, the jets vanished. Spewing curses worthy of his profession, Flinn gathered his remaining men and ducked behind an outcropping of rock just as another massive earthquake hit.

Stone formations splintered apart, throwing everyone to the ground. Waves splashed up and over the cliff, drenching them within seconds. A giant crack opened on the ground, sending plumes of dust high in the air.

"Stand back!" Breslin shouted. "The ground could break off at any moment!"

When the air cleared somewhat, they saw the section of rock they were all standing on now had a vast, jagged crack running parallel to the water.

"This could break away," Steve called out. "Let's go!" He ushered everyone off the damaged strip of land.

"What happened?" Steve asked Sarah, who was standing aside with Emily and Gareth. "Was that Usol's doing? Man alive, he must be pissed."

It seemed an eternity before the ground stopped shaking. Deez brushed by him just then, headed in the direction where the pirates had last been seen. Steve followed along, anxious to see what the pirates could possibly be doing. A quick check of the area confirmed there was nowhere for the pirates to hide.

The pirates had vanished! Steve shared a puzzled look with the guur before turning back to Sarah.

"They're gone!"

ABSENCE OF ANGRY HUMANS VERIFIED.

"I don't understand what happened," Breslin said, as he appeared next to Athos. "Those cowards were retreating."

Emily spoke up. "Sorry. It's just that…"

"What?" Sarah anxiously asked. "Did you see something?"

The paleontologist shook her head. "No, not really. I only wanted to offer an opinion as to what happened."

"We know what happened," Steve informed her. "The pirates were enhanced by Usol, and then Eion decided to enhance us."

Emily nodded. "That's right. Exactly. Don't you see? That's why they left!"

Steve scratched his chin and tried to look thoughtful. "Uh, right."

Sarah was nodding. "I get it. They weren't prepared to fight fairly."

"Exactly!" Emily said, flashing her a smile.

Steve cleared his throat. "Come again?"

"The pirates were clearly used to having the upper hand," Emily explained. "Yet, this time, Eion retaliated by doing the same thing to you guys. They were unprepared. And, when Sarah made those two vanish, they panicked."

"Where *did* you send those pirates?" Steve asked, as he turned to his wife.

Sarah shook her head. "I told you. Nowhere. I didn't specify a destination."

Steve gave her a blank look.

"Don't you remember what happened when we first got our powers? Back when we had been taken prisoner and thrown into that creep's cellar?"

"He wanted to sell us as slaves," Steve recalled. "I remember."

"Do you remember what I did to the door in the ceiling?"

"Umm, yeah. You made it go away, right?"

"That's right," Sarah confirmed. "But, I didn't know how to properly use my jhorun, so I didn't have a destination for it."

Steve shared a look with the dwarves.

"I think I sent it to… to… I don't know. Limbo? I sent it to wherever things go when I don't specify a destination."

"And that's where you put those two pirates," Steve guessed.

"Yes."

"Are they going to be okay?" Emily asked. "I mean, I guess I'm asking whether or not Limbo has an air supply."

Sarah's mouth opened with surprise and ended up shrugging when she realized she didn't know. Steve then started motioning everyone to take a step back.

"You're going to bring one of them back, aren't you?" Steve guessed. "Makes sense. Let's make sure they're okay. If they are, then you can send him back and he can just chill there until all this is over."

Sarah nodded. "Exactly. And yes, that's precisely what I'm going to do, once we verify they're safe in Limbo."

"Just don't bring back Jino," Steve gruffly added.

"Agreed. Here we go."

A split second later, the pirate with the burnt hand was standing before them, blinking with confusion. He turned to run, only to come face-to-face with Deez, who chittered a warning. The pirate cried out in terror and immediately dropped to the ground. After a few moments, when it became apparent he wasn't going to become the strange ten-legged creature's lunch, the pirate cautiously rose to his feet.

"Who are you?" Steve demanded. "What's your name?"

"C… Casimir."

"I've seen you before," Sarah recalled. She waved her hand dismissively. "That's not important right now. What can you tell us about where you were a moment ago?"

Casimir's eyes widened with shock.

"But that's what I wanna to know! How… how did I get here? Where's the captain?"

While the others conferred to figure out what happened to the missing pirates, the guur stood directly in front of the pirate, as if he was a jailer, and Casimir was an escaped inmate.

"Suspended animation," Emily concluded. "Wherever Sarah teleports these people, it would appear that no time passes for them, so they naturally don't remember anything when they're brought back."

Everyone turned to look at the pirate.

"What?" Casimir demanded, as he took another step back.

The guur took two steps in his direction and kept staring straight at the pirate.

"Okay, I think it's safe to say that he can be sent back," Steve told his wife.

Sarah nodded. "You got it."

Casimir vanished before he could protest.

"So, that's why," Steve suddenly mumbled, more to himself than to anybody.

His wife, however, had excellent hearing and turned to him, waiting for an explanation. When he didn't offer any further clarification, she nudged his shoulder.

"What are you talking about? You just said, 'So, that's why.' That's why *what*?"

"Pryllan told me earlier that, during the attack, the pirates were giving you a wide berth, as if they had been warned to stay away from you. She indicated you were more dangerous than I was." He tried to ignore the notion that his wife was more powerful than he was.

Sarah smiled and shrugged. "That sounds about right to me."

"Flinn must know that you have the ability to incarcerate his men. Once he saw you take two of his crew, he knew he had to leave. Quickly."

Precisely.

"Pryllan agrees," Steve added. "And you're welcome."

"But without locating the second temple?" Gareth asked, confused. "I would have thought they wouldn't give that up without a fight."

"They *did* put up a fight, lad," Athos corrected.

"Although, it wasn't much of a fight," Breslin admitted. "Honestly? I expected more. Lady Sarah, you have my thanks for putting an end to the skirmish before anyone was injured."

"I'm glad no one was hurt, including the griffins," Sarah said, looking up. "Speaking of which, where did our fine-feathered friends go?"

Not one griffin was visible in the sky.

"They were probably eager to return to their homes," Breslin guessed. "For all we know, the force that took them could have done so several days ago."

Steve pointed at the nearby shore.

"I want to know why the pirates avoided the water."

"Why do you ask that?" Sarah asked.

"Think about it. You've got some angry griffins on your tail. Thanks to Eion, my flames are stronger and hotter than ever, but did you see any of them run toward the water? I sure didn't. In fact, I saw several avoid it, as though they thought they'd melt if they touched it."

"That doesn't make any sense," Sarah agreed. "They're pirates. They should be used to the water."

WATER CREATURES DETERRED ENTRY INTO THE AQUATIC REALM.

"What was that?" Steve asked, as he curiously turned to the guur.

WATER CREATURES PROVIDED DETERRANT.

"What water creatures are you talking about, Deez?"

Sarah wanted to know.

Emily wandered over to the edge of the rocks and looked down at the surface of the water nearly thirty feet below.

"Umm, I'd say he was talking about *those* creatures."

The rest of the group, minus the two dwarves, gathered at the water's edge. Peering up at them from the water below was not one, nor two, but *four* sleek scaly necks topped with large reptilian heads. All four sets of eyes were trained on them, and not one of them blinked. Every couple of seconds, one of the heads would submerge beneath the surface, only to reappear moments later.

"It's the shealk!" Sarah happily exclaimed.

"We're all right up here!" Steve called down to the water dragons. "The fight is over. Thanks for having our backs!"

The four shealk nodded and then submerged, leaving a string of bubbles as the only evidence they had ever been there.

"Usol must've warned the pirates about the presence of the shealk," Steve theorized. "No wonder they didn't want to get wet. Would you want to jump in there knowing four shealk were waiting for you?"

"How long ago did the terra tremors stop?" Breslin asked. "It pains me to admit that I did not notice."

"I noticed just before Deez and I confirmed the pirates had vanished on us," Steve answered.

The wind, they all noticed, had decreased in volume and intensity, but had not disappeared. Was it simply the normal strength of the wind today, or was their all-powerful benefactor still in the area? About ready to ask his wife what her opinion was, his question was answered for him as Eion's robed human visage appeared before them. Intent on approaching the Ancient to give him a friendly high-five, Steve caught sight of Eion's face and came to an immediate stop.

"I should have known the coward wouldn't fight fair," Eion seethed, his eyes practically flashing fire. "We meet on equal terms and what happens? He flees. He should…" The Master of the Winds trailed off as he noticed that all sets of eyes were on him. "Usol never cared for a fair fight."

"What do you have over Usol, anyway?" Steve asked. "You guys are all powerful, right? If he's that annoyed with us, why doesn't he up-and-kill us?"

"Honey!" Sarah exclaimed. She punched his arm and frowned at him.

"Right on target," Steve admitted, through clenched teeth. "Your aim is dangerous, lady. As I was saying, if he's that strong, couldn't he snap his fingers and we all go *poof*?"

"His powers have been stripped from him," Eion answered exasperatedly. "He can't."

Steve raised a hand. "Umm, beg to differ, amigo. He's still using his powers. He's turned himself into that dragon, right? He's given strength and agility to the pirates. One doesn't do that if one has been stripped of powers by one's peers."

"Stop talking like a dork," Sarah scolded. After a few moments, she cocked her head. "But, Steve brings up a good point. What exactly did you do to him, Eion? Can you tell us?"

Eion sighed and lowered himself into a sitting position. A large stone appeared out of thin air to serve as the Ancient's chair.

"You have to understand something," Eion hesitantly began. "As beings of unlimited resources, life for us can become boring."

"Your life is boring?" Sarah repeated, incredulous.

Eion nodded. "Indeed. Therefore, in order to, let's say *entertain* ourselves, certain wagers are often cast."

"What kinds of wagers?" Steve asked.

"Anything. Everything. If there's a chance that one of us can gain the advantage over another, then a wager would be made."

"Have you made wagers on us?" Sarah asked the Ancient, bristling with anger.

"One or two," Eion dryly admitted. He sat back on his stone chair as his eyes started to glow.

"Now wait a moment," Steve interjected, as he snapped his fingers a few times to get the Ancient's attention. "Is that how Usol lost his stone? He lost a wager?"

Eion nodded. "Indeed. He understood the stakes and

was forced to relinquish his stone and his power."

"You guys can take each other's power?" Emily asked, amazed.

Eion shook his head. "Not in the way you believe, Dr. Benz."

"Would you stop calling me that?" Emily pleaded. "It freaks me out when you address me by my title."

"Is that not what you prefer?" the Ancient asked as he smiled at the paleontologist.

"Well, yeah," Emily admitted, "but only on my world. Not here. Anyway, that's enough about me. Back to you. What did you mean, not the way that I believe?"

"Let me consider how to best answer your question," Eion answered. His eyes closed and he became completely motionless.

"He looks like a statue when he's like that," Steve observed.

"Too lifelike," Sarah countered.

As if in response to Sarah's comment, Eion's human image shimmered and started to change. To Steve, it looked as though Eion had unwisely made eye contact with the infamous Medusa, of Greek mythology, and had become a stone statue. Steve couldn't help himself. He took a few steps toward the Ancient and then knocked his knuckles on Eion's arm.

"Well?" Sarah prompted. "Did he turn himself to stone to prove a point?"

Steve nodded. "Sure looks that way. Feels like stone to me."

The stone figure suddenly opened its eyes and, with a loud grating sound, turned to look at Steve. The thin line that was the statue's mouth curved into a smile. Everyone took a few cautious steps back.

"You humans are a very mistrusting species," Eion observed, as he turned his head to survey the group. "Even you dwarves have backed away. You do know that it's still me, correct?"

"My apologies," Breslin began. "You look so much like a statue that after seeing one come to life, it became unnerving.

Do you have an answer?"

Eion's stone head nodded. "I do. If you…"

"Sorry to interrupt," Steve interrupted, "but could you switch back to normal now?"

"Let me assure you, normal for me would be nowhere normal for you," Eion answered. "However, what I think you mean to ask was whether or not I could return to my human form. Very well." The gray texture of Eion's stony skin switched back to the normal healthy pink found on most humans' arms. "Better?"

Steve nodded. "Much. Thanks. Please, go on."

Eion turned to Emily. "To answer your question, Miss Benz, I will ask you if you are familiar with the children's game of *Jinx*, which is often played on your world."

Emily's eyes widened. "Of course I'm familiar with it. How do *you* know about it?"

"The best way to describe the circumstances in which one of us can strip the power from another, in such a fashion that a human would understand, is to reference this game, *Jinx.*"

"I am unfamiliar with this game," Breslin admitted. "Lady Emily, would you explain it to me?"

Emily glanced over at Eion, who waved a hand, indicating she could answer the question.

"*Jinx* is a game where if two kids happen to say the same word at the same time, then the one who doesn't say 'jinx' first is then not allowed to speak a word."

"Strange game," Gareth commented.

Sarah held a finger to her lips. "Hush. Let her finish."

"The person who is now unable to speak," Emily continued, "must continue to follow the rules until either someone says their name, or else they forget themselves and end up speaking before being released."

"What happens if the child speaks before their name is spoken?" Athos wanted to know.

Emily shrugged. "Well, the rules vary from family to family."

"My friends and I played that game all the time when we were kids," Steve admitted. "If the person who was jinxed spoke before their name was heard, then they'd suffer a penalty. In this case, the victor of the game would get to punch the loser on the arm."

"What does this have to do with you Ancients?" Gareth asked, as he turned back to Eion. "You guys play this game, too?"

"No," Eion admitted. "However, the rules are the same, since he who loses the wager admits they aren't allowed to use their powers and has to give up their stone. His or her powers are not restored until they are either forgiven…"

"By the winner of the wager," Breslin interrupted.

Eion nodded. "Or… would anyone care to guess what else would nullify the effect of the wager?"

"…or they somehow get their stone back," Steve quietly guessed.

Eion nodded. "Correct. Now you know why Usol is fighting so hard to get his stone returned. Only when he possesses the Stone once more will he have his full powers."

"But, he's already using those powers!" Sarah protested. "He's changing form, creating earthquakes, putting griffins in trances, and so on. Trust me, the list goes on and on."

Eion sadly smiled. "True. Usol has gone without his stone for so long now that he's had to resort to cheating in order to get it back. That's why this *must not happen*. You can all see what type of person he is. You and your companions *must* get to his stone first."

Steve noticed his wife kept shifting her weight from one leg to the next, which typically indicated something was bothering her.

"How long has it been?" she finally asked.

Eion focused his powerful gaze on Sarah.

"How long has *what* been?" the Ancient wanted to know.

"How long has Usol been without his stone?" Sarah clarified.

Eion shrugged. "A few hundred millennia, give or take."

Steve whistled. "Damn!"

"The passage of time for us is not the same for mortals. For us, a century is no more than a blink of an eye."

"Is there a time limit?" Sarah suddenly asked.

"A time limit?" Steve repeated, frowning. "For what?"

Sarah pointed at Eion. "For his wager. For example, if after five hundred millennia have passed, and Usol still hasn't acquired his stone, are the effects of the lost wager lifted?"

Eion shrugged after considering the question for a few moments.

"I believe I understand. Typically, a wager becomes null and void once fifty millennia have passed."

Steve raised a hand.

"Didn't you say that Usol lost his stone over several *hundred* millennia ago?"

Eion nodded. "You heard correctly, Mr. Miller."

"Then why hasn't Usol regained the full use of his powers?" Steve asked, confused.

"Because my brother has a history of misusing his powers," Eion coldly answered. "My sisters and I have all agreed. Usol must never regain his full strength."

"Let me see if I understand you correctly," Steve slowly began. As was the norm with him, whenever something didn't sit right with him, he began to pace. "You two placed some type of bet. Usol lost. As a result, he lost his stone and his powers, yet he clearly still has them. Plus, it looks like he's been using them for some time. Why not strip his powers away from him if you're that worried about what he can do?"

Eion's eyes dropped to the ground and he sighed.

"You can't, can you?" Sarah guessed.

"We are all evenly matched," the Ancient admitted.

"No wonder Usol is so angry," Steve said, as he looked back at his friends. "By the rules you Ancients have set in place, his, er, penalty should've been lifted, only it hasn't. But, if he gets his stone back, then he's back to full strength. Guys, we really need to find this thing before he does."

"With that being said," Eion added, "and since Usol and your pirate friends are now out of the picture, you should all now be working on how to gain entrance to the second temple."

"Is the second temple nearby?" Breslin asked, with a quavering voice. "It's not... it's not under the water, is it?"

Eion grinned and promptly vanished.

Chapter 9 — The Second Temple

"Can you believe the Ancients are that old?" Steve sputtered several minutes later. "I mean, man alive. The wager that Usol lost has lasted over several hundred millennia? What is that, at least two hundred thousand years??"

"They aren't called the Ancients for nothing, dear," Sarah kindly pointed out. "You heard it from him: a century for them can pass quicker than the blink of an eye."

"So, what do we do now?" Emily asked. "Eion confirmed the temple is in the water."

"*Under* the water," Sarah corrected. "Plus, we have no idea how far down it is."

Steve walked over to the edge of the drop-off, much to Breslin and Athos' chagrin, and looked down at the splashing water.

"It's down there. We're up here. We need to explore that temple. Okay, guys. We need to hear some ideas, no matter how preposterous it might sound."

"Bring the temple up to us," Athos decided, after a

few moments of silence had passed and no one else had volunteered any ideas.

"Yeah, that *would* solve the problem," Steve admitted, "only we have no way to make that happen. I don't even think a spell would be able to raise that chunk of land to the surface."

Sarah turned to look at Gareth. "A spell couldn't do that, could it?"

"None of mine could," the teenage wizard confirmed. "My father is strong, sure, but not even he could pull that off. Remember what he said? He tried to stabilize the land back when it was sinking, but he was unable to do so."

Steve nodded. "Roger that. Okay, good idea, Athos. Anyone else?"

Emily made a swirling motion with her right hand. "Could we somehow get the water away from the Temple? I don't know, maybe, use someone's jhorun to do it?"

Intrigued, Steve turned to look at Gareth. "Is that possible?"

Gareth sadly shook his head. "No. I mean, not unless the Temple has only sunk a few feet beneath the surface. The deeper it is, the heavier the mass of water becomes. From what I can tell, the bottom of the ocean floor must be pretty deep, 'cause I can't see anything from up here."

"I'm pretty sure we wouldn't get that lucky," Steve muttered, as he looked down at the water. "You're right. It looks deep to me, too. Okay, scratch that idea. Anyone else?"

ENTER   WATER.   EXPLORE   SUBMERGED STRUCTURE.

Steve laid a friendly hand on the guur's head. "That's what we're trying to figure out, pal. We know we need to explore the temple. The problem is, no one knows how to do it."

Gareth suddenly let out an exclamation of surprise. He hurried over to Deez and gave the large insect a congratulatory pat on his abdomen.

"Way to go, Deez! Why didn't I think of that sooner?"

Husband and wife eyed each other. Steve shrugged and

let his arms fall helplessly to his sides. Whatever the young wizard had thought of, it clearly hadn't occurred to anyone else.

Gareth's eyes closed and he began to softly chant.

"Whoa, what are you doing?" Sarah asked, as she placed a hand on the teenager's shoulder to get his attention. "Don't do anything until you tell us, okay?"

The chanting stopped and the acolyte wizard's eyes opened.

"Sure, no problem. But, I should tell you that I already found out I can do it. Thanks to Deez, our problem is solved."

Breslin shuffled closer.

"Would you care to enlighten us, lad? How are we going to bring that temple up and out of the water?"

Gareth grinned at the dwarf. "We're not. We're going to go down to *it* and check it out for ourselves."

"I don't know about you, sport," Steve began, "but I can't hold my breath that long. I don't think that'll do any good, unless you were to… wait. Now wait a damn minute! What are you proposing? You're not planning on giving us gills, are you?"

Sarah groaned and she rubbed her temples.

"What is it?" Emily asked. "Did I miss something?"

"Our young friend here," Sarah began, "is suggesting he change us to something that can breathe water, so we can go down and see the temple for ourselves. Am I right?"

Gareth beamed his approval. "That's exactly right. If you were wondering what I was checking," he told Sarah, as he turned to her, "it was whether or not I could change Deez into something so that he'd be able to join us."

"I'm sure you can," Sarah confided, "but what? Look at poor Deez. We don't know if he'd be able to cope with a new form.

Gareth looked over at the guur. "What do you say? Would you like me to change you into something that can breathe underwater?"

The large, armored insect regarded Gareth for a few seconds before he ambled over to the cliff's edge and tilted his head down. The guur was silent for a few moments before he turned back to Gareth.

YOU PROPOSE TO ALTER FORMS IN ORDER TO ENTER THE WATER?

Gareth nodded enthusiastically. "Exactly! Would you want to go with us when we go down there?

DO NOT WISH TO BE SEPARATED FROM THE HIVE. IF FORM MUST BE ALTERED, THEN FORM *WILL* BE ALTERED.

Gareth clapped his hands together. "All right. Deez is in. What do you say, guys? Are you ready to get wet?"

Steve held his hands up in a time-out gesture.

"Just a moment. I need to know *exactly* what you're planning on doing."

"Shealk," Gareth proudly announced. "I'm going to turn us all into water dragons."

"The bloody hell you will," Breslin grumbled. "A dwarf? As a water dragon? In the water? No thank you, young Gareth. I'm sorry to say, I wouldn't be much help to the mission."

"Nor would I," Athos agreed.

Both dwarfs were pale and taking great gulps of air, imagining what it would be like to be cursed with gills. However, a smile had spread across Steve's face.

"A water dragon? You want to turn us into water dragons? Negative comments withdrawn. I think we all could get on board with that."

"And you've done this before?" Sarah cautiously asked.

Gareth nodded. "Yes. I turned myself, Mikal, and Pravara into water dragons last year."

"What about me?" a new female voice asked.

Everyone whirled around and were startled to see a large green dragon, complete with a golden glow around each scale, sitting on her haunches and intently watching the humans.

"As you say, I have been a shealk before. I would not mind becoming a shealk once again."

Sarah beamed a smile at the friendly dragon.

"Hello, Pravara! It's good to see you!"

"And you," Pravara returned. "I am glad I finally caught up with you. I was starting to think my decision to journey west would be for naught."

Sarah winced.

"Because of our teleporting? Yeah, I'm sorry about that."

"Are we really gonna do this?" Steve asked, as he rubbed his hands together. "How cool!"

"There are a few things you ought to know about being a shealk," Pravara began. "They… he's no longer listening."

Sarah looked up at the dragon and then over at her husband, who was busy chatting with Gareth. She sighed and looked back up at their wyverian friend.

"Let him figure it out the hard way. What were you going to say, Pravara? I, for one, would like to hear it."

"As would I," Emily added. "To think, I'm actually going to be changed into another species! The method of locomotion must be completely different."

"It is," Pravara agreed.

While the dragon recalled what she knew about the way the shealk moved through the water, Steve was busy peppering Gareth with questions.

"How many different species have you changed yourself into? Do you have a favorite? Is this going to be like the last time you changed me into a dragon?"

"I didn't change you into a dragon," Gareth corrected, between chants. "I simply moved your consciousness into Pryllan's body. And didn't I say I was sorry about that?"

"How long until you're ready?"

Gareth held out a hand and showed Steve an assortment of small objects: rocks, coins, and a small figurine.

"I'm already done. I remembered the spell I used last time, so all I really had to do was come up with the spell to change Deez."

"What are you going to change him into?" Steve wanted to know.

"The last time we were all shealk," Gareth began, as he started setting the various objects on the ground, "I noticed all kinds of aquatic life. And let me tell you, there were some really cool things living under the sea. One of them was this really large creature that also had ten legs, although the two front legs had pincers that were so gargantuan, I was certain they could chomp a human in half. I'm thinking that should work for a guur."

Steve was nodding. "Sounds like you're describing a large crab. Yeah, that ought to work; it's fairly close to his existing form. Okay, what do you need us to do?"

Gareth pointed at the water, "Take off your clothes and jump in. I've coded the spells to activate as soon as you touch the water.'

"Excuse me?" Steve asked, incredulous. He turned to see both Emily and Sarah staring at him with bemused expressions on their faces.

"A shealk is much larger than a human," Gareth continued, oblivious to Steve's surprised reaction. "If you don't take off your clothes, they'll be ripped off when your body shifts into a water dragon. Trust me, I know. It's what happened to Mikal."

Steve felt his face flame up as he envisioned himself stripping in front of his wife and a woman he hardly knew. He heard his wife giggle and tried to hide the scowl that formed on his face. "Keep it up, Chuckles," Steve told her. "He means you two as well."

The smile melted off Sarah's face. And Emily's.

"Well, you'd better think of something else," Sarah sternly told the young wizard. "I'm *not* stripping down to my birthday suit in front of an audience."

"Nor will I," Emily vowed.

Gareth was silent as he considered. After a few moments, he snapped his fingers.

"Very well, I have it. I can delay the spell. Would five seconds suffice?"

"Would five seconds suffice for what?" Steve curiously asked. "How are five seconds supposed to help us?"

Sarah, however, was nodding.

"That'd be perfect. Thanks, Gareth."

Steve turned to his wife. "Perfect for what?"

"I can get our clothes off of us in less than five seconds,"

Sarah explained. "I can even send them back to our house in R'Tal. Or the cabin by the waterfall, your choice."

"I'm not diving into that water *naked*," Steve reiterated.

"That's not what I'm saying," Sarah protested, shaking her head. "However, if *I* wanted you to dive into that water naked, you'd suddenly find yourself without apparel in the blink of an eye."

Steve's mouth snapped closed and he blushed furiously. That's the last thing he needed to know. Sarah could teleport his clothes off of him with the snap of her fingers? Whereas he was pretty sure she had never stripped a person with her jhorun before, he sure as hell didn't want to press his luck. Not with everyone present.

"Gareth is suggesting you jump into the water, I remove the clothing, and then you transform into a shealk," Sarah explained.

"Oh. Okay. That'll work, I suppose."

Sarah rolled her eyes. "Men. Emily? Would that work for you?"

It was the paleontologist's turn to blush, Steve noted with delight. Emily looked down at the water, back at Sarah, over to Steve, then back at the water. After a few moments, she slowly nodded.

Steve looked at their two dwarf companions. "Breslin? Athos? Are you sure you don't want to join us?"

"Completely," Breslin assured him.

"Indubitably," Athos agreed.

Steve turned to look at Gareth, who held out a hand over the water in an open invitation.

"Whenever you're ready."

* * *

This sure is weird, Steve observed.

Weird good *or weird* bad? Sarah wanted to know.

Steve glanced over at his wife; the shocking image looking back at him was nothing like Sarah. She, along with himself, Gareth, Emily, and Pravara, were now water dragons. Or, as the water dragons preferred to call themselves, *shealk*.

Steve angled his neck to look once more at his body. He briefly compared his shealk body back to the time he had *borrowed* Pryllan's body while helping the dragons solve an internal crisis.

His shealk body was much longer, and much more slender than that of their winged cousins. Gone were the wings and muscular limbs the wyverians were known for, replaced by skinny, vestigial forearms and legs which were so pathetically small that they were essentially useless. He knew he had two spiraled horns protruding from the top of his skull, which was sitting on top of a neck that had to be over a dozen feet long. His coloring was a two-tone green.

Steve's eyes shifted to his wife.

Sarah's own shealk body was somewhat smaller, had curved spiral horns, and her coloring was purple. Sarah later confided that she had been asked what their favorite colors were, and Gareth had obligingly made sure their shealk bodies matched their preferences.

Steve also couldn't help but notice just how fast Sarah had acclimatized to her new body. In less than two minutes, she was able to jet around the water with what looked like practiced ease. He, on the other hand, had to remember his experience in a dragon's body.

Kahvel had instructed him to not overthink the problem, but instead, just *imagine*, or *think* where he wanted to go. The body, Steve later learned, already knew what to do. He just had to stop overthinking every movement.

With that memory fresh in his mind, his erratic movements had smoothed out and his swimming had become much more efficient. Pravara, Steve noted, also had no trouble in her shealk form. Her coloring was a soft yellow for the upper portion of her body, while her lower half was salmon-colored.

Emily assured him she finally had the shealk method of locomotion figured out. With all five of them swimming as normally as they could, Steve turned his long neck to regard their last companion, who was—oddly enough—perched on his back.

Deez? How're you doing, buddy?

Looking like a large gray crab, the size of small bulldozer, Deez sensed he was being watched. After a few moments of silence, the crab waggled a large pincer.

I am unfamiliar to this form. I? Steve wondered.

It's the spell, Gareth explained. *We're not in mental contact anymore. What you're hearing is Deez's actual voice, spoken in the language of the shealk. Since we're all shealk, we can all understand one another. And that includes Deez.*

Gareth's black shealk form swam up next to Steve.

Once we get so deep the light is gone, don't worry. The shealk can see images even when it's practically pitch black, Gareth explained to them all. *We all have a parietal eye, a reptile's third eye.*

Exactly, Pravara agreed. *The light has decreased enough that I believe we can start using our third eyes. If everyone would close their eyes, and wait a few moments, I believe you'll be surprised at what you see. Including Deez.*

If everyone is done chatting about their new bodies, Pravara's dry voice said, *perhaps you'd like to begin your search? Behold. We're here.*

A mass of tumbled rocks and thick seaweed appeared below them, outlined in a strange yellow-greenish glow. Steve bent his neck around to watch Deez detach himself from his elongated back and settle onto the seabed. The crab's legs sank nearly two feet into the soft floor of the sea before coming to a stop. Deez's right pincer prodded the ground, which kicked up a large cloud of silt.

The floor is alluvial, but I believe it to be only a few feet thick. My legs have encountered a very stable foundation beneath the detritus that has settled here.

Steve glanced over at Emily's teal form.

Doc? Would you translate?

The seabed floor has several feet of earth and sand, but beneath that, he believes there is solid rock.

The crab snapped its pincers together a few times.

Precisely, Deez agreed.

So, how are we supposed to find anything? Steve wanted to know. *If this is the temple, how in the world are we supposed to find the entrance, let alone how to open said entrance?*

Pravara swam close and snapped her tail, like the crack of a whip, which they all felt. A huge brown cloud rose and hovered several feet above the sea floor. Nodding, Sarah mimicked the gesture, which pushed the cloud of debris a dozen or so feet away. In this manner, the five of them were able to clear a large patch of seabed floor, revealing a large smooth rock directly beneath.

That's encouraging, Steve observed. *I can see some symbols here. They don't really mean much to me. Emily, do you recognize them?*

The teal shealk sank lower and brought its nose to within a few feet of the slab of rock. After a few moments, the large aquatic head swung from side-to-side. Evidently, their paleontologist friend didn't recognize any of the marks.

Let's clear off some more, Sarah suggested. *Let's see what we're working with.*

For the next half hour, working as a team, the five shealk cleaned as much of the seabed as they could, revealing the outline of the temple. And, it was quite different than the first they had encountered.

It looks to be Egyptian! Emily exclaimed, delighted.

Egyptian for this one and Mayan for the last, Steve observed. *What are those influences doing here, in Lentari?*

The only answer I have to that is to remind you about what Eion told us, Sarah answered. *He said he's been to our world on more than one occasion. Clearly the others have, too.*

Do we know whose temple this one is? Emily asked.

Not yet, Steve reported. *Has anyone seen any of those triangle symbols? Right-side up, or upside down, it doesn't matter.*

Spread out, Sarah ordered. *They must be here somewhere.*

Deez, busy waving his two large pincers as close to the ground as possible in an effort to 'sweep' the floor clean, suddenly started sinking. Within a matter of moments, the large carapace that was Deez's outer shell vanished from sight, leaving only his two eye stalks poking up out of the sand.

Steve hurriedly swam over to investigate.

Deez? Can you hear me?

Not well, but I can see you.

Oh. What happened?

The foundation appears to have vanished.

Are you going to sink anymore? Sarah wanted to know, as she swam up beside her husband.

The eye stalks shifted a few feet to the left, then reversed course and moved to the right.

The ground appears solid here, Deez reported.

Emily appeared next to Sarah.

Of course! This structure, this temple… *I think it might be a recreation of the* Temple of Hatshepsut. *That area above us was large enough to be the third courtyard. Leading outward, in front of us, would be the large second courtyard, and finally way out front, the first.*

That sounds really big, Steve complained. *Like, needle-in-a-haystack big.*

Not really, Emily countered. *The courtyards are big, yes, but the inner temple, where I'd expect to find any artefacts, or treasure, would be at the top and it is by far, the smallest section of the temple.*

Suggesting what we're looking for is on this third level? Pravara asked.

Emily nodded her head. *Right. And the entrance? In the* Temple of Hatshepsut, *the entrance could be found by following the ramp from the second courtyard.*

I think I found it, Pravara reported. *The sediment is thicker here, but not here. Do you see? There's a walkway here, and it appears to lead deeper into the seabed floor.*

Emily swam excitedly around the area where Deez was currently standing.

The entrance has to be here. Hurry! Let's see if we can clear some of this muck away. The way in must be here somewhere!

Once they had enough of the sea floor exposed, they could, indeed, see a ramp angling down. As with the first temple, carved reliefs, pictographs, and runes were everywhere. Gareth was the first to spot one of the symbols.

Over here! I found one of those triangles!

The five shealk—plus one crab—crowded close together to study the triangle. And that's all it was, a simple triangle, pointing up. There were no lines to be found, nor were there any other triangles nearby.

$$\triangle$$

What does this tell us? Steve asked. He looked over at Emily.

Do you know which element this one is?

One you should know well, Emily answered. *Fire.*

This is a fire temple, Steve quietly mused. *Underwater. Go figure. All right, what do we do to open the door?*

We have to find the door first, Sarah interjected.

Deez, having finished sweeping the area clear of sand and mud, was now swinging his large pincers back and forth as he struck the face of the wall comprising the temple's third level. In fact, to Steve, it looked like the enormous crab was trying his hand at taiko drumming. Having the perfect physique to naturally walk from left to right, the crab kept hammering at the walls, while slowly walking the length of the temple.

About thirty feet later, Deez paused. One pincer had landed a blow, while the other was ready to strike, only Deez wasn't moving a muscle. Encouraged, the others crowded close.

Did you find something, pal? Steve hopefully asked.

The composition of the stone has changed here, Deez announced. *Listen.*

The giant crab back stepped a few paces, struck the wall several times, then returned to the spot where he had hesitated. He hammered the wall a few more times before turning triumphantly to his companions.

Tonal echoes confirm composition has changed.

Sounds the same to me, Steve observed, *but I trust you, amigo. Okay, assuming this is the door, there must be more of those triangle symbols around here. Let's see what we can find, okay?*

The shealk spread out while Deez, in crab form, continued to explore the immediate vicinity of the sealed door. While they all did an admirable job of scouring every square inch of the exposed structure, including floors *and* walls, no other elemental symbols could be found.

Maybe we need to clean more of this area off? Steve suggested, after searching fruitlessly for nearly an hour. *Emily, didn't you say there were several courtyards, and they were much bigger than this?*

I did, Emily confirmed. *It's just that…*

What? Sarah asked, after the paleontologist trailed off.

I expected to find the symbol in more places than only the one.

Sarah's purple shealk head lifted and turned to look at

the level above them, which would be the first area they had cleaned.

If there's only one symbol, then that must be what we're looking for. I say we go back up there and take a closer look.

Once they were all crowding around the symbol once more, husband and wife looked helplessly at each other.

If that's a button, how are we supposed to press it? Steve asked. *I mean, look at these teeny, tiny arms we have. I couldn't reach that thing even if I tried. I can't even scratch my own nose with these toothpicks. And if, by some miracle, I was able to get my arm that close to the symbol, I wouldn't be able to see what I was doing.*

Sarah contemplated the predicament for a few moments before letting out a soft growl. Before she could say anything, though, it was Gareth who came up with the winning suggestion.

Wait a minute. Our tails!

Four shealk heads turned to study their long, sinewy tails. Steve looked back at Gareth's black shealk body and scowled, which unfortunately, came out as a growl. Just then, something slammed into him, sending Steve careening into the nearest wall. Sarah appeared at his side first.

Oh, no! Honey, are you okay?

Yeah, I think so. What hit me? Are we under attack?

Gareth snickered loudly. Steve glanced over and noticed the other three shealk were each looking in different directions. Suspiciously, he turned to his wife.

Was that you? Did you hit me with something?

I'm so sorry! I wasn't thinking. I went to smack you on your arm and, before I knew what was happening, my tail lashed out and caught you on the side of your head. Are you sure you're okay?

Steve gave his dragon head a shake and tried to shrug.

Don't worry about it. Now, what about that symbol? Is it a button? Has anyone pressed it?

Pravara turned herself around and expertly touched the tip of her tail to the floor. After a few moments, it became evident that this temple was not like the first and that the method used to gain entry to the first would not work this time around. Steve sighed.

It was worth a try. Wait. Emily, didn't you say this was a fire temple? I wonder. Could it be that simple?

What are you thinking? Sarah wanted to know.

Fire. What if all it takes is to touch that symbol with some fire?

Sarah doubtfully looked at Emily. Could it be that easy? The teal shealk looked down at the symbol, over at Steve, and then swung its head in a wide arc, as if taking in the situation they were in.

Sarah nodded. *Good point. That may be a problem.*

What's the problem? Steve asked.

Honey, we're underwater. If what you say is true, we'll need to start a fire. Under water. Is that even possible?

Steve nodded. *Sure. They have flares which will burn under water. You're talkin' to the Fire Thrower. If anyone can make something burn under water, it's me. The only question I have is, what should I burn?*

Deez scuttled off, only to return moments later, clutching a piece of driftwood in one of his claws. He held out his pincer and waited for Steve to take it, which he did, using only his mouth.

Damn, freakin' tiny-ass arms, Steve grumbled. *What I wouldn't give to have opposable thumbs right about now.*

Steve focused his jhorun on the broken plank and ordered it to ignite, all while recalling a picture of a submerged, burning flare. The tip of the wood burst into flames and started sizzling and hissing something fierce. He also noted, with dismay, that the wood was being rapidly consumed by his jhorun. He needed to act fast.

Out of the way! Out of the way! This wood is burning faster than I wanted.

Holding the wood, and looking for all the world like he had a lit stogie in his mouth, Steve swam over to the symbol and brought the sputtering driftwood into contact with the floor.

The blackened wood died out right then, like a spent sparkler. At that moment, a powerful wave rushed by, and they all heard a very welcoming sound: the grating of stone.

Steve and his companions raced back and were rewarded with an open doorway. Visible through the opening was a shimmering translucent wall, stretching from the floor to the ceiling.

Now we're playing with fire! Steve happily exclaimed.

Chapter 10 — An Ancient Surprise

Don't you think you ought to wait to see what that is before you go swimming through it? Sarah asked, as she watched her husband line himself up with the temple's entrance. *We really don't have any idea what lies behind that shimmery wall.*

Well, we'll never know until one of us tries it, Steve replied. He locked his eyes on the strange glistening barrier and felt his tail bracing for a powerful kickoff. *If something does happen, I'll trust you guys to know what to do.*

I don't like this idea, Steve heard Emily whisper.

Neither do I, Sarah's voice admitted.

Steve sighed, *Will you two relax? Everything will be fine. Watch this.*

Steve ordered his shealk body to swim through the large entrance, on a direct course for the strange flickering object. Almost immediately, he felt his tail flex and in a split second he made contact with the unknown phenomenon.

In a blink, Steve found himself on the other side of the shimmering wall. His body convulsed. Coughing, swearing, and coughing a bit more, Steve finally managed to sit up. He realized three things. First, he was breathing air. Second, upon glancing down at his hands, he was shocked to discover he was back in his human form. And finally, he was mortified to discover he was buck naked.

"What the hell!" he managed to wheeze out.

He rolled over to look through the doorway, back toward the sea. There, looking as confused as he felt, were four pairs of shealk eyes. And one crab's. Muttering a curse, he ignited his hands and allowed the flames to encompass his entire body.

"Anyone care to explain what happened here?" Steve grumbled, as he slowly rose to his feet.

The four water dragons were silent as they continued to stare at him.

"You guys can't understand me. Oh, this is just peachy." Steve singled out the purple shealk and pointed at her. Then he touched his chest and pointed straight up, to the surface of the water. "I don't suppose you could teleport me some clothes, could you?"

Evidently, his pointing in various directions had the desired effect. A few seconds later, his bundle of wet clothes materialized in front of him. Steve applied his jhorun to the sodden pile and, a few minutes later, he donned his mostly dry attire. He turned to look at his wife's shealk form and gave her a thumbs-up.

He watched his wife swim up to the shimmering barrier and tilt her head to the side. She wiggled her tail, rocked backward a few feet, and then inched forward again. She wanted to join him!

Steve pointed at each shealk in turn and spun his finger, indicating he wanted them to turn around. Then he pointed at Sarah and waved her through. He positioned himself to catch her once she breached the barrier.

As soon as she appeared, wet, naked, and choking on the water still in her lungs, Steve shielded her from sight by generating a wall of flames. He held her hair away from her face as Sarah fought to remove the excess water from her system. As soon as she was able, he helped her to a sitting position.

"That was unpleasant," Sarah whispered. She looked down at herself and cringed. "Oh, please tell me they can't see me like this."

Steve shook his head. "They can't. Fetch your clothes so I can get them drying for you."

Five minutes later, Sarah was on her feet and looking back at their friends on the other side of the wall.

"I don't get it," she was saying. "Why is this here? Why would it nullify Gareth's spell like that?"

Steve shrugged. "I really don't know. I can only imagine how it must've looked when I went through it."

"You looked like a fish out of water," Sarah admitted, giving him a coy smile. "Not pleasant. Now that I've gone through that, I would have to agree."

"You ought to bring Gareth's and Emily's clothes here. I can get them drying, then if they're willing, they can join us in here."

"What about Pravara and Deez?"

"Well, we don't have to worry about Deez. I would imagine he'll revert to his normal guur body."

"And Pravara?" Sarah prompted.

"She'll be more of a problem," Steve admitted. He turned to see Gareth staring at him. Steve pointed at the young wizard and beckoned him through the barrier. "We need Gareth in here. He might be able to do something for her."

"Wouldn't it be nice to be a wizard?" Sarah idly commented. "That way, whenever a problem presents itself, we could… look out! Here he comes!"

Steve was ready. He caught the teenage boy the instant he emerged through the barrier and then snapped his firewall back into place. He hooked an arm around Gareth's waist and waited as the teenage wizard coughed his way through the change-over process and pulled on his dry clothing.

"Any idea why, or *how*, your spell could have been nullified by the wall?" Steve asked, as soon as Gareth rose to his feet. He pulled his jhorun inward and watched the wall of fire poof out.

Gareth shrugged. "Well, it could be…"

As soon as the fire was gone, Deez hurried by Emily and Pravara, and dove *sideways* through the Temple's entrance, since that was the only way his large crab body would fit, and only by tucking all ten of his legs close to his body. Half a moment later, Deez's inert form thudded to the ground next to Steve's feet.

Unsure how to help, Steve hesitantly patted the misshapen rock that Deez had become.

"Come on, buddy, you can do this. Cough up the water in your lungs. Clear out your airways. You'll be just fine as soon as you do."

A muffled cough sounded from somewhere within the 'rock'. A small puddle of water appeared under Deez's inert form. After a few moments, the guur hesitantly rose to his feet. His armored head turned to Steve and remained there.

TRANSITIONING BETWEEN BREATHABLE MEDIUM WAS MOST UNPLEASANT.

"You can say that again, pal," Steve agreed.

TRANSITIONING BETWEEN BREATHABLE MEDIUM WAS MOST UNPLEASANT.

Steve groaned. "I walked into that one, didn't I?"

Together, husband and wife turned to look at the two last remaining members of their party. Two sets of shealk eyes stared impassively back at them. Sarah turned, pointed at Emily's clothes, and then up at the teal shealk. She made a beckoning gesture with her arm, indicating she was tasking the paleontologist with being the next to make the transition to human.

Emily's shealk eyes widened with alarm. Sarah patiently smiled and again gestured for her to come through the wall.

"Oh, that was terrible," Emily softly moaned, four minutes later.

Steve immediately turned to the young wizard and

nudged him on the shoulder. He pointed at Pravara, who was still floating in the water on the other side of the shimmering wall. Gareth fell silent as he thought about what best to do for the transformed dragon.

"Obviously, we can't have her swim through that," Sarah was saying. "She'd revert to her normal body, and she's way too big to move around in here."

"I suppose I could shift her to something smaller," Gareth said, as he mentally reviewed the spells he had memorized.

Not necessary. I am perfectly fine waiting out here. Good luck to you all.

Steve tapped the side of his head. "Feel free to eavesdrop."

Acknowledged.

Sarah seemed about to speak but froze.

"Hey, are you okay?"

"Does anyone else hear that, besides me?"

I can.

"Hear what?"

"There's someone moving around," Sarah whispered, pointing at the hallway leading deeper into the Temple. "Aren't we the only ones down here?"

Steve ignited his hands. "Gareth and I will take the lead."

Gareth's eyes widened. "Now I hear it. Sounds like someone is talking."

"Chanting," Emily corrected. "They sound like you, Gareth."

"Someone's chanting? Another wizard?"

Steve grinned. "Then it's a damn good thing we have a wizard of our own."

"That's not funny," Gareth muttered as the two started down the passageway.

They hadn't made it more than a few steps before Deez zipped by, upside down. Sarah appeared at Steve's side.

"The chanting sounds similar to that of Benedictine monks," Steve said.

The group arrived at the end of the hallway, made a right turn, and came to a halt.

"What do these monks look like?" Gareth asked, staring ahead.

"Ummm, they look a lot like that, actually," Steve admitted, as he pointed at a figure, wearing a long white tunic with a dark leather belt at the waist, who had his back to them.

They were now in a large chamber, complete with lit torches lining the walls. A raised stone rectangular table stood in the center of the room. The robed figure was pacing beside the table.

A recessed shelf encircled the entire room, and it held nearly a hundred small knee-high statues. The figurines were in various poses, and every one of them had one or both arms extended with open palms.

"That can't be good," Steve muttered, as he looked around at the small figurines. "Somehow, and in some way, this is gonna come back to bite us in the butt."

Sarah and Emily both giggled.

"Umm, excuse me?" Steve called out to the monk. No reply. He cleared his throat and raised his voice. "Excuse me? Are you real? Can you hear me?"

"And why wouldn't I be real?" a soft voice inquired.

The monk slowly turned to face the group. He appeared to be in his mid-fifties, was bald except for tufts of gray hair above his ears, but towered over Steve by at least a foot. The strange monk gave each of them a small bow, and then turned to look up at the ceiling, where Deez was perched.

"Good afternoon to you, young guur. Please come down."

Deez immediately did as he was told. As soon as the five of them were standing before the rectangular table, the monk sat, where Steve was certain a chair didn't exist five seconds earlier. About ready to say something, Sarah held a finger to her lips.

"I must admit," the monk was saying, "that it's been a long time since I've entertained any guests here."

Steve cleared his throat. "Um, er, that may be because this place is now at the bottom of the sea. Speaking of which, how are you even here? And what's with that liquid-y, sparkly wall thingy that nullified Gareth's spells?"

Sarah groaned and placed a hand on Steve's chest before

turning to face the strange monk.

"Honey, I've got this. Okay, what my husband is trying to ask you is, how is it possible that you're here in this place? There's water outside, held in place by some unknown force that, once you pass through, will nullify any existing spells. Did you have a hand in that?"

The monk gave her a cryptic smile and remained in place, staring impassively at her.

"It doesn't seem like he's willing to answer that," Steve grumbled. "Okay, let me try one. Mr. Monk, is there another way to the surface besides having to grow a set of gills?"

The monk bowed low. "No."

"So, *that* he answers," Sarah whispered to herself. She looked up at the monk and was startled to see the gentle, kind face staring straight at her. "How long have you been down here?"

"At times," the monk slowly began, "it feels like I am always here."

Steve pointed at the many statues encircling the room.

"Do you know what we're supposed to do with all of those?"

The monk turned to scrutinize the figures. With a grunt, he looked back at Steve.

"It would almost appear as if they're wanting something, isn't it?"

"What do they want? Can't you tell us?" Gareth asked.

"I would imagine," the monk slowly answered, "they want whatever is in here."

The monk reached inside his robes and produced a small, bejeweled box. He placed it on the altar and gently slid it over. Sarah, being the closest, was the first to reach for the chest.

"Are you sure you want to open that?" Steve asked, concerned.

"It's okay," Sarah assured him. She looked at the monk and smiled. "I can't explain how I know it, but I *know* that he wouldn't put us in harm's way."

The monk simply smiled and shrugged.

"Fine," Steve sighed. "Open her up. Let's see what we're working with."

Everyone crowded close as Sarah gently undid the tiny pewter clasp and opened the box. What lay within had them all gasping with surprise. Four small objects, each of which were a different shape and color, met their gaze and beckoned invitingly from within the velvet confines of the tiny chest. Sarah reached in and gently took one of the objects out. It was a slightly oval shaped sapphire.

Sarah stared at the gem, unblinking.

Steve reached past his wife and withdrew another of the gems, this one emerald green and pyramid shaped, a trilliant cut.

Gareth, not wanting to be left out, reached into the chest and selected the gem that resembled a gently squashed diamond cube. The acolyte wizard whistled with amazement as he held the jeweled cube, turning it to admire the many cut facets. Noticing that there was one jewel left in the small box, Gareth turned to Emily and nodded his head.

Emily shrugged, reached in, and closed her fingers around the final gemstone: an unusual ruby. In fact, Steve decided, this ruby outshone the spiraled ruby from the Narian power hammer. This particular gem had been deliberately fashioned into a perfect blooming rose, complete with rows of delicate petals, each looking more fragile than the next.

Sarah, catching sight of the flower-shaped gemstone, immediately returned hers to the container and crowded close to their paleontologist friend.

"Ooooo, how pretty!"

"Right?" Emily agreed. "Look how delicate it is. Someone made this? Wow. The jewelers in this world are much better than ours back home."

"So, what are these for?" Steve asked. His gaze suddenly fell upon one of the many statues in the room and its single, outstretched hand. Then, realization dawned. He let out a loud groan and sighed heavily.

"What is it?" Sarah asked. "What's the matter?"

"I knew those things were gonna come back to bite us in the ass," Steve grumped as he pointed at the statues. "Look at all of the hands. The statues want something. *These* things."

"Look how many there are," Sarah argued. "That's a lot

for differences. He even cited previous examples of finding something different."

"He's one smart guur," Gareth commented.

"How many has he checked so far?" Sarah wanted to know.

"I think he's made it around the room," Steve decided. "It doesn't look like he found anything, unfortunately. It's okay, Deez. You tried, buddy. It… now what are you doing?"

The guur chittered excitedly and tapped the ground with its two front legs, like it was playing the bongo drums.

"Deez found something!" Sarah excitedly exclaimed. "Way to go! Now, what is it? Did you find something different?"

STONE IS NOT STONE. WAS STONE BEFORE.

Steve and Sarah each touched the statue nearest the guur.

"Feels like stone to me," Sarah offered. "However, we're clearly not geologists. On the other hand, Deez has lived around stone his entire life. I trust him. If he says this one isn't stone, then it isn't stone."

Deez's armored head turned until he was looking at Sarah.

THANK YOU.

Sarah smiled and patted the guur's head. "You're welcome. You're really starting to get used to thinking for yourself, aren't you?"

YES.

Steve pointed back at the statues. "See if you can spot any others that stand out, ok?"

COMPLIANCE.

"That's one way to do it."

Everyone turned to see the monk standing behind them. The old fellow had his hands clasped behind his back and was regarding them with a neutral expression.

"What's the problem?" Steve asked.

"Of all the people who have attempted to gain entry to that chest," the monk began, "no one had ever thought to consider the statue's composition as a determining factor as to which statues should be awarded stones."

Steve straightened and looked back at the altar, where the four jewels sat glittering in the torchlight.

"Stones. Stones? Wait a minute, is that what those are? Replicas of the Alchos Stones?"

The monk groaned and sadly shook his head. "I shouldn't have said that."

Steve stared at the tiny replicas.

"Do we know which one Flinn has?"

Sarah pointed at the sapphire. "This one."

STONE IS NOT STONE.

Everyone turned to Deez. The guur had stopped by a kneeling figure of a robed woman. The statue's hands were cupped together, and it appeared as though the woman was staring at her hands.

"Gareth, go stand by that one. Deez? Keep going, buddy."

COMPLIANCE.

"So far, that's one on each wall," Sarah quietly observed.

"Do you think each wall has one of the statues we need?" Emily whispered back.

"That's my guess," Sarah confirmed. "He… look! That didn't take long. He's stopped again."

Steve heard a slight hiss of irritation come from his left.

"I can't help but feel we're on the right path," Steve softly muttered.

The monk scowled. "There has never been anyone who managed to find all four statues, yet that infernal insect has found three of them."

"Oh, he'll find the fourth," Steve assured the monk. "Deez has proven himself invaluable during this trip. Hey, can I ask you something?"

The monk gave a slight nod of his head.

"Do you know what powers Usol's stone possesses?"

"Why do you ask?" All traces of irritation had vanished from the monk's voice.

"Flinn's stone has the power to conceal, so I can only imagine what the Earth Ancient's stone will do. No wonder he wants his stone back. I wouldn't want to lose those kinds of powers, either."

"Usol abused his powers," the monk said. "He was only interested in his own entertainment. Never once did he care about helping others. Why are you so interested in this subject?"

"Something about this whole situation doesn't sit well with me. It's like… well, it's like the other three Ancients ganged up on him. Yes, it sounds like he was being a real jerk, but to take away his powers? One would think that a different solution could have been found."

"We have the last statue!" Sarah happily exclaimed.

Steve hurried over to see Deez standing in front of a male warrior figure, with a shield strapped to his left arm and holding out his right. His hand was cupped, as though he was simply waiting for someone to return the appropriate replica stone to him. From the altar, Sarah had retrieved the other three jewels.

"We've narrowed down our list," she began, as she gave Steve an encouraging smile. "Deez has indicated which four need the jewels. All we have to do now is figure out who gets what."

MELTED CUBE'S RESTING PLACE DISCOVERED.

Steve turned his attention back to Deez and the warrior figure.

"What? How can you be so sure?"

OBSERVE. STATUE TREMBLES WHEN CUBE PLACED ON APPENDAGE. STATUE DOES NOT TREMBLE WHEN OTHER STONES PRESENT. PLUS,

CUBE NOW GLOWS.

Four sets of human eyes stared at the small diamond cube that was now resting in the statue's cupped hand. None could tell that it was glowing.

Emily spoke up. "Deez lives underground, so it's not too hard to believe that this creature, sensitive to the tiniest bit of light and the faintest vibrations in the rock, would be able to see and feel something that we cannot."

"An oversight that will not be overlooked in the future," a quiet voice added.

Steve was the only one who heard the comment. Turning, he grinned at the monk, who rewarded him with a wink and a smile in return.

Sarah handed Deez another of the replica Alchos Stones and waited for the efficient guur to locate the proper statue. As soon as all four had been placed, they heard a distinct click. The chest on the altar was now slightly ajar.

"Ooo, let's see what we've got!" Steve eagerly exclaimed.

Sarah reached into the chest and gingerly pulled out … a glittering silver key, similar to an antique skeleton key, but untarnished. The bow was flat and circular, the shaft at least three inches long, and the bit resembled a curved fang. Upon closer inspection, Steve could see small grooves cut into it, suggesting the existence of tumblers inside the lock. And there, on the flattened bow of the key, was a single rune:

Chapter 11 — Perils of Piracy

The gentle swaying woke him. The constant creaking was familiar, yet he couldn't remember why. The smell of brine was back in the air, and the sudden cry of a gull prevented him from slipping back to sleep. Opening red, bloodshot eyes, Captain Flinn cursed with disgust and slapped both hands over his face. The bright sunshine sent daggers of pain straight through his skull, which throbbed mercilessly. Flinn screwed his eyes shut and tried to remember if he had passed out drunk the night before. That would certainly explain what had to be the worst hangover ever.

Wait. Why did it feel like he was back aboard the *Emberbrand*? Hadn't they been hundreds of leagues away, on the opposite coast of this blasted kingdom? Hadn't they been battling the blasted Lentarians? How, then, could they suddenly be back on board their vessel?

Pushing aside the pain, Captain Flinn rose unsteadily to his feet. When his eyes were finally able to focus, and he noted—with dismay—that he was, in fact, back on his beloved ship, he groaned aloud. He left his cabin in the stern and carefully stepped out onto the main deck. The sea was calm, but the ship was leaning much too far to the starboard. Making it to the guardrail, he braced himself as he waited for the nausea to pass. He also noticed that the rest of his crew, the ones who had fought with him against the Lentarians, were strewn about the deck, just beginning to awaken. Like him, they were grumbling as they slowly awoke to the bright sunshine streaming in through the canopy of trees ringing their hidden inlet.

"Where... where are we, Captain?" Rusty hesitantly asked. The *Emberbrand's* quartermaster pulled himself to his feet, clutching the deck railing, lest he topple into the water. "Why does it feel like I've had one ale too many?"

"Yer on the ship, Q," Flinn announced. "We all are."

"But, we hid the ship on the eastern coast, less than two leagues from the Lentarian Castle. How did we make it back here?"

Flinn automatically thrust his hand inside his jacket pocket. What if the stone wasn't there? What if one of the crew... wait. There it was. He couldn't remember the last time he had passed out in front of the men. In the privacy of his own quarters? Sure. Never in front of the crew, though.

"It's about time you're awake, Cap'n," came a surprisingly chipper voice.

Flinn turned to see a thin, short man in his mid-thirties looking at him with evident concern. The crewman bowed his head as soon as he noticed the captain was looking his way.

"Cap'n? Are you okay?"

"Arik. Have ye been on the ship all this time?"

"I've never left, Cap'n," Arik assured him.

"Were ye awake when we arrived?"

Arik nodded. "I was, Cap'n. Strangest damn thing I ever saw."

"Go on," Flinn urged. "What did ye see, mate?"

"It happened just after sunset. I remember I was lookin' forward to restin' my jhorun, 'cause it ain't easy hiding a ship as big as this, when I heard a splash on the starboard side. I hurried over, fully expectin' to see the locals, yet there was nothing there. When I turned back, I made it no more than three steps when I tripped on somethin' and landed flat on my face. That's when I saw that I had tripped over Q."

Rusty absent-mindedly rubbed his chest. "That explains much."

"Never saw anything like it before, Cap'n," Arik continued. "One minute, Ferris and I be the only ones aboard, and the next, the deck became littered with bodies. I… I thought the worst, Cap'n."

"Are ye responsible for takin' me to my cabin, mate?"

Arik nodded sheepishly.

"Why didn't you take us to our bunks below deck?" Von demanded. "My back is stiff as a board. Could've avoided that had you…"

"That be enough, ladies," Flinn spat out. He nodded appreciatively at Arik before turning to the rest of his crew. "Think I care where ye spent the night? Do none of ye care that the blasted Lentarians drove us away?"

"How *did* we get back to the *Emberbrand?*" Rusty wanted to know. "The last thing I remember was trying to hide from that infernal monster they keep as a pet."

"It scared the bejeezus outta me," Grenden admitted. "It was able to run along the walls, like a spider. Nothing I could do would make it go away."

"Yet, here we are," Flinn announced, spreading his hands wide.

"Do ye know what happened to us?" Puck suspiciously asked.

"Better yet, do you know what happened to Jino and Casimir?" Rusty interjected. "They're not here, Captain!"

Flinn sighed and sank down on the closest bench. "Truth be told, lads, I be warned about this."

There was a collective gasp of astonishment.

"I was no' honest with ye, and I regret that," the captain continued, before anyone could protest. He pulled his left hand out of his pocket and slowly unwrapped his Alchos Stone. "Some of ye know I have this. Some do not."

"What is that thing, Captain?" Rusty asked. "Is it a jewel?"

"That's gotta be the biggest sapphire I've ever seen!" Arik added. "It's gotta be worth a fortune! How long have you had it, Cap'n?"

"Q, would ye care to enlighten 'em as to what this is?"

"How would I know what it is?" Rusty stammered.

"Because ye were the one who told me about the Alchos Stones."

There was another round of gasps, and a few curses. Rusty's eyes bulged. His quartermaster pointed a shaky finger at the stone and practically squealed with fright.

"Out with it, man," Flinn snapped, rounding on Rusty. "Ye got somethin' to say? Then, say it!"

"Is … is *that* one of the four Alchos Stones?"

Flinn nodded proudly. "Aye. It even has a name: *Essence of the Sea.*"

"Aeus," Rusty whispered, his eyes going wider still.

Flinn shrugged. "So?"

Rusty swallowed nervously. "Captain? You don't want to mess with an Ancient. That? That belongs to the Water Ancient. He's gonna want it back!"

"She," Flinn corrected. "This particular Ancient be female."

"All the more reason to get rid of it," Rusty groaned.

Flinn angrily shook his head. "Absolutely not, Q. This be the reason we have avoided capture. This be what allows us to vanish, right from under everyone's noses. This be how we stole the fang from beneath the dragons."

"Why are you telling us this?" Arik curiously asked. "You had your reasons for keeping it to yourself, Cap'n. Why tell us now?"

"Because it has been brought to my attention that one o' the Ancients be more than likely helpin' us out."

Rusty gasped again, but refrained from saying anything after Flinn's look dared him to speak.

Von approached next and, surprisingly, didn't give the large jewel a second glance.

"I want to know what happened to Jino. He and Casimir are missin', Captain. How do we get 'em back?"

"That accursed Teleporter," Flinn scowled. "She zapped

'em outta existence."

There was a collective snort of disgust among the crew.

"Well, then she can simply zap 'em back," Rusty decided, earning himself grunts of approval from the men.

"It be no easy task," Flinn admitted. "All she has to do is look at ye, and ye are toast. The Ancient warned me 'bout her. I do not know why she waited so long to use her blasted powers, but..."

"Maybe she didn't know how?" Puck suggested.

"Pssht," Rusty scoffed. "She's a woman. What does a woman know?"

Flinn leveled his gaze at the quartermaster.

"Care to tell that to her face, Q? I can guarantee ye, ye'll find out for yerself where she put our men."

"What... what about Pedr?" a timid voice asked.

Everyone turned to the remaining cabin boy, Ferris.

"He was my friend, Captain. Do you think this woman will give him back?"

Flinn shrugged. "Who knows, boy."

"What do we do about her?" Rusty asked, in a fit of exasperation.

"Avoid her," Flinn instructed. "Be sure ye know where she be at all times. If ye see her, then make yerselves scarce. Be that understood?"

A chorus of 'ayes' sounded from the group.

"Do we know which Ancient is helping us?" Rusty asked, once the crew had quieted down.

"Does it matter?" Flinn snapped.

Rusty shrugged. "I would think so. Legends say that each Ancient favored different animals, activities, and so on. If we could keep ourselves in his favor, then perhaps the Ancient would be willing to do us a favor or two."

"Like?" Flinn prompted.

"Returning our missing crewmen," Rusty promptly answered.

"He hasn't told me his name," Flinn admitted. "But, now that I think about it, I do have my suspicions."

"Who is it?" Grenden asked.

"I'd like to know, too," Arik added.

There's no need to tell them who I am.

Flinn blinked with surprise.

So, ye be listenin', are ye? The time for keeping secrets from my crew be long gone. The only way we are gonna beat the Lentarians will be if we be workin' as a team, like we used to.

"Captain?" Rusty asked, clearing his throat. "Are you okay?"

"Aye. A moment."

It's time to be honest with my crew. Since I saw and experienced the strongest terra tremors I have ever felt, along with some of the most powerful winds I have not had a hand in making, I would say ye are either Earth or Air. I be thinking Earth.

Correct. I am Usol.

Why did ye transport us back to the Emberbrand?

It's where you need to be.

What? Why?

When a response wasn't forthcoming, Flinn scowled and returned his attention to the crew.

"Our benefactor—and I use the term loosely—be Earth."

"Usol?" Rusty whispered. "Usol has been helping us?"

"Which means Air be our enemy," Flinn continued.

"Oh, not good," Rusty moaned.

"Why is air an enemy?" Puck asked.

"Not the air ye breathe, ye daft moron," Flinn scolded. "Air, the Ancient. Don't ye remember the battle? Ye all felt the terra tremors, did ye not?"

Heads were nodding.

"Do ye also remember the wind?"

Rusty pointed a finger at Flinn. "Well, you handled all the wind, right?"

"Not then, I didn't," Flinn informed him. "I can handle more than any man can, 'tis true. However, what we saw yesterday be stronger than anything I can create. And that tells us...?"

"Air," Rusty miserably confirmed. "Eion. He's powerful, Captain."

"They all be powerful," Flinn argued. "For now, ye must listen to me. Some of ye have been askin' what we be doin' here, in Lentari. Well, if ye have not figured it out yet, there be another one of these magical stones here."

"In the second temple?" Rusty guessed.

Flinn shook his head. "No. It's in the next one. The third temple."

"And where's that?" Rusty hesitantly asked.

Flinn focused on the stone. *Do ye know where the last temple be located?*

Of course. However, we have some time. In fact, you are ill-equipped to gain entry.

What are ye proposin'?

Let the Lentarians gain entry first. Just before they take possession of the stone, you and your men will take it.

Just tell me where the blasted temple be located and we'll be on our way.

The stone grew warm.

Listen to me, simpleton. You do not have the ability to open the temple. The Lentarians do. Let them do the work.

Blast. Fine. What would ye have us do now?

Wait. Be patient. You have the ability to observe in stealth. Do so. Wherever the locals go, be sure to follow so that you can strike at the most opportune time.

Patience be not one of my virtues.

You think? Now go. Settle your crew. Several are contemplating returning to the string of pathetic islands you call home.

Flinn tuned back in to the crews' conversations in time to hear that Usol was right. Several of the crew, mainly Arik and Von, wanted to return home to the Seven Kingdoms. His quartermaster, while unwaveringly loyal, appeared to be considering the offer.

"What is this talk of abandoning our mission, lads?" Flinn demanded. "Have ye lost that much faith in me? Is not the acquisition of a second stone worth the price?"

"Price?" Von sputtered. "What price could be higher than death itself?"

"Death?" Flinn repeated. "Who be talkin' about death, mate?"

"Where's Jino?" Von challenged. "Where's Casimir? What if we need to scare someone away? What will we do?"

"Hmm," Flinn grunted. *Can ye tell me what happened to my*

men? Where did the Teleporter take 'em? I can only assume it be some remote prison somewhere?

Worse. She, unfortunately, has figured out how to nullify a person. That is, until she chooses to restore them.

Restore 'em? What the blazes does she do to them?

Where? The question should be, where does she put them? Unfortunately for you, the Teleporter has learned how to access Grimere.

Grimere? Never heard o' it.

Of course you haven't. It's the world between worlds. Somehow, and I don't know how, the woman has the ability to place something from this world into Grimere.

Well, if she can place someone into Grimere, then she sure as blazes can take someone out *as well.*

Flinn heard nothing but a wry laugh as Usol's presence faded from his mind. Scowling, he turned back to his crew, only to discover them, once more, in a heated debate, something about divvying up the profits from the sale of his Alchos Stone. Growing angrier by the second, Captain Flinn generated twin jets of air and slammed them together. He smiled with satisfaction when the air jets knocked everyone off their feet.

"I grow tired o' sayin' this," Flinn slowly began, "so this'll be the last time. I be the captain here. Ye follow my orders. If ye think ye can fare better on yer own, fine. Ye can go with my blessing. However, the *Emberbrand* stays here until this blasted mission is over. We've succeeded thus far…"

"…except for yesterday…" someone muttered.

"True," Flinn reluctantly admitted, "but that was at the behest of our benefactor."

"Usol ordered us to leave?" Von asked, incredulous.

"I would not consider it an order," Flinn began, "but more of a strongly worded piece of advice. He saw what happened to poor Jino, and told us that if we all did not leave, we would be finished."

"Because of the woman," Puck grumbled.

Flinn nodded. "Aye. Because o' the woman."

Puck turned his head and spat. "That woman must pay."

"And pay she will," Flinn promised. "But, on our terms only."

The crew of the *Emberbrand* let out a series of angry whoops.

"Now," Flinn continued, "we must talk. I have been advised that we be unable to open the last temple. Only…"

"Balderdash," Rusty interjected. "Get us to that temple, Captain. We'll get inside it, or die trying."

"Still yer tongue, Q. Only the Lentarians can get inside, so…"

Rusty was shaking his head.

"I know Usol is an Ancient, Captain," the quartermaster began, "but are you sure you believe that? Why wouldn't we be able to get inside this temple? The Lentarians don't have anything over us. I say we press on. Who's with me?"

"What part of the word 'Ancient' are you having trouble with?" Puck wanted to know, as he rushed to the captain's side. "He is the Earth Ancient. If he says we are to let the Lentarians do the dirty work, then who are we to argue? There must be a reason, so just let the matter drop."

Flinn gave Puck an appraising stare. Did he have a hidden agenda?

"Raise yer hands, lads," Flinn instructed. His men complied. "Raise yer hands if ye want to go back to the Seven Kingdoms."

Every single hand was forcefully yanked down.

"Good. Now, I do not want to revisit this topic again, be that understood?"

There was a chorus of 'ayes.' Flinn nodded approvingly and reached for the dwarf hammer on his belt and set the tool down on a nearby bench, on its head. Once he had everyone's attention, he slipped his hand inside his jacket, intent on pulling out the fang, but his pocket was empty. Stifling a curse, Flinn was startled to discover a sizeable hole in the pocket.

"What's the matter, Captain?" Puck asked. "Are you looking for something?"

"I was plannin' on settin' the spoils of our battles out here, for all to see, but I no longer have the fang."

"Where is it?" Grenden asked, frowning.

"It would seem that it slipped through a hole in my pocket."

"Oh, that's just *great*, Captain," Von grumped. "Are you tellin' us the damn Lentarians have it back?"

Flinn was silent as he considered the absence of the fang. After a few moments, a grin appeared on his face.

"What does it matter? It served its purpose. We don't need it anymore."

"We won't need it to get into the third temple?" Rusty asked.

"If we did, and if we could, do ye think Usol would've told us to let the Lentarians enter first? No, ye saw for yerself how it protected us from the falling rocks in the second temple."

"Then how did the Lentarians make it through?" Puck asked. Actually, Flinn decided, it sounded like more of a whine.

"I know not," Flinn confessed. "Again, why dwell on the past? What's done be done. What we have to focus on now be the future. We need to be one step ahead of the locals. We need to… what, Puck? Speak."

"How are we supposed to be ahead of the Lentarians when they have whatever was in the second temple? Do we know what was waiting for them?"

"No," Flinn answered. "Not yet, anyway."

"What's the plan, Captain?" Rusty eagerly asked.

Flinn walked over to the bulwark and pointed northwest. There, visible through the line of trees, was one of the turrets from the Lentarian castle. The crew fell silent as they studied the distant capital.

"If they only knew we're hiding right under their noses," Von chortled.

"Be silent," Flinn snapped.

"What's your plan for spying on the Lentarians?" Rusty asked. "Will you use your jewel again?"

Surprised that his prized Alchos Stone was being so openly talked about, Flinn grunted as he realized he didn't know. It was certainly the logical move to make. Use the stone, spy on the Lentarians, and learn their plan.

"Let me, Captain. I can do it."

Flinn turned to see Arik standing before him.

"I can stroll through their city, unobserved."

"So can I, mate," Flinn told him.

Arik nodded. "True, but you're needed here. You have the ability to cloak the ship much better than I can. Let me do it. No one will ever know I was there."

"Do ye know what to be listenin' fer, lad?" Flinn asked.

Arik nodded. "Aye. I am to learn what I can of the temple."

"The third temple, mate," Flinn told him. "We don' care 'bout numbers one and two. The third be the important one. It be holdin' the second stone."

"Got it. Has any of us been inside their castle?"

"Most of us have," Flinn answered. "I have the most experience."

"Can you give me a sketch of the castle's layout? Anything you can remember could be helpful."

Flinn thoughtfully stroked his chin.

"Probably."

Arik nodded. "That'll do, Captain. When should I get started?"

Flinn turned to look back at the castle.

"Yer test begins as soon as the map be drawn, lad."

"Test?"

"Ye expect me to turn over so much responsibility without knowing what ye can and cannot do?"

"What would you have me do, so that I can prove myself?" Arik asked, growing concerned.

Flinn was already nodding.

"I have just the thing, mate."

* * *

"You want me to do *what?*"

"Ye heard me, mate."

"But, Captain… a sword?"

"Not just any sword, Arik. I want the blue one."

"You saw a blue sword? In the castle? Where?"

"It be in the library, in a display cabinet. Ye saw the shade of blue on my Alchos Stone. The blade and the stone are almost a perfect match. I want it."

"A blue sword?" Arik skeptically repeated.

"Aye. Will ye do it or should I do this myself? Ye have been doing a remarkable job of hiding the ship during daylight hours, mate. Ye have earned the right to be given more responsibility. Opportunity be knockin'. Will ye answer?"

"I'll get it, Captain," Arik promised. "Wait here."

"I'll meet ye back at the *Emberbrand*," Flinn told his chief lookout. "If ye are not back by sunset, then…"

"I'll be left behind," Arik sullenly finished, after the captain trailed off.

"See that ye get back on time, mate."

Arik eagerly nodded, then climbed down to the waiting skiff. Once he was on land, he bade his crewmembers goodbye and trudged off to the castle. The skiff immediately turned around and headed back toward the much larger ship, but not before Arik heard a question.

"Think he'll be able to do it?"

"Five pieces of gold says he doesn't."

"Make it ten!"

"Deal."

Grunting irritably, Arik pushed through the trees and bushes, and very nearly stumbled directly into the path of a group of soldiers. Hurriedly activating his jhorun, Arik peeked through the trees lining the cobblestone road and watched, mesmerized, as line after line of soldiers marched by in perfect formation. Noticing that the soldiers were headed in the same direction as he, Arik groaned inwardly.

"Maybe this wasn't such a good idea after all."

Nearly an hour later, the pirate—and the group of soldiers he was following—crossed through one of R'Tal's extensive and heavily fortified gates and into the city. Being careful not to allow anyone to touch him while he was disguised, Arik kept the imposing castle in his sights and angled toward it. What should have been a simple twenty-minute walk ended up taking twice that, since vendors, entertainers, and swarms of people were everywhere. At times, Arik felt as though he was executing a complex dance, to avoid them.

Arik watched the soldiers pass under the portcullis and

disappear down a large hallway on the right. Hugging the walls as best he could, the pirate scampered past numerous storage rooms, private offices, and through an immense room with two (empty) thrones. Now, which way was the library?

Arik ducked through a nearby open door. Once he verified he was alone in a storage room, he allowed his jhorun to rest. Just like that, he was able to see his hands and arms again. While many of his companions viewed his jhorun as being the best and most useful, little did they know how difficult it was to move around when he was cloaked. The last person to make the comment, the new cabin boy Pedr, had only made it a few steps before tripping over his own feet. Walking without seeing your own feet, was a daunting task.

He pulled out the rudimentary sketch of the castle Captain Flinn had provided him. According to this, the large chamber he had passed through was the Great Hall. All he had to do was take the northern hallway there, and stay to the right. It would dead-end in another larger hallway, which would then take him straight to the entrance of the library.

Arik tucked the map away. A library. Why in the world would someone want to display a sword in a library? Sure, the blue blade made it a fairly unique weapon. He could also understand why the captain would want it. But what would possess Captain Flinn to instruct him to steal the sword out from their very noses, to possibly give away their presence?

Convinced he was following a foolhardy plan, Arik carefully worked his way north. Treading quietly through several long hallways, he was eventually rewarded with discovering the entrance to what the locals evidently called, The Archives. And there, sitting behind a semi-circular desk, as though she was a jailer charged with keeping her prisoners in the dungeon, sat an old woman with frizzy white hair.

As he approached the counter, intent on tip-toeing past the grouchy-looking old woman, Arik hesitated as, inexplicably, the jailer's head snapped up and looked directly at him. Arik sucked in a breath and held it, terrified that, somehow, the woman knew he was there.

After a few moments, the woman rose to her feet and walked around her desk. She put her bony hands on her hips and glared at the empty lobby. Too scared to do anything else, Arik remained rooted to the spot, holding his breath. His chest burned.

Apparently satisfied, the old woman returned to her chair and resumed her work on a pile of tiny slips of papers. What they were, or what they could be for, Arik didn't know. The only thing he *did* know was that he had to make it past her so he could finally breathe again.

Leaving the frail librarian behind, Arik ducked behind a stack of thick, dusty books, and allowed himself to fill his lungs with air. Exhaling loudly, Arik sighed with contentment. That had been much too close.

"Is someone there?" a female voice suddenly asked.

Arik silently cursed and, with extreme reluctance, took another deep breath. Hopefully, this person would leave him be. Making certain his jhorun had concealed his entire body, which led to an errant thought—could he only hide part of himself?—he waited to see who would come around the corner. Already feeling his cheeks puffing out, he waited in misery.

A woman in her late thirties appeared, followed by an older thin man. The old man's outfit was entirely orange, from the floppy hat, all the way down to the slippers. All orange. Arik cringed, not having ever recalled seeing such a garish outfit in his life.

"Did you hear something, Lady Sarah?" the old man asked the woman.

"I thought I heard someone sigh," the woman—Sarah—confessed.

"Well, there doesn't appear to be anyone here," the old man replied, as he looked straight at the spot where Arik was standing. Thankfully, the old man was staring *through* him.

"It's just weird. Oh, well. Maybe I only imagined it. Come on. That last book Andra pulled for us has turned out to be more useful than the rest combined. Who would've thought that a codex for ancient runes would exist *and* the Archives had such a pristine copy?"

"That's my Andra for you," the old man cooed. "She knows her books."

"That she does," the woman admitted, as she turned away.

Arik made a mental note not to sigh. That was too close. Now, where was this sword he was supposed to find? Find and steal, that is.

He slowly emerged from the shadows of the many bookcases and entered the large open center of the library. Tables were everywhere, and unfortunately, so were people. Didn't the Lentarians have anything better to do than sit around and read all day? Trying to navigate through such a crowd was dangerous. One slip-up and the people would know that a stranger was here, spying on them. He had to be careful!

He smiled as he saw that one table, directly in the middle of a group, held a large glass display case. There, laying horizontally on a bed of white felt, was a large, two-handed broadsword, with a striking dark blue blade. That was obviously what he had come for!

Arik's scowl returned when he realized he must create a distraction in order to make off with a sword that big. Sure, his jhorun could easily accommodate him holding the unique two-handed sword, but the problem was, it made for an even bigger challenge of trying to leave the area without bumping into anyone. Or running anyone through, Arik sourly added, as he gazed down at the three-foot long blue blade.

Whatever he did, it had to be enough of a surprise that it would pull everyone away from the sword. Arik glanced around the table and silently cursed. There were no fewer than a dozen people present, and they were all huddled around the sword. The pirate squinted. They were all school children. Older school children, mind you, but still children. What were they doing here, anyway?

"For this next part," a voice was saying, "I want you all to look at the blade. I'm sure you've noticed the distinct coloring? Well, forget about the color for now. Focus on the runes. Who can tell me what type they are?"

Several hands shot skyward.

The teacher singled out a child. "Very well, Merla. I saw your hand go up first. What do you think?"

"The runes are dwarfish by nature, Mr. Quinn," the girl

immediately answered.

The adult male—Mr. Quinn—nodded. "Excellent. And how do you know for certain?"

The girl pointed at the sword and drew a rune on the surface of the glass cabinet with her finger.

"Because the first rune is the clan identifier. Do you see how it resembles a bug? This sword was made by none other than the Kla Guur."

The teacher clapped his hands with excitement. "Top marks, Merla! Now, if we all focus our attention on…"

Arik tuned out the lesson and turned to regard the surroundings. Aside from this group of school kids, the large chamber was predominantly quiet. It shouldn't take much to create a distraction. The only question was, what should he do?

The answer came in the form of a hushed conversation happening nearby.

"Why would he be watching us now?" a young man hesitantly asked his companion, as he nervously eyed the surroundings.

"Why wouldn't he?" a second young man countered. "You've already angered him with your blatant disregard for that book's condition."

"All I did was put a little crease here, on this page," the first man whined. "Besides, you've got no proof this place is haunted. You and I both know it. They're only stories."

"I've heard that Miss Andra Alwyn keeps him locked up in her desk," the second man continued, eliciting a low moan from the first man. "She lets him out when she wants to instill fear in someone. Look what you did to that book. I'll bet she already knows you've done it. I'll bet she's already sicced ol' Estin on you."

"Has not."

"Has so!"

"No way."

"I feel so sorry for you."

"Would you stop that? Nothing is going to happen to me. All I did was put a little mark on this book. Nothing bad will come of it, mark my words."

Arik smiled and stepped forward. An opportunity had presented itself. He moved close and gently closed the book. Both men fell silent as they stared, aghast, at the (recently) closed book. The first man's eyes sought out his friend's.

"Tell me you did that. Tell me that was some trick."

The second man, as surprised as the first, had no comment. He reached for the book, but gasped in shock as the book—inexplicably—slid several inches to the right in an effort to keep its distance from him. Two sets of scared eyes stared at each other for a few moments before the first man built up his courage and tried to pluck the book from the table.

They both sat, horrified, as the book suddenly tipped itself up, lifted off the table, and deposited itself on a nearby empty table. The two friends stared—wide-eyed—at the book before turning to look at each other. Nearly five seconds of silence passed before each of them calmly pushed themselves away from the table, rose to their feet, and then let out twin blood-curdling screams as they fled.

People scrambled to clear a path to the door, as the two men fled from the 'haunted' book. The old woman with the white frizzy hair appeared at the doorway and opened her mouth to deliver an angry scolding. However, both fleeing men caught sight of the woman and screamed even louder. They deftly ran around her and disappeared down the large hallway.

Nearly thirty minutes later, Arik emerged into the tiny clearing, which ringed the hidden inlet. He couldn't see the *Emberbrand*, but he knew it was there. He ran to the water's edge and waved his arms to signal his presence. A split second later, a sheepish grin appeared, as he realized no one would be able to see him until he ordered his jhorun to allow him to be visible once more.

Now, fully visible to everyone, Arik triumphantly held the blue-handed broadsword high in the air. A split second later, the ship appeared. Arik could also see Flinn, standing at the prow. The captain had a grin on his face as he looked down.

"Damn glad t' see ye, boy. Nice job. Nice job, indeed, mate. Congratulations. Ye just became our spy. Now, hand over that sword and get yerself back to the castle. I want to know what the locals are gonna do before they do, be that understood?"

"Aye, Captain."

Chapter 12 — The Key is the Key

What in the world was Rhenyon's sword doing out here, in the open?" Steve asked, bewildered, as he stared at the empty display in the Archives. "I mean, look at this thing. There's no lock. There's nothing to prevent someone from opening it and absconding with the sword. But, I'm glad they did."

"Why would you say that?" Sarah wanted to know.

"By taking that sword, we'll be able to track him," Steve victoriously explained. "Do you remember Rhenyon lost Mythron during the attack against the queen? My sword actually dragged me over to where it had fallen."

Sarah smiled. "I remember."

"You're assuming the pirates are responsible for this?" Emily asked.

Steve nodded. "Who else would have the brass to pull this off? This has 'Flinn' written all over it."

"It doesn't make any sense," Sarah complained. "We already know where he is."

"I know that. You know that. *They* don't know that."

"Do you think their captain was the one who took the sword?" Gareth asked.

Steve shook his head. "No, I don't think he'd be foolish enough to try to sneak in here again. I'll bet he sent someone else. I can't believe Rhenyon didn't take the sword with him when he accompanied the king and queen on their travels."

Sarah shrugged. "Maybe he felt he didn't need it as much as he used to, and wanted to make it available for others to study?"

"Maybe he forgot it?" Gareth suggested.

Surprisingly, Mikal smiled.

"Whatever the reason may be, we already know where the sword has been taken."

"We do?" Steve asked, surprised.

"Probably back to their ship," Sarah decided. She looked at Gareth. "You said you had located the ship and it wasn't far from here?"

Gareth nodded. "Aye."

"Then *that* is where we'll find Rhenyon's sword," Sarah decided. "We really ought to see about getting it back for him. That sword means a lot to him."

Mikal was shaking his head.

"There's no need. I know exactly where the sword can be found, and it's in Straosia. With Rhenyon."

A sea of confused faces turned to the pro-tem king.

"It was suggested to me that the pirates are still spying on us," Mikal confided. "So, I wanted to run an experiment, just to find out."

"And you had a copy of Rhenyon's sword just laying around?" Steve asked, impressed.

"No," Mikal disagreed. "A few of our blacksmiths fancy themselves on the same level as the dwarves, so they took it upon themselves to create replicas of Rhenyon's sword. We have one other, in storage."

"And they're as good as the dwarves?" Steve asked, nodding. "I'm impressed."

Mikal frowned. "Don't be. They were able to fashion a reasonable facsimile of the sword, but couldn't reproduce the blue coloring."

"Then, how did they do it?" Sarah wanted to know.

Mikal grinned. "Paint."

"Let's hope the pirates don't figure that out," Steve laughed. "Okay, experiment confirmed. The pirates are still watching us. Umm, how do we know they aren't watching us right now?"

"Working on it," Gareth mumbled.

The companions whirled around and saw their young wizard friend sitting at one of the tables, eyes closed. And, unsurprisingly, he was chanting. After a few moments, a smile spread across his face and his eyes opened.

"Well, that ought to do it."

"What?" Sarah asked. "Gareth, what did you do?"

The acolyte wizard held out a hand. "Before I answer that, I need everyone to place their hand over mine."

Puzzled, but willing to trust the teenager, Steve and Sarah immediately placed their hands over Gareth's. Emily was next, followed by the two dwarves and then Mikal and Lissa. Steve glanced over at Deez's rock shape.

"Latch on, pal. You're part of the Hive, remember?"

The rock sprouted legs and hurried over. Deez gently placed the tip of his right foreleg on top of Mikal's hand.

THANK YOU FOR INCLUDING ME.

"So, what are we doing?" Steve asked.

"I shared one of my spells with you," Gareth proudly announced.

"Which one?" Breslin cautiously asked.

"The pirates have hidden their ship," Gareth explained. "We know Flinn can use his Alchos Stone to conceal the ship, but we also know that he hasn't been on the ship every day since he arrived. That means someone else on that ship is also able to conceal it, and I assumed—correctly, I might add—that it had something to do with that person's jhorun. This spell is the one I used to counteract that jhorun and allowed me to find the ship. I simply added another facet to the spell, specifying the caster was more than one person."

"Meaning, as long as it isn't Flinn doing the spying by using his fancy gem," Steve began, "we should be able to spot someone who shouldn't be here?"

Gareth nodded. "Exactly. Be on the lookout for red people."

Sarah giggled. "Red people? Literally?"

"My spell will identify concealed people—or items—by casting them in a red hue. I don't know why it's always red. I've tried other colors, but red is always the one that appears. I'm sure it's something minor I've missed. I'll just have to figure it out later."

"When does it start?" Steve wanted to know.

"It already has," Gareth answered.

"And what if we see someone who is red?" Breslin curiously asked.

"Then you chase them out of here," Steve replied.

Sarah shook her head. "No, I don't think we want to do that."

Confused, Steve turned to Sarah. "What? Why not?"

"Think about it, honey. If we let on that we can see a disguised person, then the pirates will inevitably change tactics and try something else."

Mikal nodded. "That's a good point. Okay, umm, what do we do if we spot someone?"

"Can we use some type of code word?" Lissa asked.

Sarah had the winning suggestion.

"I have it. I did this once with the king, when I had to let him know what we were doing without telling him specifically."

"You lost me," Steve told his wife.

"Listen, everyone. If any of us spot a disguised pirate, then we need to immediately say something that is a blatant lie. For instance, if I see someone that isn't supposed to be here, then I'll say something like, 'Mikal, now that your parents have retired, how are you handling the responsibility of being the permanent king?' Something like that."

Emily nodded. "I get it. You say something that clearly isn't true. For me, I could say that I was a natural born citizen of Lentari. Everyone here knows that isn't true."

Sarah smiled. "Exactly."

"Are you planning on giving false information to the pirates?" Steve asked, as he deliberately dropped his voice, as though he believed the pirates could be listening.

Sarah nodded. "Doesn't it make sense? Make something up. If a pirate appears in here, it's clear he's trying to figure out what we're doing. They were driven away from the second temple, which means that Flinn is probably upset…"

"…very upset," Steve interrupted.

"Exactly," Sarah continued. "So, he'll be craving information, and we're going to see that he gets it."

"Just not the right information," Breslin added knowingly.

"Right. Now that we have that out of the way, we can talk about the key. It's safe to say no one recognizes the symbol, right?"

Everyone nodded.

"Then, I guess we have to head back to the Archives. Perhaps Andra will…"

MONOCHROMATIC BIPED DETECTED.

"What does that mean?"

"Monochromatic means one color," Emily translated. "Deez is saying that he has detected a one-color biped? Er, he's spotted a one-colored human? I'm not sure what he means by that, either."

Sarah's eyes went wide. "There's a pirate here! Deez, where is he?"

MONOCHROMATIC BIPED APPROACHES FROM THE SOUTH.

"The south?" Steve repeated. "The main entrance."

Their entire group turned to look in that direction.

"No, not all of us at once!" Sarah hissed. "It'll look too suspicious! Everyone, back in the huddle, like we're discussing important details. Now, one at a time. Steve, you're first."

Steve pretended to stretch his back, and in doing so, glanced south, toward the Archives' main entrance. A faint reddish glow caught his eye. "You're right. Red guy near the door."

Sarah raised up to take a look.

"Where's he headed?" Steve wanted to know.

"I'm not sure," Sarah admitted, as she watched the pirate carefully pick his way around the tables and people milling about the floor of the Archives. "I thought I'd seen all of Flinn's crew, however, I don't recognize him."

"Neither do I," Steve admitted.

Gareth watched for a moment. "I've seen him before," the teenager admitted. "He's the one who usually stays on the ship."

"He must be the pirate who keeps their ship hidden when Flinn isn't around," Sarah guessed. "No wonder Flinn chose him to poke around. He thinks he's invisible."

"He *is* invisible," Steve pointed out. "The only reason we see him is thanks to Gareth's spell."

"Doesn't that mean his ship has been left unprotected?" Breslin asked, frowning.

"Maybe your pirate captain is back on his ship and is the one doing the protecting?" Lissa suggested.

"How would he be able to get back there so quickly?" Steve asked. "I mean, we were just on the other side of the kingdom."

"We're here," Sarah reminded, "so you know it's not impossible."

"It's possible for us," Steve argued, "because we have you, the world's strongest teleporter."

"I'd say that Usol character is helping them," Emily suggested.

"I wouldn't put it past him," Steve eventually decided. He turned to watch the concealed pirate slowly move amongst the various tables.

"We should let him know we're the ones he needs to spy on," Breslin announced.

"Why?" Steve asked. "Let him find us on his own."

"And if he wanders away?" Breslin prompted. "What then? One of us would have to go after him."

"We have to assume Captain Flinn has told him who to

watch for," Steve decided. He looked over at their insectoid companion and a smile appeared on his face. "And I know just how to attract his attention. Who's got one of those small slips of paper Miss Alwyn is so fond of?"

Sarah pointed at a nearby table. "I don't have one, but I see a few over there."

Steve retrieved one of the slips and began scribbling out a message. "Perfect. Okay, Deez? Would you kindly hand this to Miss Alwyn? She's over there, at the front desk."

The guur took the slip of paper and nodded.

COMPLIANCE.

"What did you do that for?" Sarah asked. "You know she is still frightened of Deez."

"What do you want to bet that Flinn told his man to be on the lookout for Deez? How many bugs do you see running around here? If we want to get the pirate's attention, this is the way to do it."

"It's working," Breslin quietly hissed. "Behold. He's now following Deez."

Sure enough, they could all see, thanks to Gareth's spell, the unnaturally hued pirate following close behind the guur. Deez scuttled around tables and navigated between patrons, all with the pirate in hot pursuit. As soon as he had rejoined their group, Deez settled back to ground, looking like a large stone once more.

Husband and wife eyed each other. Steve knew that, in order to maintain the illusion that they didn't know the pirate was there, they were going to have to come up with something believable that could be reported back to Flinn. The question was, what could it be? He glanced helplessly at his wife, but noticed she was staring at a nearby table.

"So, now that we've identified who made the goblet," Sarah slowly began, "we can move on to what we're supposed to do with it."

Steve's eyes flitted across the room to the table he had seen Sarah studying. There, lying discarded on the table's surface, was a large book dedicated to the study of goblets and chalices. With a smile, Steve suddenly realized how he could help his wife.

"We found it underwater," Steve announced, as he tried valiantly not to look at the strangely hued man standing behind Breslin, "so it stands to reason we need to place another liquid in it. The temple was made up entirely of … Emily, what stone did you say the temple was made of again?"

Emily's eyes widened with surprise. "Oh, er, that would be, uh, dolomite."

"And how does that help us?" Athos glumly asked. "If we … oof!"

"Oh, my apologies," Breslin said, with a contrite expression on his face. "I didn't see you there. Lady Emily, do go on."

"Well, dolomite is a sedimentary stone. It's typically formed over thousands of years by the accumulation of various organisms and deposits on the surface of the land."

"I'm not sure if that helps or hinders," Athos softly grumbled, earning him another thump in the gut from Breslin.

"And what about that goblet thingamajig?" Steve continued. "Did you say that you saw something on it, like a mark?"

Emily started to shake her head but then quickly nodded. "Yes, I, uh, noticed something etched onto the surface. It was, erm, looked like a, uh, let's see. How do I describe this?"

"Anything will do," Sarah quietly whispered.

Emily held her hands apart and bent several of her fingers, creating the four corners of a square.

"It was kinda like a square, with the bottom of it bent in, as though something had pushed up from beneath it."

Silence fell around the table.

"And," Emily continued, as a smile appeared on her face, "there was what looked like a spike hammered through the middle of it."

"That's…very descriptive," Steve decided, after he had paused for a few seconds. "Any idea what it means?"

Emily nodded knowingly. "I sure do. It was an ancient symbol for earth and fire. Do you know where we can find that?"

"Earth and fire?" Steve repeated. "What's that supposed to mean?"

"Lava," Sarah guessed. "Hmm, if I didn't know any better, I'd say you were suggesting we need to find a source of magma, like a volcano."

"Precisely! Now, does anyone know where we can find one?" Emily asked.

"Are there volcanoes in Lentari?" Steve curiously asked, as he turned to Sarah.

"I know there are some under the water," Gareth added. "My father has warned me time and time again to stay away from what he calls vents. They're very dangerous to shealk."

A tube was suddenly thrust in his hands. Steve looked up in time to see Miss Andra Alwyn head back to her desk. Curious, Steve uncapped the tube and pulled out the large piece of rolled parchment. It was a map! And, he thought excitedly, it focused on volcanic activity.

"Here," Steve decided, as he tapped several dots in the middle of the Selekai Mountains. "There are four volcanoes right here, and it looks like two of them are still active. That's where we've got to go next."

Sarah was nodding.

"Perfect. What's our time frame? Think we can get there before the pirates do?"

Steve nodded. "Absolutely. You've been to this valley, and this part of the forest. We can easily be there in a few hours. Tell you what. The sun is going to set within the hour. Let's start for the mountains first thing tomorrow, okay? Is everyone on board with that?"

Heads were nodding, and both dwarves were grinning.

"That'll allow us to get something to eat," Breslin added. "Splendid. I'm famished."

"And… he's gone," Sarah quietly reported. "Well, that was interesting. Think it'll work?"

"We essentially told him where we were planning on going," Steve said, nodding. "Of course it'll work."

Sarah turned to their guur companion. "Deez, I have a new job for you. Would you please alert us if you see any more of those monochromatic bipeds? We would really appreciate it."

COMPLIANCE.

Sarah held out an open hand and watched as the key from the second temple materialized. She hefted its weight a few times before passing it over to Steve. Eager to learn more about the key, everyone crowded close and took seats.

"Okay, everyone. Here we go. This is the key we recovered from the temple. It clearly unlocks something, so…"

"What if it's simply ceremonial?" Sarah interrupted.

Steve's mouth closed with a snap. "Oh. Didn't think about that. Damn. How are we supposed to know?"

Sarah tapped the symbol. "Our answer lies right here. We need to identify this symbol. Is it some artist's personal mark? The only thing I do know about it is that it isn't a rune. I skimmed all the way through the codex Andra gave me. I have to assume it's some type of pictograph, but what it represents, I don't know. Come on, guys! We need to find out as quickly as possible, so if anyone has a suggestion, now's the time to hear it."

CONSULT MANIACAL FEMALE BIPED.

Steve snorted with surprise before letting out a hearty laugh. He turned to Deez and grinned. "Maniacal. Man, I love it. Although, I do have to admit she's been behaving better."

"That's because we've been showing her some respect," Sarah scolded.

Everyone at the table suddenly turned to Steve and started smiling.

"Oh, swell. You all think I should be the one?"

"Lissa, Mikal and I have already asked her for help on several occasions," Sarah reminded him.

Steve pushed his chair away from the table. "Fine. Be right back."

Several minutes later, Miss Alwyn was back at their table.

"I knew something was up," the elderly records keeper

confided. "I saw Lady Sarah notice the encyclopedia of stemware on the adjacent table and incorporate that into her lie."

"You knew I was lying?" Sarah asked. "Wow. I'm impressed, Miss Alwyn. You're way more observant than I originally gave you credit for. For that, I apologize."

Andra smiled at Sarah and gave a slight bow of her head. "No apologies are necessary. So, what do you need help with now?"

Steve held out the key to the archivist and waited until Andra's arthritic hand had taken it.

"That's what we found at the second temple. Obviously, it's a key. Do you recognize that symbol?"

Andra Alwyn turned the key over in her hands. "Hmm. The most obvious conclusion is that the symbol is a reference to the sun, only I've never seen it depicted like this before."

"Lovey Poo!" a shrill voice suddenly exclaimed.

Steve turned in time to see Andra cringe. Shardwyn appeared and rushed to the record keeper's side.

"There you are, my dear! I wanted to tell you that I have finished restoring order to the, er, little mess that happened earlier. I... what's that? A key? How delightful! What does it open?"

"That's what they're trying to figure out, you nitwit," Andra scolded, as she swatted away Shardwyn's questing hand. "I was about ready to lend my expertise in the matter. Now, we're looking to identify this symbol, then..."

"...you should look no further than right here!" Shardwyn cried. "Maker's marks on keys? Why, I did a paper on the very subject not too long ago. If I'm not too much mistaken, I have it here. Somewhere."

With that, the eccentric wizard began emptying his pockets on the table.

"Balderdash," Miss Alwyn harrumphed. "I assure you that no one has seen this symbol in the last hundred years. I would pit my knowledge against anyone. Even you, my dear. You're old, but you're not that old. You wouldn't know what this is, any better than I would. The answer lies here, within my books. I'll be the one who identifies the symbol."

Two bushy gray eyebrows shot up as Shardwyn slowly turned to the elderly records keeper. "Have my ears betrayed me? Does my Lovey Poo think she can identify a key's maker before I can?"

"It's a symbol," Andra countered. "And you know I can. By the way, I've asked you to refrain from calling me that while I'm here."

"Of course, Lov… er, Miss Alwyn. However, a symbol on a key, I'm quite certain, is nothing more than a manufacturer's mark. I think you will find yourself surprised to learn that I will be the one to identify it first."

"A piece of gold on the wizard."

Everyone turned to Athos.

"What?" the dwarf sputtered. "Does this not have the makings of a wager? I say the wizard will identify the mark first."

Andra threw the dwarf a frown and scowled. "Your confidence is misplaced, dwarf."

"Methinks not, human," Athos returned, giving the archivist a smug smile in return.

Andra and Shardwyn eyed each other for a few brief moments before the frizzy-haired old woman hurried off. Shardwyn, for his part, resumed yanking things out of his pockets. Within a matter of moments, he had covered an entire table with various bits of junk: papers, bottles, bits of metal, and so on.

"Be a dear," the wizard said to Sarah, "and hand me any bits of paper you see, would you?"

"But, that'd be cheating," Sarah calmly answered. "If I did that, you wouldn't have won the wager. You need to find whatever it is you're looking for before she does."

"Fair's fair," Mikal jovially told the elderly wizard.

Shardwyn bowed. "Of course, Your Majesty. I don't know what I was thinking. I wouldn't want to be caught cheating now, would I?"

"Who do you think will win?" Breslin asked Steve, dropping his voice to a whisper.

"She may be old, and she may be a pain," Steve quietly began, "but one thing I'll give Andra is that she knows her

Archives. If the answer is here, then she'll find it. I have to go with Miss Alwyn."

"I'm going to tell her you said that," Lissa softly teased.

Steve gave the young queen a grin and returned his attention to Shardwyn's puttering around the table. He was now trying to sort the items as rapidly as he could. The piles, as far as Steve could tell, were bits of herbs and plants in one corner, various pieces of metal in another, small devices and contraptions in the third, and a vast collection of bottles in the fourth. In the direct center was what couldn't be classified as any of the four. As for bits of paper, there was, unfortunately, not much to be found.

While Shardwyn was preoccupied with emptying his pockets, a guard appeared and passed a folded piece of paper over to Mikal. The pro tem king opened it, read the contents, and groaned. Lissa immediately took his hand.

"Is everything all right?" she quietly asked him.

"Another group of peasants has requested my presence. This group is from Donlari, and they apparently have a matter they cannot settle on their own."

"Does it have to be dealt with now?" Lissa asked.

"This group was caught fighting, which forced the constable to incapacitate all of them."

"I think you mean incarcerate," Lissa softly corrected.

"Whatever," Mikal crossly agreed. "If there's one thing I do not enjoy, it is listening to bickering people."

Lissa rose to her feet and held out her hand.

"I'll go with you, my love. Steve? Sarah? Would you keep us posted on your progress?"

Steve nodded. "You bet."

Once the two of them were gone, everyone's attention returned to the elderly wizard, who was now holding various sections of his robes upside down and giving them a vigorous shaking.

"Blast," Shardwyn grumbled, as he studied the latest bits of junk that were added to the growing collection on the table. "It *must* be here somewhere."

Steve held up the key and waggled it. He kept gently shaking the key, hoping to get Shardwyn's attention and figured, sooner or later, the quirky wizard was going to look up. When he did, however, he smiled patronizingly at Steve, and returned to his search. Only when Steve cleared his throat did he look up a second time.

"Perhaps you'd like to take a look at this mark," Steve suggested. "I can't help but notice you really haven't examined it yet."

Steve was certain Shardwyn was about ready to wave a dismissive hand in his direction when the wizard's eyes widened. He dropped the various bits of bric-a-brac he had been holding and gently held out a hand. Smiling profusely, Steve passed him the key.

"Well?" he prompted.

Shardwyn had fallen silent as he turned the key over and over in his hand. He traced a finger around the symbol before he scowled and thrust his hand into a pocket. Discovering it empty, Shardwyn scowled again and started poking through the various bits of debris on the table.

Steve cleared his throat as loudly as he could. "I, er, is there something I can help you look for?"

"My spectacles. I need them."

"I didn't know you wore glasses, Shardwyn."

"Only for reading, I assure you," the wizard explained, turning back to the table and sweeping various items aside. "I cannot imagine what I've done with them."

Steve held up his hands in a time-out gesture and gently plucked the hat off of Shardwyn's head.

"What did you do that for?" Shardwyn wanted to know.

Steve spun the hat until a certain item came into view. How the glasses ended up being hooked through the tall, conical hat, Steve didn't know.

"Well, I'll be. I wonder how long they've been up there. I am surprised that no one noticed earlier."

"Maybe they did," Steve offered. "But, more than likely, people thought you *meant* to put them up there."

Shardwyn pulled his spectacles free and returned to studying the key. "I do believe I was in error, my dear boy. This isn't a maker's mark at all, but a symbol as my Lovey Poo originally suggested. Do you see here, on this flat part of the key, this symbol?"

Steve sighed. "It has caught my attention, yes. Have you seen it before?"

Shardwyn was silent for a few moments before he gently shook his head. "I have not, I'm afraid."

"Damn," Steve swore.

"But…"

Steve eagerly looked up and saw a smile forming on the old wizard's face.

"I have seen the like before. This is a…"

Andra Alwyn appeared; arms full of books. She selected the next table over and started organizing her selections. She looked up at Shardwyn, gave him a rather condescending smile, and returned to her work.

"She doesn't know nearly as much as she thinks she does," Shardwyn confided to Steve as he dropped his voice.

"That may be so," Steve returned, "but I would highly advise you to keep that to yourself. No matter what she says, just smile and go along with it."

"That is sage advice," Shardwyn acknowledged. "Now, about this key. Do you see how this looks like a sun? But, the rays are curved instead of straight?"

Steve nodded. "Yep, I see that. What does it mean?"

"Well, a curved ray could indicate…"

"You think that's a representation of the sun?" a shrill voice said from behind them.

Steve turned to see Miss Alwyn standing there, with her hands on her hips. She pushed by Steve to stand next to Shardwyn. She tapped the symbol.

"This is an elemental symbol," Andra said. "I'm certain of it. I need to know which one."

"Elemental?" Steve repeated.

Sarah nodded. "Sure. That makes sense. Based on the earth, air, fire, and water motif that seems to be prevalent, I'd say we're right on track."

"If that's elemental," Emily began, "then it's on a periodic table I'm not familiar with."

"We're in a kingdom where fire is considered an element," Sarah quietly reminded her paleontologist friend.

"Good point."

Shardwyn's face suddenly lit up. He snatched the key out of Andra's hand and let out an exclamation of surprise.

"Hah! I knew I had seen this symbol somewhere. Lovey Poo, do you remember that large book you found just the other day? The one pertaining to all things alchemy? Didn't it also have a list of failed experiments performed throughout the ages?"

About ready to object to the elderly wizard's term of endearment, Andra's mouth closed. From the way she tilted her head, Steve figured she must know the book Shardwyn referenced. Miss Alwyn finally nodded.

"I do. You're referring to *Alchemy: From Concept to Conclusion*, are you not? It was one of the volumes I pulled while I was trying to identify the creator of that ghastly idol."

Shardwyn was nodding. "Aye, that's the one. Do you still have it handy?"

"What's on your mind, Shardwyn?" Steve wanted to know.

The wizard tapped his fingers on the counter as he closed his eyes. "I seem to recall seeing that symbol before, and I believe it was in that book."

"I'll personally eat my hat if that's true," Breslin grumbled.

Athos grunted by way of acknowledgment.

Andra vanished back among her shelves and returned moments later, holding a thick, dusty reference guide which looked as though it hadn't been opened in decades. The archivist produced a piece of cloth from somewhere within her robes, reverently wiped the cover and spine clean, and then placed the book on the table.

Shardwyn gently opened the cover and eagerly began skimming through the pages.

"That's gonna take him some time," Steve decided, as he eyed the wizard's progress. He turned to Andra. "While he's working on that, do you have any other tricks up your sleeves?"

Surprisingly, Andra gave Steve the tiniest of smiles. "Perhaps. We can't let him win now, can we?"

Miss Alwyn hurried off, only to have Sarah take her place.

"You two seem to be getting along better, wouldn't you agree?"

Steve shrugged. "Possibly." He lowered his voice and cast a quick look at Shardwyn, who was completely engrossed in his book. "As much as it grosses me out to say this, I think Shardwyn's involvement with Miss Alwyn is an important part of it."

Sarah smiled mischievously. "Well, do you think that maybe the two of them... you know, maybe they...?"

Steve jammed his fingers into his ears and started singing the first tune he could think of. "Just sit right back and you'll hear a tale, a tale of a fateful trip..."

Emily burst out laughing.

"I'm surprised, Steve. You don't strike me as the singing type."

"That's because he's not," Sarah confirmed. She nudged Steve and gently pulled out his fingers. "You can stop singing now. Please. We don't need anyone to start bleeding from their ears."

Steve pointed accusingly at his wife. "You started this. Oh, man. What a thought. Blech. Okay, if..."

"I knew it!" Shardwyn victoriously exclaimed. He pulled husband and wife close and beckoned for the others as well. "Do you see this?"

"I'll be damned, amigo," Steve sighed, as he verified for himself that Shardwyn had won and Andra had lost. "That's the symbol all right. So, what's it mean?"

"It's on the heading for this chapter," Shardwyn pointed out, "which deals with alchemical experiments. I've checked. This is the only place in the book where this symbol is displayed. That has to mean something, doesn't it, dear boy?"

Steve nodded. "I'd say so. I..."

"What's going on?" Andra asked, as she reappeared next to Sarah.

This time, the archivist was holding a small book no larger than the size of an ordinary paperback, bound in a striking green cover embellished with a single, unfamiliar, rune in the center.

"Shardwyn found the symbol, in the alchemy book"

Sarah announced, drawing a gasp of surprise from Andra. "He found it on the chapter pertaining to experiments."

Andra nodded as she gazed down at the book. Without speaking a word, she offered one of her rare smiles and held the small green-covered book out to Sarah, as though it held the secrets of the universe.

"I think you'll find that useful."

"What is it?" Sarah asked, as she studied the rune embossed on the book's cover.

"What you're holding is the biography of a little-known wizard by the name of Calibrun. Calibrun was someone who was fond of experiments. His interests were varied, as most tend to be when it comes to wizards…" At this, Andra glanced over at Shardwyn and, shockingly, gave him a smile, too. "Calibrun was obsessed with turning one thing into another."

"Do we know what he was trying to create?" Gareth hesitantly asked.

"It didn't specify," Andra answered. "I only skimmed a few pages, and from what I've learned, his experiments ranged over a wide variety of items."

Steve took a breath.

"But," Andra hastily interjected, before anyone could interrupt her, "from what I read, many of his experiments focused on precious metals."

"Gold," Steve guessed.

Andra nodded. "Precisely. Attempting to turn iron into gold, without using his jhorun."

Ten minutes later, they heard the snap of the book being closed. Emily rose from her seat, rubbed her eyes, and handed the book back to the archivist.

"So, what did you learn?" Steve asked.

"That's about it, I'm afraid," Emily said. She shrugged. "One thing I *did* learn was how much this Calibrun always felt hot and disliked the feeling. But, how that helps us, I don't know."

Sarah pushed away from the table and started pacing.

"Let's review what we know. I feel confident we're on the right track to finding the third temple, so we just need to piece together where we need to go."

"First, this wizard was known for his experiments in alchemy, which definitely fits in with an Alchos Temple dedicated to either earth, air, fire, or water."

Heads were nodding.

"Second," Sarah continued, "this wizard apparently shared Shardwyn's fondness for blowing things up. That would suggest Calibrun would probably have chosen to carry out his work in seclusion. He disliked being hot, so he would choose a cold place."

"I can get on board with that," Steve decided. "I…" Pravara's voice interrupted his thoughts. He listened carefully and then turned to the others.

"Okay, get this, guys," Steve began. "Pravara told me that Kahvel and Pryllan have the oskorlisk fang back."

"What?" Sarah exclaimed. "How? When?"

"We think Flinn lost it during the battle at the second temple. The shealk were the ones who found it."

Gareth nodded. "Unsurprising. If Flinn lost the fang during the battle, and it fell into the water, then I definitely think they would have investigated."

"Hey, it's a good thing," Steve decided. "It doesn't matter how you look at it. The pirates no longer have it and that's all that's important."

Sarah nodded and hurriedly sat back down at the table and grabbed a blank piece of parchment from a nearby stack.

"I agree. Now, moving on. We need to find someplace cold. We need someplace remote."

"Someplace where there are no people," Emily guessed.

Sarah nodded. "Right. We have to think of safety and security."

"Security?" Steve repeated, puzzled.

"Yes. Think about it. What if Calibrun was successful? What if it became known that his workshop had discovered how to make gold?"

"That's a very good point," Emily praised. "You'd make a fine professor, Sarah."

Steve frowned. "What about me?"

"Moving on," Sarah said, as she winked at Emily, "we

have to ask the question, 'How do you hide a temple?' That's the question we need to be asking now."

"I thought we were looking for a wizard," Steve reminded his wife. "I mean, I know we're looking for the third temple, but it sounds to me like we need to find this wizard first, right?"

"The clues are the same," Gareth announced, drawing everyone's attention. "Since, once again, I cannot use jhorun to find this temple—and believe me, I've been trying—we have to assume that the clues we're discovering will lead us there. Aye, there's a chance that Calibrun's workshop and the temple are two different places, but I doubt it."

"As I was saying," Sarah began again, "we have to figure out how this temple has remained hidden for so long."

"The second temple was underwater," Steve reminded her.

"But that wasn't intentional," Sarah argued.

"It could've been," Gareth added. "It wouldn't take much to create a terra tremor and focus its energy on one place."

"People lost their lives when Capily sank," Sarah recalled. "I don't think the Ancients would have willingly done that."

"Okay, fine," Steve grumped. "How would *you* hide a temple?"

Sarah shrugged. "Up on a floating island? Like, maybe, Ranal?"

"I have no intention of ever stepping foot back on that island," Steve vowed. "You remember what it was like trying to get there, don't you?"

"I do."

"So, push that little notion out of your head. No floating islands. What else do you have? Breslin, Athos, you've been awful quiet. What do you guys think?"

"Underground," both dwarves replied, in unison.

"A very distinct possibility," Sarah decided. "We might end up going for that if nothing else pans out. But, I honestly think the answer is here. We're looking for somewhere remote. Remote *and* cold. Hmm. Andra, is there anywhere in Lentari that's located well away from people and... and covered with snow? I mean, it's *always* covered with snow?"

Emily nodded excitedly. "Of course. Miss Alwyn, look for a remote region that never gets warm enough to melt the snow. That's why the temple has never been found. It's buried under the snow!"

"But where?" Steve demanded.

Andra hurried off. In less than a minute, she was back. She quickly unrolled a large map of the kingdom and encouraged everyone to help hold it in place. Then, she leaned over and tapped an area in the extreme northern area of the Bohanis.

"Here. Up here, it never warms. The weather is inhospitable. Only the strongest jhorun would keep a person from freezing solid up there. You, Fire Thrower, would be the only one I can think of that should be unaffected if you go there."

Sarah smiled victoriously. "There's our answer!"

Chapter 13 — Dragon Riders

Really? Are you serious? Are there really close to a dozen riders now? Wow. It really makes me wonder what Rinbok Intherer would have thought about that."

"It is no longer his concern," a calm, female voice told him.

"It must be nice that Kahvel is more open-minded than his predecessor."

The great wyverian head nodded. "True. Although, Rinbok never had to worry about being asked to tend the nest before."

"Is Kahvel going to be okay watching Pylaria?"

Pryllan chuckled. "He should be. I have asked Yamira and Lamira to stop by in an hour or two, just to check."

"Do you really think Kahvel will need the help?"

"The female zweigelan wouldn't necessarily be checking on Pylaria, but Kahvel. It's *him* I worry about."

Steve laughed, sighed deeply, and once again admired the view. The two of them were skirting the tops of fluffy white clouds as they headed northwest. The border of Anakash Forest had long since passed beneath them, and now, Steve noticed, they were smack dab in the middle of the Bohanis. He had no idea how far from Ylani they still were, and since he knew they had to focus their search along the extreme northwest borders of Lentari, he had been sitting up in his seat to try and see if they were close to the shores of the Erudian Ocean. So far, unfortunately, there had been no signs of water, provided you didn't count the half dozen or so small lakes they had flown over.

We're not seeing anything over here, Darius reported.

Steve automatically looked up. With the soft wispy clouds passing all around them, and having it so quiet that they could've heard the flapping wings of a passing insect, Steve could easily forget that they were not the only ones in the sky at the moment. In fact, there were several sets of dragon riders nearby, and all of them were all doing the same thing: looking for a suitable location to hide a temple.

He checked in with Pheron.

Not a blasted thing, Sir Steve, came Pheron's thought. *We passed over a small valley half an hour ago. I wanted to go in for a closer look, but Rhamalli assured me that there was nothing there.*

WE MUST GO FARTHER NORTH, Rhamalli's powerful thought confirmed.

Acknowledged, Steve told the friendly dragon.

He yawned, stretched his back, and stared down at the passing shapes of peculiar rock formations, somewhat reminiscent of the Grand Canyon,

Whether boredom was setting in, or it was just the sight of the amazing rock formations below them, Steve asked Pryllan if she'd like to challenge the other dragons and their riders to a quick game of dodge-the-peaks. Without a specific response, she tucked her wings and took off at high speed. Rhamalli uttered a dragon sound that must have meant 'you're on!' and followed. Malth and his rider couldn't resist. Around the ridges, over ravines, and through narrow confines, the three dragons raced. Steve whooped and shouted, having the time of his life.

A cloud bank appeared before them, and the dragons

zoomed into it. Suddenly, the temperature began to drop, and when they broke free of the cloud, there were snow-covered peaks, much higher than those they'd been playing around.

"Okay, guys. Now that we're all fully awake, you'll see that we're now ascending higher into the Bohanis," Steve said, catching his breath.

"As evidenced by the presence of snow," Pheron sarcastically added.

Steve nodded. "Right. Time to be on the lookout now. If you spot a suitable cave, or a suspicious hill, please report it. We're far enough north now to be over areas that are covered with snow year-round. That damn temple has gotta be here somewhere."

You should inquire whether or not the others are cold.

Why?

You are a fire elemental. Of course, you won't feel the cold. But your companions are most certainly feeling the effects of this altitude.

Ah. Got it. That's a good idea, Pryllan.

Steve called out to Pheron and Darius. Both assured him the cold was bearable.

"Wait," Darius said, "I feel heat. Are you doing that?" Steve grinned. "Yep. I've got a few mimets with me, in case my jhorun runs low. As it is, I'm fully charged, and I can barely tell I'm using anything to keep you guys warm."

"You have my thanks, Sir Steve," Darius called, from his position on Malth's back. The others added their thanks, as well.

"All right, it's time to split up again. Let's see who can find this temple first."

Darius angled off to the west, while Pheron and Rhamalli banked east. Steve leaned over Pryllan's side and watched the passing scenery below. Nothing but inhospitable mountainsides as far as the eye could see.

"This wizard must have really liked his isolation," Steve muttered, after nearly an hour and a half had passed. "There's nothing out here. How could he have built something so far away from civilization?"

"He was a wizard," Pryllan casually answered.

"Hey, there's something," Steve said, growing excited. "Look to your right, Pryllan. Do you see that depression? That's the first locale I've seen that might possibly work."

Dragon and rider dropped several hundred feet from the sky and slowly flew over the small, flat section of snow. Could the temple be buried there?

"Can your vision penetrate snow?" Steve asked, as he looked up at his wyverian friend. "I know it can penetrate the forest canopy, so hopefully it can, here."

"It can," Pryllan admitted. "And no, I see nothing but stone."

"Stone structures?" Steve hopefully added.

"No."

"Damn. Well, moving on."

"I see another location worth investigating."

Steve sat up straight on Pryllan's back. "You do? Where?"

"Look to your left and perhaps three leagues away. For that matter, look further west and you'll see a second option. And a third."

Steve fell silent as a wave of concern swept over him.

"Pryllan? Let's head back up. I want to see this from a higher vantage point."

"Very well."

Ten minutes later, Steve was cursing silently to himself. This area of the Bohanis was *riddled* with small mesas, depressions, and tiny plateaus, well over forty. Steve groaned and slouched in his seat.

"There's too many to check," he glumly reported.

"It would seem we are in the right area."

"How are we supposed to know which one it is? And, the temple might not be under any of them. So, why in the world would you say we're in the right place?"

"Does this not appear to be a puzzle that has to be solved?"

"All right, that's a point for you. Should we bring Pheron and Darius over here?"

Pryllan nodded. "A wise decision. Very well, the connection has been opened and shared."

Pheron? Darius? I think you guys need to come over here. We found a whole slew of possibilities. It's gonna take us hours to check them all unless we pool our resources.

Sir Steve? Captain Pheron here. Funny you should say that.

We have found a myriad of potential sites, too.

As have we, Darius added.

Swell. Okay, there's nothing else we can do but to start checking.

We're on it, Pheron told him.

We've already started, Darius added.

Steve looked down and sighed. "Let's head for the first one, shall we?"

Pryllan nodded and angled into the turn. Just then, dragon and rider were nearly upended by a strong gust of wind. Steve sat forward and clenched his fists. Flinn? Had he somehow already beat them here? Perhaps they were in the right area. However, after a few minutes of silence, it became evident it wasn't the pirate captain.

"What was that all about?" Steve asked. "I mean, you felt that, too, right? I thought it was Flinn."

"As did I," Pryllan admitted. "It was more than likely an errant gust of wind. We must be near a storm. Do you see those clouds? Look at the mists that are swirling nearby. They are full of snow."

Steve watched Pryllan tuck her wing and start her turn. This time, movement from the clouds attracted his attention. The swirling snow-laden mists coalesced into what looked like a hand. Then, without preamble, the hand swung back and struck him across the face.

Hard.

Steve tumbled backward, off his seat, down the dragon's left flank. Pryllan whipped her tail around in the nick of time.

"I've got you." She reached beneath her belly and flicked her tail forward, placing him on her wing so he could climb back to his seat. He wiped his nose on his sleeve and saw the tell-tale red smear. "Man alive, that hurt like hell. If that wasn't Flinn, then who was it? He's the only person I've seen who can form a jet of air into a fist."

"I can think of one. Bacaed."

"You mean Eion? Why?"

"Clearly, the Master of the Winds does not want us to alter course."

"Eion?" Steve called out. "Dude, was that you?"

In his peripheral vision, he noticed the churning mists were back. Right before his eyes, the mists pulled away from the mass of clouds and headed straight for him.

"Heads up, Pryllan. Those damn mists are coming back!"

Nearly a hundred feet away, the mists stopped, coalesced once more, and formed… an arrow. The vaporous arrow gently spun in place, pointing northeast.

"Eion?" Steve tremulously asked again. "Is that you?"

The arrow pulsed once before falling still. Then, a second arrow formed farther in the distance, also pointing northeast. Then a third appeared. And a fourth.

"Pryllan? I'd say we follow Eion's directions."

"Should we alert the others?"

Steve nodded. "Yes. Okay, let's see where this damn temple is hiding."

They followed the ghostly arrows for nearly fifteen minutes before they began to descend. Directly ahead of them were four possibilities. The arrows bypassed a small plateau and a moderately sized valley, veered again, and led them straight to a small mountain with a crater-like top.

Up and over the rim of the mountain, down into the empty crater, Pryllan followed and touched down on solid ground; Steve slid down her wing and landed next to his wyverian friend.

"Well, would you look at that? I think we're in a volcano."

"Expecting trouble?" Pryllan inquired, as she noticed his crouched position.

"I landed a little harder than planned," Steve painfully explained, as he rose to his feet. His knees were protesting angrily. "You're higher off the ground than I remembered."

"Sarah was right."

Steve crossed his arms over his chest. "Oh? How so?"

"She mentioned to me that you were getting older, and were incapable of…"

"Oh, knock it off," Steve grumbled, as he gave the dragon a playful swat on her leg. "What do you think? Does this look like the insides of a volcano?"

"It would certainly be one way to keep a temple hidden," Pryllan decided.

"Only a batty wizard would choose to create a workshop in a place like this. What if the volcano started to awaken?"

Pryllan looked skyward, spotting Malth, who was circling high overhead as Rhamalli glided in and set down next to them.

"Are you sure about this, Sir Steve?" Pheron asked.

"Quite sure, actually. The temple is here, somewhere. I say we should spread out. Look for an opening of some sort. There's gotta be a way down."

"I can feel the strain on your jhorun," Pryllan announced. "How much longer can you maintain this?"

"I'm fine."

"But if Rhamalli, Malth, and I were to leave, and you only had to see to the safety of Pheron and Darius, how long could you fare?"

"Considerably longer," Steve admitted.

The three dragons launched themselves upward, leaving the men standing in knee-deep snow in the crater of an inactive volcano. Steve immediately felt his jhorun grow stronger. At this rate, he should be able to last for hours!

We just reached the northern border of the forest. We will wait here for your signal.

Steve clapped his hands together and then rubbed them vigorously, eager to start searching.

"Okay, guys. I figure we're looking for a tunnel, a cave, or maybe a concealed door. Maybe something like a dwarf door. This crater is only a quarter of a mile across. Come on. Let's start looking."

An hour passed. Then two. Steve was beginning to lose hope. Darius and Pheron joined him and reported no luck either. Had Eion led them to the correct place? Or, more disturbingly, was this the correct place and they were simply unable to find the entrance?

"Come on, blast it," Steve grumbled, as he felt along the crater wall. "There's gotta be something here."

Darius took a step back, staring at the mouth of the crater

some two hundred feet above their heads. But, just then, he slipped and fell heavily onto the snow.

"Are you okay, Darius?" Steve asked, as he pulled the soldier to his feet.

"Aye. I must have slipped on ice. I tell you, I'm tired of the snow, the ice, the wind, the…"

"Just a moment," Steve interrupted, staring at the surface.

"Let's clear some of this snow. I want to see how big of an area this ice encompasses."

The three of them dug furiously and saw that the ice extended in all directions. Had the crater filled with water at some point and then frozen solid?

"Well, I'll be a monkey's uncle," Steve muttered. "The third temple. No wonder we can't find it. It's buried in the ice down there!"

Chapter 14 — Aeia's Temple

Pheron knelt on the ground and swept another armful of snow out of the way. "If you're right about the temple location, how are we supposed to get to it? We can't sit out here and chip the ice all day."

"We should get the others up here," Steve decided. "We can use their help."

Pryllan? Are you there?

Aye.

We need to get the others.

I will contact Sarah and ask that she use her jhorun.

Less than a minute later, Sarah popped into the crater. Steve wrapped his arms around her to keep her warm.

"So, is this it? Have you found the third temple?"

Steve nodded and pointed straight down. "Pretty sure we have. It's down there."

Sarah knelt and tried to peer through the dark slab of ice.

"What's the plan? How are we supposed to get through it?"

"Bring the others, would you? And make sure they're dressed warmly."

Sarah nodded once and promptly vanished. Ten minutes later, they were back.

ENVIRONMENT INHOSPITABLE, BUT ABLE TO WITHSTAND CLIMATE. GRATEFUL FOR HIVE LEADER.

"Hive leader?" Sarah sputtered. "Who said he was the Hive Leader?"

"You heard him," Steve gloated. "I'm the boss. You have to do what I say!"

His wife threw him a look.

Steve gave a quick briefing, pointing out the location of the temple in the ice.

"You're the Fire Thrower," Athos pointed out. "Could you not just melt this blasted ice?"

Steve nodded. "Yeah, I can, but that creates another problem. Look, I'll show you."

Steve took a few steps back and blasted a jet of fire at the ground below.

After a few moments, the ice started to melt, but it wasn't a fast process, and the melted ice simply pooled up and began to refreeze.

Steve scowled and let his flames extinguish.

"I'll admit, I never would have thought of that," Pheron admitted.

Sarah spoke up. "All right, Steve's flames are out. What about teleporting? Gareth, is there anything you can come up with that would allow me to see inside the temple down there?"

"I've been working on that," the teenager admitted. "Not surprisingly, there aren't any familiars down there I can use. I'm still trying, though."

"Good. Keep on it. I…"

May I offer a suggestion? Could you simply make your flames hotter?

Steve was silent as he considered. "We can always bring

Mikal up here. Remember what happened to me when he touched me during the battle with Celestia?"

"You burned down half of R'Tal," Pheron chuckled.

Sarah burst out laughing, Emily gasped with surprise, and Gareth's mouth fell open.

"The Great Fire of R'Tal?" the teenager exclaimed, shocked. "The one from a few years ago? Wow. I had no idea that was you."

"I was kinda defending the castle against an evil sorceress hell bent on kidnapping Mikal," Steve grumbled. "It's ancient history."

"We're not bringing the king here," Pheron flatly stated. "There must be another way."

Sarah suddenly stood taller.

"I, er, have a suggestion. Now, dear, before you shoot me down, I need you to listen, okay?"

"Out with it, woman," Steve groaned. "What are you trying to get me to do?"

His wife raised both of her arms, opened her hands, and teleported something from their world. Once Steve saw the chain dangling out of each of his wife's hands, he paled and immediately started backing away.

"Oh, hell no. No way. You can't possibly think that's a good idea."

Sarah shrugged helplessly. "You wanted to know what would make your flames hotter, right? Well, this would certainly do it."

"What is that?" Emily asked, as she peered over Sarah's shoulder. "What are you holding? It looks like two pieces of jewelry."

Pheron moved closer to Steve. "That was placed on your world for a reason. Its power is too great. Do you really think it wise?"

"Wizards be damned," Breslin muttered, as he caught sight of the items Sarah was holding. "I've seen them before. Captain Pheron and Sir Steve are right. They're much too dangerous to use."

"Will someone tell me what I'm looking at?" Emily asked again.

"These are the two broken pieces of the Amulet of Aria," Sarah reverently said. "Even one of these pieces is enough to amplify a person's jhorun by, what, ten times?"

"Probably more," Steve murmured.

Emily stared hard at the two unremarkable pieces of jewelry.

"And if you happen to have both pieces?"

"No idea," Steve admitted. "And I sure as hell won't start experimenting now."

Sarah shrugged. One of the pieces vanished. "Look. I know you don't want to use this. Neither do I. However, what choice do we have? We have to think about the pirates. They're more than likely on their way here right now. We have to get inside the temple first."

"I'd wager they're already here somewhere," Gareth sullenly said. "They're probably waiting for us to do all the hard work."

"We can't take the chance," Sarah argued. "If an Alchos Stone is down there, and I'm inclined to think there is, then we have *got* to be the ones who take possession of it. Allowing Captain Flinn to take possession of two stones is out of the question."

With a groan, Steve stepped forward and took the unremarkable piece of jewelry. As soon as he closed his hand around half of the Amulet, his jhorun started buzzing so strongly that it felt like he was standing in the path of a fire breathing dragon, and he was absorbing every ounce of the flames.

Steve looked down at his hands. Both had turned dark red. He cast a look back at his wife.

"Are you sure you want me to do this?"

"This will work," Sarah insisted. "Go ahead."

"Alrighty then. Get as far away from me as you can."

Breslin and Athos ushered everyone well away from him. Steve stared long and hard at his clenched hand, back at the bulky slab of ice he was standing on, and then back at his hand. Bracing for the worst, and unsure what was going to happen, he ordered his hand to ignite.

A blast of fire jetted out of his hand and slammed into

the ice, sending up a cloud of mist and vapor. The force of the blast had knocked Steve off his feet and sent him sliding along the ice to slam into his companions, knocking over Breslin and Emily in the process. After disentangling himself, he painfully regained his feet.

When the clouds cleared, he could see a gaping hole big enough to swallow a car. Also of note, the flames had instantly vaporized the water, resulting in no residual run-off.

Sarah appeared next to his side. "Well, I told you this would work."

Steve turned to her and raised his clenched fist, which was still clutching half of the Amulet of Aria. "This thing is dangerous as hell. Do you have any idea what it's doing to my jhorun right now?"

"I'd say it's giving it a major boost," Sarah decided, as she looked down at the hole in the ice. "Did you mean to make the first hole that deep?"

"Hon, the only thing I did was ignite my hand."

Sarah sobered. "Oh. Wow. Damn."

Steve frowned. "This thing is so dangerous that … that…"

Sarah suddenly nodded. "That thing is dangerous if it comes into contact with you."

"Thanks, Captain Obvious," Steve snorted.

"Hey, I have more experience with the amulet than you do. Trust me. When you don't want to use it, put it in a pocket, or wrap it in something."

Surprised, Steve could only nod.

"I'm going to take all of us someplace safe, like our cabin at the waterfall. I'll give you, say, fifteen minutes and then I'll bring everyone back, okay?"

Steve nodded. "That'll work. I'd hate for any of you to get hurt. It isn't worth the risk."

Once Sarah and his companions were safely out of the way, and presumably on the other side of the kingdom, Steve threw the chain holding the amulet around his neck and tucked the powerful talisman beneath his tunic.

"All right, let's see what we can do, shall we?" he said to himself.

Holding his arms up over his head, he gave his hands the order to ignite once more. This time, two powerful blasts of fire, one from each hand, spiraled into the sky. Steve smiled fleetingly. No one could possibly throw fire better than he could. With his right hand still held high, he purposefully let out a bout of flames.

The jet of fire that emerged from his hand illuminated the entire interior of the dormant volcano.

"Cool, but oh-so-freaky," Steve muttered, as he dropped his eyes to the ground. "Here we go."

He gave his jhorun strict orders to keep his flames as weak as possible, but it really didn't make any difference. In less than five minutes, he had expanded his original ice hole to nearly thirty feet across and twice that in depth. Holding his arms perpendicular to the ground, he activated both hands and blasted twin jets, spinning quickly in place as he did so.

The thirty-foot hole tripled in diameter.

Steve nodded, satisfied.

"Now we're getting somewhere."

He repeated the spinning trick and watched as more of the ice vanished before his very eyes.

There! What was that? Something was jutting out of the ice. It had four sides, was nearly three feet tall, and tapered to a point at the top.

Steve hurried over and squatted next to the object. Running a hand across the surface, he blasted away the surrounding ice and dropped the depth another twenty feet. Once the clouds of vapor had cleared, Steve's eyes widened with surprise and a grin appeared on his face.

A capstone. It was the tip of an honest-to-goodness pyramid, straight out of Egypt, and now it loomed more than twenty feet above his head. It had to be the third Alchos Temple! Forgetting his wife was nowhere close, he eagerly reported his findings.

"I found something! Pryllan, please relay the message to Sarah."

Sarah and Emily appeared a few moments later. Sarah looked up at the pyramid, whistled softly, and then turned to look for him. Steve cleared his throat as loudly as he could.

"Ahem! I'm over here. No, don't come any closer. My hands are still lit, and I don't seem to be able to extinguish them as long as I have this damn amulet around my neck."

"You found a pyramid, honey! Nicely done!"

Emily nodded her approval as she gazed up at the temple.

Steve gave a light cough. "Doc? I was hoping you could help out."

Emily turned to give him a quizzical look.

"You helped Deez find the entrance to the first temple, right?"

Emily nodded.

"If you could tell me which side has the entrance, I'll only melt the ice on that one side. It would save us a lot of time."

"If this is a representation of an Egyptian pyramid," Emily began, "you won't find the entrance at the bottom."

"Do you have any ideas which side has this entrance?"

Emily nodded. "Actually, yes. As it turns out, each pyramid is aligned with the four directions: north, south, east, and west. Pyramid entrances are always located on the north."

"But that's assuming the people who made this one also are members of the same union who built the ones in our world, right?" Steve asked.

"The same union?" Emily repeated as she giggled. "That's a strange way to put it."

"That's only the tip of the iceberg," Sarah told their paleontologist friend. "Don't get him started on Star Wars."

"I've never seen it," Emily admitted. "Any of them. I've never been able to figure out why some dopey space movie holds so much appeal to so many people."

Steve started singing at the top of his lungs to drown out her words.

Sarah laughed and threw him a dismissive wave.

"Not everyone is a fan, okay? Obviously, Emily has some taste."

Steve cast the short blonde woman a dark look. "Hmmph. Just when I was starting to like you, lady."

Emily giggled again. Sarah wordlessly hooked her arm through Emily's, blew him a kiss, and prepared to teleport.

"Wait!" Steve called. "Which way is…"

The two women vanished.

"…north," he grumpily finished. "Swell. That's just peachy. But, it is to be expected."

What is?

Never mind. Will you tell me which way is north?

Of course.

Can you please tell me, right now, which way is north? Seriously? Was Pryllan ganging up with Sarah and Emily?

Face the structure.

Done.

You are looking at the eastern face of the structure.

Okay, thanks. I'll take it from here.

Mindful that people would have to climb down the pyramid from the frozen surface above, Steve carefully angled his blasts so that the resulting tunnels had a gentle slope. He cleared a path to the surface of the pyramid itself, then kept clearing away the ice until he found a corner. In this case, it was the northeastern corner of the temple.

Another angled blast, and the depth came down another twenty feet. In this manner, Steve zigzagged his way down the surface of the pyramid. Emily had said the entrance was typically found above the ground level, so he paid close attention to the stones themselves.

His luck held.

Ten minutes later, he was facing something different, and anything different had to be worth investigating. Leaning close, Steve's eyes widened. The flat, square stones were smaller! Could he have finally found the beginnings of an entrance?

Keeping his flames as weak as he could make them, he began clearing away about five feet of ice at a time. Yes! He had found what looked like a large rectangular door—currently closed, of course—in the middle of the current row of stones he was on. Glancing up, Steve guessed he was probably three hundred feet or so from the surface. How much farther to the base of the pyramid, he didn't know.

Pryllan?

Yes?

I found something that I think is worth checking out.

Five minutes later, the entire group had joined him in staring at the closed door. Joyous exclamations echoed noisily inside the dormant volcano. Steve was one of them until he caught sight of their paleontologist friend. She was frowning.

"What's the problem, Doc? Why aren't you smiling?"

"I've never seen a pyramid with a closed door before."

Everyone sobered instantly.

"Never?" Sarah asked.

"Not once," Emily confirmed.

Breslin shrugged. "The other temples had obstacles we had to overcome. Why should this one be any different? Look around, my friends. The solution is here. We just have to find it."

"And where the ruddy hell would you have us start?" Athos demanded. "There's nothing here but rock and ice."

Steve looked over at Emily.

"I've got the door cleared off, Doc. Would you care to take a look and see if there's anything that jumps out at you?"

Emily nodded. "I can only try, provided there really isn't anything that *will* jump out at me."

"I second that notion," Sarah echoed.

"Over here," Emily called, nearly twenty minutes later. "I think I found something."

Everyone eagerly crowded around the paleontologist. Emily was standing to the left of the large, sealed door, gesturing at something embedded in the wall.

"Whatcha got?" Steve eagerly asked, keeping his distance.

Emily turned to point at a one-foot by one-foot beige square stone that was sunk into the wall.

"The stone is different, as is the pattern, which makes it stand out. I think... I think it may be a control panel of some sort."

Sarah peered closely at the insignificant square stone.

"Do you see any of those elemental symbols anywhere?"

Emily shook her head. "Not yet, and I've checked every square inch of this door. There must be something we're missing."

"Perhaps Sir Steve could simply cut his way through the stone?" Breslin inquired.

"We don't have that kind of time," Steve told the dwarf. "I mean, sure, I have the amulet, but I don't have that kind of control. Not yet, at least. Hey, you're a dwarf. Couldn't you guys tunnel through it?"

"As with you, my friend," Breslin began, "it would take time."

"Wouldn't cutting through the stone be faster than digging?" Darius asked.

All eyes turned toward Deez. The armored guur turned his head to stare at the temple's entrance. Deez crept forward until his long front forelegs were within striking range. After giving the wall an experimental tap, the guur leaned forward and started to dig.

No one saw the flash of light.

* * *

Pryllan?

Yes?

Would you let Sarah know that I've found something? Tell her that the third temple looks to be a pyramid, and I'm going to start clearing away the ice that's surrounding it.

Very well.

Wait. Why does this suddenly feel familiar?

What does?

It must be nothing. Never mind. Please let her know that I've found something. Tell her to bring Emily, too, okay?

I will.

Once the two women had arrived, and it was revealed that the third temple was, in fact, a pyramid, Steve grinned. Now they were making progress! However, he could make faster progress if he didn't have to clear away ice from the entire structure. All they needed was the entrance.

"North," Emily told him, before the two of them teleported back to safety. "Pyramid entrances are on the north side, usually around a hundred feet or so from the bottom."

There's something awfully familiar about this, Steve quietly mused to himself, as he worked his way down the pyramid.

What was that?

Oh, it's nothing. I'm having a strong feeling of déjà vu right now.
I'm not familiar with that term.
It means that it feels like I've done this before.
I see. Well, if you need me to relay any additional messages, let me know.
I will. Thanks, Pryllan.

Once Steve had uncovered the temple's sealed entrance, and everyone was standing beside him, they started brainstorming ways to open the door.

"Perhaps Sir Steve could simply cut his way through the stone?" Pheron inquired.

Surprised, Steve looked over at the tall Lentarian soldier.

What is it? Your pulse has increased. Are you in danger?

No. It's just that feeling of déjà vu again. I can't seem to shake it.

Certain that it was only a coincidence, Steve turned on his heel and joined the others to think of a way inside. Because of this, he didn't see Deez approach the door and raise his forelegs. Once more, no one saw the flash of light.

* * *

Pryllan?
Yes?
Would you let Sarah know that I've found something? Tell her that the third temple looks to be a pyramid, and I'm going to start clearing away the ice that's surrounding it…

Steve shook his head, trying to get rid of the weird sense of déjà vu again. Once more, everyone arrived to study the sealed door and offer suggestions. As before, since the events went unchanged, their large insectoid companion decided to take it upon himself to create an entrance into the temple.

The flash of light happened the instant Deez's front forelegs dug into a large slab of granite.

* * *

When the events began to repeat for a third time, Steve called a halt and explained it to the group.

"It has to be déjà vu," Sarah suggested. "That's all. I don't think there's anything worth becoming so agitated. Now, as far as what you've found … you're right. I think this is the entrance."

The women went on to discuss the composition of the stones, when Pheron straightened with alarm.

"Where's Darius?"

Steve automatically looked up the sloped tunnel he had carved through the ice from above. No sign of Darius, even when Steve called out.

Athos raised a hand. "I believe I saw him right before Sarah teleported us."

"Did he not make it back?" Emily asked, concerned.

"You misunderstand, Lady Emily," Athos said. "I last saw the human soldier *here*, not there."

Sarah frowned. "Now that I think about it, I don't remember seeing him at the cabin, either. Did he not get teleported with the rest of us?"

Pheron scowled. "Wizards be damned."

Steve watched the captain disappear up the ice tunnel, but movement in his peripheral vision attracted his attention. Deez stood before the door with both of his forelegs extended.

Steve held up a hand, anxious to get the large insect's attention, when a loud commotion sounded from within the ice tunnel. Pheron came running full tilt, waving his arms and shouting something. Shockingly, his Lentarian friend dove out of the tunnel, performed a neat somersault, and landed on his feet. He gestured frantically at Deez.

"Stop him! Someone stop the guur!"

Before Deez could make contact with the sealed door, something grabbed him, as if lassoed by an invisible rope and physically yanked away. Confused, Deez looked at Steve.

YOU DO NOT WISH ENTRY INTO STRUCTURE?

"Something *is* very wrong," Pheron wheezed, as he straightened to his full six and a half feet height. "Lieutenant, tell them what you told me."

Darius appeared, also winded.

"I was standing on the surface and was watching you make ready to melt the ice. Lady Sarah suggested she would teleport everyone to safety, when this mountainous pile of snow appeared out of nowhere and fell on me. I have been digging myself out of the snow for the past hour or so."

"For the past hour?" Steve repeated, frowning. "I've only been blasting away at this ice for no more than twenty minutes. How is that even possible?"

Sarah turned to look at the pyramid's sealed door. She looked over at Deez, who still seemed as though he was itching to try his luck at digging, when her eyes widened.

"Have we discussed the ramifications of what will happen should we mess something up?"

"Like what?" Steve asked.

Sarah pointed at the door. "Like trying to open the pyramid the wrong way. You were telling me that you felt as though you have done this before, right? Well, what if you have?"

"You mean that whole déjà vu thing?" Steve shrugged. "How would we know?"

"I think the temple was protecting itself. If Deez had started digging through that door, what do you think would have happened? There are clearly obstacles in place. He would be bypassing the obstacles the other Ancients put in place to guard the stone."

"Such as the snow that immobilized Lieutenant Darius," Pheron said.

Husband and wife eyed each other.

"Think it was Eion?" Steve asked.

Sarah nodded. "I think it was. Did anyone else experience any feeling that you've done the same thing before?"

Emily answered, "Yes, I did. Before we went to your cabin, Sarah, I felt as though I had been there before."

"Then that means we probably *were* there before," Sarah said, nodding. "We must have been caught in some type of loop, and Eion sent that snow to break one of us out of it."

"Okay, so, what does that tell us?" Steve asked.

Sarah looked at Deez. "Were you going to tunnel your

way into the pyramid?"

YES. QUICK WAY TO GET THROUGH DOOR.

"Right. Okay, everyone. Important safety tip: no doing anything without talking to the rest of us. Clearly, there are ramifications in place if we screw something up."

COMPLIANCE.

"It's not safe to force the door to open," Steve said. "Got it. All right, how *do* we open it?"

Emily strode over to the left side of the sealed door and pointed at the small, beige square stone. She bent down next to it and fell silent as she considered.

"We had to use Steve's fire to open the last temple," Emily recalled.

"I had to direct a jet of air over that statue to open the first," Sarah added.

Steve was nodding. "So, that means this temple is either going to be earth or water. I'm leaning toward earth, since we're looking for Usol's stone."

Sarah shook her head. "No, it's water."

"How can you be so certain?" Steve asked.

"If this was earth," Sarah began, "then why would the other Ancients choose to store Usol's stone in his own temple?"

"That's a fair point," Steve conceded. "However, we know Lentari only has the three temples. There are four Ancients. How do we know one of them isn't repeated?"

Sarah sobered. "Damn. I hadn't thought of that. Good point, dear."

"Hey, I have them every once in a while."

Emily and Gareth snickered.

"For now," Sarah decided, "let's assume this temple is for water. I'm starting to think that each of the Ancients once had a temple here in Lentari. I'd bet that Usol's temple was destroyed. Either way, I don't think it matters."

Breslin nodded. "I concur. Based on everything Eion

has said about the Earth Guardian, I do not think the other Ancients would have allowed a temple to co-exist with their own."

"Meaning, they were still ganging up on him," Steve quietly whispered.

"What did you say?" Sarah asked, dropping her voice to match his.

"Doesn't it strike you as odd that the other Ancients were treating Usol like crap?"

"You heard what Eion said," Sarah quietly reminded him. "He was a bully, and was always misusing his powers."

"True, but based on what Eion said, Usol should have been released from his jinx by now."

"These guys are basically gods," Sarah argued. "They can set whatever rules they want. It's not for us to decide."

"I don't like it when people don't play by the rules," Steve grumped.

"Their rules, not ours."

"I know. All right, if we are to assume this is the water temple, er, this is Aeia's temple, how does that help us?"

"I'd say we need to make an offering of some water," Sarah said.

Steve looked left, then right.

"There's ice everywhere. Ice is only frozen water. Why didn't the door open for that?"

"Perhaps the offering has to be water and not ice?" Emily suggested.

"Easy enough," Steve said. He retrieved a chunk of ice from the ground and held it in his hand. "Instant water, coming right up."

He held his fist next to the square panel and as gently as he could, applied his jhorun to the ice. The jagged piece of frozen water was instantly transformed to water, which drained through his fingers. However, due to the extreme cold, the water froze before it could reach the ground.

"I think we're missing something," Emily said.

Steve pointed at the panel. "Even if I can keep the water thawed, what are we supposed to do with it? That panel is on the wall. Typically, there was something to place the offering in. I agree that we're missing something."

Sarah peered intently at the panel before she experimentally poked a finger at it. When she pulled her finger away from the surface, she gasped with surprise. There was a dot on the panel, exactly where she had rested her finger!

"Look! Do you see that?"

Everyone crowded close. Steve automatically stepped back so that the two dwarves could be included. He looked over his wife's shoulder.

"What am I looking at?" Steve asked. "There's nothing there."

Surprised, Sarah looked back at the panel. Yes, Steve was right. The smooth-as-glass surface of the stone was blank!

"It was just there!" she complained. She reached forward to touch the panel again. Sure enough, as she pulled away, the dot was back. "There! Do you see that? It's responding to my touch."

Steve reached forward and tapped the panel twice, then swung his finger in a curve.

"Stop drawing smiley faces all the time," Sarah instructed. "We clearly have to draw something, but what?"

A few seconds later, the grinning face disappeared as the panel reset itself.

Emily snapped her fingers. "The symbol! What do you want to bet we have to draw the symbol for water?"

Sarah shrugged. "Okay. I'll buy that. Umm, how does it go?"

Emily pushed forward. "Here, I'll do it. The symbol for water looks like an upside down pyramid. Like this:"

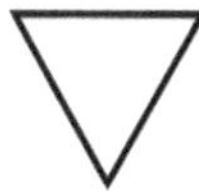

"It's a simple triangle?" Steve asked, confused. "There aren't any lines through it?"

Emily shook her head. "No. There's ... omigod! Look! Something's happening!"

The ground trembled at the base of the panel. Loud cracks could be heard as residual ice started cracking. A pedestal rose out of the floor. Reaching a height of maybe three to four feet, a depression formed on the top of the pedestal.

Steve grinned. "And I do believe we finally have somewhere to place our offering. Nicely done, Doc!"

Emily, however, wasn't smiling.

"What's the matter?" Sarah asked.

Emily pointed at the pedestal. "What if … what if I drew the wrong design? What if I drew fire instead of water?"

"It probably wouldn't have brought that pedestal out of the ground," Steve guessed.

There was a loud grating sound as the top of the pedestal leveled off, and slowly sank back into the floor.

"Let's find out," Sarah decided.

"Are you sure it is safe, Lady Sarah?" Breslin nervously asked.

"I've got my safe zone ready, just in case," Sarah assured the dwarf. She looked over at Gareth. "In case something bad does happen, are you ready?"

Gareth opened his clenched hand to show her an assortment of small figurines.

"I'm ready. For what, I'm not sure, but I think I have most situations covered here."

Sarah nodded. "Good. Here we go."

She drew the same symbol Emily did, but this time, she added a line.

$$\bigtriangledown$$

"Earth. Let's see what … hmm. Look at that. The pedestal is coming back up."

Once the rudimentary bowl had formed into the pedestal's top once more, Steve looked helplessly at his wife.

"Why do I get the feeling that it'll do that for the other two symbols, too?"

A few moments later, the pedestal returned to the floor.

"Which symbol do you want me to use?" Emily asked, as she turned to husband and wife.

Steve looked at Sarah. "I'd say you should give it your

best guess."

Sarah nodded affirmatively and placed a reassuring hand on the paleontologist's shoulder. "I agree. Use water. I'm pretty sure this is Aeia's temple."

Emily nodded and drew the same symbol she had drawn earlier. Once the pedestal had returned, she looked over at Steve, who was ready. He was resting his hand inside the bowl, and was clutching a chunk of ice. Moments later, the ice melted as Steve applied his jhorun to his hand.

The ground began to shake. Everyone could hear the telltale sounds of ice cracking all over the pyramid. Steve nervously eyed his wife.

"Do you think that's good or bad?"

"It's a terra tremor!" Gareth decided, concerned. "We need to… hey, would you look at that? The door is opening!"

The gang whirled about and reeled in shock. Gareth was right. The heavy stone door receded into the wall for several feet then slid up into the ceiling and vanished completely.

Sarah tapped his shoulder. "Let's have some light, dear. I see some torches scattered along the wall. Will you light those for me?"

"Gladly."

Once the interior chamber was lit, they were dismayed to see it was no larger than their foyer at home, in Idaho. Inside, another door stood on the wall to their left. Sarah walked up to the imposing ten-foot-high door and sighed.

"We should have known it wasn't going to be this simple. None of the other temples were. They all had multiple obstacles in place. Now, let's see what we can learn about this one."

"I don't see anything," Steve reported.

"Spread out," Sarah ordered. "Look around. The key to getting through this door is here somewhere."

It was Deez who provided the answer.

ANOMALY DISCOVERED.

Steve appeared by the large insect's side. "Whatcha got, Deez?"

The large, sealed door turned out to be inset in the wall, by nearly a foot and a half. The guur was looking at a section of the narrow wall, tapping one of his large forelegs against it. There was a familiar looking square stone, complete with the same light beige color and texture.

"You found another panel? Way to go, pal!"

"I wonder how we activate this one," Sarah quietly mused. "Does it respond to touch?"

Steve placed his palm on the stone, waited for nearly five seconds, and then pulled it off. He let out a grunt. No marks were visible.

"What does that tell us?" he asked, as he straightened back up.

Sarah shrugged. "I'm not sure."

Athos pointed at Emily. "Perhaps she should try touching that stone."

"I agree," Gareth added, pleased.

"Why?" Steve asked.

"She's the one who drew the mark which got us into this temple in the first place," Sarah said, turning to Emily. "Ready whenever you are."

Emily approached the panel and laid her hand on it.

"Well, it's warm."

"It wasn't for me," Steve told her. "And you'd think it would be, since I'm the Fire Thrower."

The paleontologist pulled her hand away and was rewarded with a dark outline of her hand, which quickly faded away.

"What should I draw?" Emily asked, as she turned to Sarah.

Sarah pointed back at the panel. Words were starting to appear, written in a stylish, neat script:

An old man greeted a boy as follows: "May you live long—as long again as you have lived so far, and as long again as your age would be then, and then to three times that age; and let the Ancients add four years more and you will be 104." What age is this boy now?

"What the hell is this?" Steve demanded. "What, this is

a riddle? You've got to be kidding me. Breslin? Athos? Got any ideas?"

Both dwarves shook their heads. Steve looked over at Gareth.

"Math was never my favorite subject," the teenager helplessly told him.

Steve turned to Pheron and Darius. "Guys? Tell me you've heard this before."

Both soldiers were shaking their heads.

"I have not," Pheron confirmed.

"Neither have I," Darius added. "Hopefully, it shouldn't be too difficult to figure out."

Pheron nudged his lieutenant on the shoulder. "Behold. Both of the ladies have their eyes closed. Perhaps they know the answer?"

"Working on it," Sarah quietly muttered.

Emily nodded. "Me, too."

"If they can do it," Steve decided, "then so can I. Let's see. The first part says… crap. It vanished. Emily? Could you touch that thing again?"

"Shush," Emily ordered. "Don't break my concentration."

After another five minutes of silence had passed, both women opened their eyes, looked at each other, and gave their answer:

"Eight."

"He's eight years old," Emily echoed.

"You guys got the same thing," Steve observed. "Fan-freakin'-tastic. Emily? Would you do the honors?"

Emily approached the panel, drew a large number eight into the pad and stepped back. After a few agonizing seconds of silence, the grating noise began.

Quickly, the second door split down the middle and swung inward, revealing a dark tunnel leading deeper into the pyramid. Steve tuned his fire down and victoriously led their group through the doorway. After a few seconds of darkness, they saw a light ahead. Whistling merrily, Steve reached the tunnel's mouth and froze in place.

They were staring at the interior of the volcano and a smooth *unbroken* sheet of ice, which stretched across the entire crater's floor. Confused, Steve turned to look behind him, to see that they were standing next to the outer perimeter wall of the volcano. His eyes dropped back to the ice and he groaned as realization dawned.

Breslin sighed. "I think we got the answer wrong, lad."

Chapter 15 — Divine Humor

"Oh *hell* no," Steve groaned, "We're right back where we started from. This has got to be a mistake! We answered that riddle right, so why did we end up here?"

Sarah sighed. "Emily and I will figure out where we went wrong with the riddle. In the meantime, you'd better get going. You have some ice to clear."

"But I've already done this," Steve complained. "Do I really have to do it again? I mean, come on! You've been inside this temple. Can't you just zap us all back there?"

"It's already been proven that this place defends itself," Sarah reminded him. "We have to do this right, or we don't progress any further. You didn't think this would be easy, did you?"

"Fine. You'd better back away."

"At least this time you know where the entrance is," Emily helpfully added.

"Hmmph," Steve snorted, as he ignited his hands.

As soon as he had melted his way back to the entrance,

and cleared away all the ice surrounding the door, Steve glanced over at their guur companion. Sure enough, it looked as though he was studying the sealed door.

"Nope. Back away, Deez. No digging through that. Do you remember what happened last time?"

CHAIN OF EVENTS REPEATED?

Steve nodded. "That's right. So, let's get Emily to open the door and we'll try our luck at that riddle again. This set us back, what, about half an hour?"

"Less," Sarah told him. "It took longer the first time. Since we know what we have to do now, and where to go, we're able to do it a lot quicker."

"Our own version of *Groundhog Day*," Steve observed. "I'm just not sure why we were allowed to retain our memories this time, not that I'm complaining."

Sarah shrugged. "Think it was Eion?"

"Probably. Whatever. Emily? You're up."

Emily drew the symbol, and once more, they were walking into the small foyer-sized chamber with the second obstacle. Sarah pointed at the panel.

"Any chance the riddle has changed?"

Emily laid her palm on the panel and waited for the writing to appear.

"It's the same," Emily reported.

"Did you guys figure out where you went wrong?" Steve asked. Then he pointed at the panel. "Maybe someone ought to write it down. Perhaps you two remembered it wrong?"

Both Sarah and Emily shook their heads.

"Between the two of us, we have it memorized. Besides, we both worked out the math and we both came up with the same answer. Again," Emily told him. "Eight. I'm not sure why it isn't accepting it."

"If 'X' is the age of the child," Sarah began, "and we…" She trailed off as Steve held up his hands in a time-out position. "What is it?"

"Can't you work backward?"

Sarah shared a blank look with Emily.

"Huh? Is that how you'd solve this problem?"

"That's the first way I'd tackle it," Steve confessed.

Both women crossed their arms over their chests.

"Fine," his wife decided. "Let's see what you come up with.'

"No pressure," Steve grumbled. "Okay, going backward. The final age is one hundred four, right? Take four years off that, one for each Ancient, and you get a hundred."

Sarah was nodding. "Right."

"The next part of the riddle, working backward, said something about three times that age, so take one hundred and divide by three."

"You'd get thirty-three and a third," Sarah answered. She frowned. "That wouldn't work because you don't have a whole number."

Steve grinned. "Who says the answer has to be a whole number? Okay, continuing on, if we take thirty-three and a third and divide that in half, we get… um, we get…"

"Sixteen and two-thirds," Emily said. "Sarah's right. That can't possibly be the right answer."

"Oh, it isn't, because we have to divide that number in half one more time. What do we get?"

"Eight and one-third. I will give you credit. You did come up with eight."

"Eight and one-third," Breslin corrected. "Could that be the problem? The remaining third?"

"Tell it, 'eight years and four months'."

Emily shrugged and entered the answer on the panel. The grating began anew and, as before, the door swung inward as it opened.

"If that wasn't the right answer, then I'm going to just apologize right now," Steve offered.

"You're the one who has to clear away all the ice," Sarah reminded him. She offered her arm to him. "Ready to try again?"

"What the hell. Here we go. Get ready for whatever lies that way."

PRESENCE OF OMNISCIENT HUMAN?

The dwarf nodded. "All-knowing, or all-powerful."

Comprehension dawned on the teenager's face. "Deez thinks Eion is nearby?"

"Or Usol," Athos said. "I heard you say before, lad, that your spells won't work against an Ancient."

"It's true," Gareth sulked. "I don't like that."

"I'd let it go, wizard. They have more power in their little finger than the rest of us combined."

Fifteen minutes later, they were still walking through the tunnel. Steve could hear several of his companions grumble, and he couldn't blame them. He had started to scowl, too. Was this supposed to happen? Was this another of the temple's defense mechanisms? To simply walk through this tunnel for ages without ever reaching the end?

"On the bright side," Sarah suddenly announced, "we've made it farther than we did the last time, right?"

"This tunnel just keeps going and going," Gareth complained. "Are we ever going to make it out of here?"

"We didn't answer wrong again, did we?" Emily asked, with her voice full of concern.

Sarah shook her head. "No. Even Steve got the same answer we did. It clearly didn't like our answer, and when we added the 'four months' on the second try, we get the never-ending tunnel. Plus, we really don't know how big this pyramid is, so for all we know, we're heading toward the center of it."

Steve smiled. "You got the same answer I did?"

"Of course I did. Emily and I both did. Why?"

"Oh, nothing. And you claim you're better at math than I am."

"That's because I *am*," Sarah clarified.

Emily laughed.

"How long have the two of you been married?"

Both husband and wife grinned at each other before turning to the short blonde woman.

"A few years now. Why? Do we sound like an old, bickering couple?"

"You do," Emily clarified. Then she pointed at Sarah. "She doesn't."

Sarah hooked her arm through Emily's.

"And you're my new best friend!"

Emily laughed again.

"But seriously, you two, how long have you been married? I'd like to know, if that's okay."

"This year marks our twentieth anniversary," Sarah answered.

"That's really impressive, you two. You're clearly meant for each other."

Steve's brow furrowed. "I'm not certain if that's an insult or a compliment."

"It's a compliment," Sarah decided. She looked back at Emily. "Right?"

"Hey, look!" Emily exclaimed, as she pointed down the tunnel. "I think we're approaching the end."

"She didn't answer," Steve whispered to his wife.

Sarah swatted his arm and shushed him.

True to Emily's observation, the passage was starting to brighten.

"I swear," Steve began, "if we're dumped back on the top of the ice again, I'm going to be super pissed." All he wanted was to find Usol's Alchos Stone, and to survive this without the pirates catching them.

They emerged in an unremarkable, perfectly square room that had to be over a dozen feet high. Two lit torches were on each of the four walls, flickering as though a brisk wind was fanning their flames. What caught their attention, however, was the empty stone dais in the center of the chamber No stone, no box, and no puzzle.

"Did we goof it again?" Steve asked.

"This isn't the surface," Gareth pointed out. "The answer had to be right."

"I concur with Master Gareth," Breslin added. "Had we supplied an incorrect answer, then we'd be faced with another session of tunneling our way down through the ice."

Sarah and Emily approached the empty dais, while the men waited.

"I don't like this," Steve began.

"Nothing has jumped out at us," Pheron observed. "And

it doesn't appear we're in any danger."

"Yet," Darius quietly added.

"What are we supposed to be doing?" Athos gruffly asked.

"We don't know," Breslin told him. "Lady Sarah and Lady Emily are inspecting the pedestal now."

Steve glanced back at the mouth of the tunnel, intent on observing Deez, but he wasn't there. A clattering sounded from above his head. Looking up, Steve watched as Deez carefully picked his way across the ceiling.

"See anything up there?" Steve asked.

NO ANOMALIES DETECTED.

"If you find anything, let us know, ok?"

COMPLIANCE.

Steve turned to his wife. "Sarah? How's it going over there? Have you guys figured out what we need to do?"

His wife sighed. "There's nothing here. I've pressed every stone. I was hoping to find a key hole. We have that key from the second temple, remember? It has to unlock something."

Steve turned to Emily, who was studying the wall opposite the tunnel's mouth. "Hey, Doc, have you touched this thing yet?"

Emily's long blonde hair shook from side to side. "No. Sarah performed an exemplary inspection of the dais."

Steve scratched his head. "You drew the water symbol to get past the first door. Then, you answered the math problem from the previous door. What if … what if this temple thinks you're the one who is in charge?"

Sarah patted his arm. "I see where you're going with this. Emily? Come here. Maybe, for the first time ever in his life, Steve is right."

Steve let out a snort.

"For the first time ever? Really? You're a snot. A cute snot, but a snot nonetheless."

Sarah blew him a kiss. Emily approached, looked down

at the empty dais, and shrugged. She raised a slender arm and gingerly poked one of the stones on the pedestal's top.

They all heard a loud *click*, followed immediately by what sounded like a bucketful of rocks tumbling to the ground.

"Well, *something* happened," Emily reported, "but I'm not sure what to make of it."

Steve rushed around the pedestal and joined his wife. There, strewn across the ground, were a number of small stones in varying shapes and sizes. Confused, Steve picked up a marble-sized stone that looked as though it belonged on a Tetris board.

"What's this supposed to be?"

Sarah shrugged and selected her own stone from the floor. It had a complex shape, too. She held it up next to his.

"I'd say we're supposed to build something with these … these … what do we want to call them? Blocks?"

Emily was nodding. She was holding several of the stones and comparing them to one another. She placed the blocks on the pedestal, knelt to retrieve a few more, then added them to her growing collection. After a few moments of holding each of the pieces next to each other, she looked up.

"I think Sarah is right. I've seen these types of puzzles before."

"It's a 3-D puzzle," Sarah happily exclaimed.

"Wipe that smile off your face," Steve ordered. "We have no idea what all those pieces build."

"True," Sarah admitted, as she selected another block. "But, I think it's safe to make a few assumptions."

"Like what, Lady Sarah?" Pheron wanted to know.

Sarah pointed at the dais. "The other two temples we explored each dealt with that Ancient's element. For example, wind for Eion and fire for Oro. We're pretty sure this is Aeia's temple, so somehow water is involved. I'd say we need to build something to hold an offering."

"You're totally guessing," Steve accused.

Sarah smiled. "Only a little. The more I think about it, the more I'm convinced I'm right."

"Who is best at completing these types of puzzles?" Breslin asked. "For the record, I am *not*. I lack the patience."

"As do I," Athos added.

Sarah sighed, and looked at Emily. "Based on this crowd, I'd say solving this thing is going to fall on the two of us."

"That's fine by me," Emily said, offering her a smile. "I enjoy puzzles."

"Put your feet up, boys," Steve drawled. "This might take us a bit."

Sarah grunted as she sank down to the ground and started sorting the pieces. Without looking up, she held out her right hand and waited. Two seconds later, a bottle of perfume appeared in her open hand.

"What's that for?" Emily asked, confused. "Do you really think we'll need perfume?"

Sarah passed the bottle over and pointed at Steve.

"It's for him. If he acts up, or makes a snotty comment, then you have my full permission to soak him in this. It's his favorite, isn't that right, dear?"

Steve shook his head. "You're not playing fair. Leave Emily out of this."

Emily looked at the perfume bottle, over at Steve, and then back to Sarah. A smile appeared on her face as she set the bottle on the ground beside her. Steve waggled a finger at her.

"No taking sides, Doc."

Emily flashed him a smile before returning to work.

"What do you think they have to build?" Breslin asked, as he unhooked his axe from its holder on his back. He sank down next to Steve and rested his back against the wall. "A bowl, perhaps? Maybe a chalice?"

"Did you see how many blocks there were?" Steve asked. "It'd be one walloping, ugly chalice, that's for sure. Based on the shapes I saw, this water-holder-thingy has to have a rudimentary shape."

The rest of his companions joined him on the floor. Gareth chose to settle a few feet in front of the adults, while Deez lowered himself to the ground in his usual rock shape. Steve looked over at the guur and smiled.

"I never thought I'd call a guur my friend, Deez. Thanks for making a believer out of me."

WHAT IS TO BECOME OF ME ONCE WE ACQUIRE THE TREASURE?

Steve slowly looked over at their guur companion. Deez was staring straight at him. After a few moments, Deez's head tilted, like a dog's, and then tilted back. Steve wondered if Eion had allowed the mental connection between the humans and guur.

A tiny dust devil appeared in the doorway. It circled the room, gathering dust, sand, and small debris. As quickly as it appeared, it zipped back through the doorway, but not before the swirling sand dropped back to the ground in two neat letters: NO.

"No?" Breslin said, confused. "What just happened? Was that the Master of the Winds?"

"Yep," Steve confirmed. "I was wondering if it was Eion allowing us to talk to Deez, since he connected us once before, and maybe he had forgot to turn it off. Clearly, he's left it in place. Intentionally. Well, if you're listening, thanks, buddy. Deez, to answer your question, I believe you'll be living with Gareth here. He'll look after you."

THE HIVE WILL DISPERSE?

"We all have our separate lives, Deez," Gareth tried to explain. "I know you'd like us all to stay together, but that isn't possible. That isn't how things work for humans."

I AM NO BIPED.

"We know, pal," Steve told the friendly guur. "However, it doesn't mean we can't all stay in contact. That's what friends do. We enjoy spending time with one another. Plus, you can make new friends."

REPLACE HIVE? I ... I DO NOT WISH TO REPLACE THE HIVE.

Unsure of what he should say to his guur friend, Gareth

gave Steve an imploring look.

"Think of it as an ever-expanding Hive," Steve suggested. "You'll always have your Hive, but if you're willing, others would like to join it. Gareth's parents will become your friends once you meet them."

"I wouldn't count on that," Gareth muttered. "My mother is not a fan of bugs."

"Most people aren't, sport," Steve agreed. "Especially big ones. But, Deez is an exception. If he can make a believer out of me, then he can do it with anyone."

"I think we have something," Sarah suddenly announced.

"You're done? Awesome!"

"No, it isn't done," Sarah contradicted, "but I think what we have is the base of a large goblet."

"There weren't any circular pieces," Sarah explained, as she pointed at the remaining pieces. Clearly, jhorun is at play here."

"We're dealing with an Ancient," Emily informed the men. "There are a lot of things that don't make sense."

Sarah looked at Steve. "Watch what happens when I hold this piece right next to this other. Do you see how easily they fit together?"

"Whoa! The pieces change shape when they're attached to one another. A moment ago, it was all ninety-degree angles and square shapes, but when you fit the two pieces together, it kinda melted into that shape. See how it flares at the bottom and tapers at the top now? If what you say is true, then I'd say that piece is part of the stem."

Sarah nodded. "Let's see if … yes! Look! It just attached itself right there. Emily, I think we have this thing licked."

"Give them some space," Steve ordered. He gave Sarah a peck on her cheek. "We'll be over here, out of your hair."

Sarah blew him a kiss and reached for another block.

* * *

"I wouldn't have called it," Steve said, as he inspected the newly finished silver goblet.

"It changed to metal once Emily and I put it on the

pedestal," Sarah clarified. "Do you still think we're *not* on the right track?"

Steve shook his head. "Nope. I think you and Emily are a helluva team."

His wife and the blonde scientist both grinned and gave each other a high-five.

Pheron turned to Sarah.

"We are going to need some ice, milady. Do you think you could teleport some here?"

She sank to the ground and rested her back against the wall. She rested her open palms on her knees and waited for her mind to clear. Once it did, she brought up an image of what she had in mind and teleported it to her lap.

A split second later, she screamed in surprise as nearly twenty pounds of ice, transported all the way from their refrigerator back home, appeared on her lap. The cubes were already starting to melt, so she hastily scooped up handfuls and dumped them into the large goblet.

"Honey, start melting this. Now that I look at it, I think all this ice will fit. You have to start making room."

Steve shrugged, ignited a hand, and held it over the goblet. Within moments, the ice began to melt.

"Keep feeding the ice in until we either run out of ice or fill up the cup."

Gareth dumped in another handful when the goblet began to glow. Then the dais started to tremble. Gareth nervously looked back at Steve.

"Something is happening! It's glowing! Do you see that?"

"I can *feel* that," Sarah corrected. She hurried over to stare at the goblet. "What's it doing?"

"I think it's melting," Steve decided, as he extinguished his flames. "Look, I swear I didn't get it that hot."

At that moment, the goblet actually turned to water. The clear liquid ran harmlessly down the stone pedestal and collected on the floor. Then, one of the identical square stones in the floor tilted, draining the water away, then righted itself.

"What just happened?" Steve asked, perplexed. "Did everyone see what I did?"

"It looked to me as though the floor was thirsty," Gareth decided, eliciting a snicker from Athos.

"Honey!" Sarah suddenly exclaimed.

Steve glanced at his wife. She was clapping her hands and pointing at the now empty dais. He squinted at the top. There, if he wasn't mistaken, was a hole. A keyhole!

"Who's got the key?" Steve asked, as he turned to look at his companions.

"No one does," Sarah reported. She held out a hand and watched as a sparkling silver key appeared. She took the key and handed it to her husband. "Would you do the honors?"

Steve grinned. "I'd love to. Okay, let's see what happens."

He inserted the silver skeleton key into the hole and gave it a twist to the right. As with the goblet, the key suddenly shifted its composition to water and flowed away. The trembling began anew, and right before everyone's eyes, the pedestal itself shimmered and turned to water. It splashed down onto the floor, only to be swallowed up by two of the moving stone tiles.

Where the pedestal had been, Steve was shocked to see an old-fashioned wooden treasure chest sitting in its place. The chest, Steve figured, must have been concealed within the pedestal and, with the stone pedestal turning to water, had appeared to them for the first time.

He gingerly lifted the latch and opened the chest. Inside was any pirate's dream: magnificent jewels. He counted seven. Two large, glittering diamonds, one spiraled ruby, one smooth-as-glass opal as large as his fist, a pyramid-shaped emerald, and a glittering purple jewel that had been crafted to resemble a single rose.

"There was only supposed to be one. We have to choose," Sarah said, as she looked in the chest. "The problem is, how do we decide?"

Before she could shout a warning, Steve reached into the chest and plucked out the sparkling green emerald.

Chapter 16 — Elemental Battle

What did you do that for?" Sarah complained. "How do you know that's the right one? It could have been one of the others. Did you see that purple rose? It could have been that one."

Steve was shaking his head as he held up the emerald tetrahedron.

"Don't you remember? From the second temple? The big dude who looked like a monk gave us that box of four jewels. Those four gemstones were tiny replicas of the real thing. As such, the only one that matched any of those four jewels was this green one."

Emily was nodding. "You have a good memory. I remember that now."

Steve pointed at his wife. "Be sure to tell her that, okay? Now, if this is Usol's stone, which I'm inclined to believe it is, what do we do with it?"

"We take it from this place," Pheron announced. "Far from here. It should be secured in the castle."

Steve palmed the green jewel. "I actually thought Flinn might have been hiding somewhere nearby."

Sarah held out her hand and looked at the others. "So did I. We're going back to the castle. Everyone grab on. The Lentarian Express is leaving in about five seconds."

Once everyone was in physical contact with Sarah, the dismal confines of the treasure chamber was replaced with … books. Sarah had chosen to deposit them in the Archives.

Several patrons recoiled with surprise.

"What are you doing back here?" Miss Andra Alwyn was standing before them, but for once, she wasn't wearing her trademark frown. If anything, she appeared concerned. Before Andra could ask a question or two, Steve turned to his wife.

"Are you okay? I just assumed you'd shoot for the Antechamber."

"I *did* shoot for the Antechamber," Sarah argued. "I don't know why we ended up here. I haven't had a misfire of my jhorun in, well, forever."

"Something is amiss," Pheron quietly announced. "Do any of you hear that?"

Everyone fell silent.

Pheron spoke up. "Can you not usually hear what's going on in the rest of the castle from here? Troop movements, Shardwyn blowing himself up in his tower, and the like?"

"I don't hear anything, either," Steve added. "Pheron's right. Something's wrong."

"Come on. We need to see what's going on."

Sticking close together, with Deez leading the group from his position on the ceiling, they edged out into the hallway. No guards, no servants, and no people. What was going on?

It was as if the castle had been deserted! Surely, there must be a staff member or two *somewhere* on the grounds. They didn't encounter anyone until they approached the Antechamber.

There were so many guards crowding around the Antechamber's two front doors that it was standing room only. No one was moving, and no one was speaking. As one, every soldier in the room turned at their approach.

Pheron stepped forward. He singled out the closest soldier within grabbing distance and pulled him close.

"Report, soldier. What is going on here? Why have all the posts been deserted?"

"They… they have them, Captain!"

"They?" Pheron repeated, confused. "Who?"

"The pirates, Captain!"

"And they have *who*?" Steve asked.

"Kri'Mikal and Ny'Lissa," the guard miserably answered.

Steve swore loudly. Alarmed, he looked down at his hands. His clenched fists had turned a dark red.

"Whoa, no you don't," Sarah hastily said, as she took his hands in hers. "Calm down, dear. We don't need any explosions going off in here. Let's figure out how to get Mikal and Lissa to safety, alright?"

Steve's hands returned to a healthy pink color.

"Fine. So, what do we do? Can't we teleport in there?"

Sarah shook her head. "No. I mean, I could, but should I? What if trouble is waiting for us on the other side of that door?"

The Antechamber's doors suddenly burst open. A jet of wind blasted out of the king's private chamber, knocking soldiers over as though they were bowling pins. The wind continued to bounce off walls and windows as it looked for anyone still standing. Then, almost on cue, it singled out Steve and sped straight toward him.

Steve raised a hand, intent on using his own jhorun to counteract Flinn's. However, before he could fire his own jet, Sarah was there, holding his arm.

"Don't forget about what you're holding," she whispered in his ear, as they both ducked low to avoid being struck by the wind.

Steve pulled the piece of Amulet from around his neck and promptly handed it to his wife.

"Good point. Here. I have a feeling you'd have a better use for that than I would."

"I'm referring to the *other* thing."

Steve automatically dropped his hand down to his trouser pocket and felt the large lump that was the pyramidal emerald.

"Umm, will this do anything to my jhorun?"

Sarah shrugged. "I honestly have no idea. Please be careful."

"Will do. I … hold on!"

The concentrated air jet changed course and headed straight for him. Steve ignited his hands and waited for the jet to approach. Once it was less than ten feet away from them, he blasted it with a well-timed burst of fire. Air and fire met head on, canceling each other.

"That confirms ye be out there, Fire Thrower," Captain Finn's voice drawled out. "I knew ye would come. If ye try anything stupid, then any blood spilled will be on yer hands! Do ye hear me, mate? If I see one blasted soldier, then we start cuttin' throats!"

Steve's face hardened. "I'm going in. Come on guys. Pheron? Darius? You're with me. Breslin? Athos? Be on the lookout for anyone that's trying to get the drop on us." Both dwarves eagerly nodded. "Sarah? You and Emily stay behind us. Be ready, if you catch my drift."

"I do, and I will," Sarah promised.

"What about me?" Gareth asked. "What should I do?"

Steve pointed at the ladies. "You're with them. I'm trusting you to keep them safe."

About to protest, the teenage wizard sighed and solemnly nodded. He pulled several small objects from his pocket. Clutching them tightly, he nodded his readiness.

Steve looked up at Deez.

"Stick close to Gareth. Protect Sarah and Emily, okay?"

COMPLIANCE.

Two pirates suddenly poked their heads out of the Antechamber, checking. They took one look at Steve's flaming hands, let out a cry of alarm, and disappeared back inside.

"Come, come, Fire Thrower," Flinn taunted. "Don' keep us waitin', mate. Ye don' want nothin' to happen to this boy who be wearin' the crown, do ye?"

"Wizards be damned," Pheron cursed under his breath. "How the blazes did those damn pirates take the king and queen prisoner?"

"They *could* be bluffing," Steve murmured. "But, I kinda doubt it."

"Steve?" Mikal's shaky voice called out from within the Antechamber. "Do not worry about me. I implore you to do whatever it takes to save … oomph!" His sharp cry was followed by a brutal round of coughing.

"Someone just hit Mikal," Sarah whispered, horrified. "Honey, we have to do something!"

"And ye will do something, lass," Flinn's voice told her. "Ye can bring me the second stone. Now. I want all of ye in here, where I can see ye. Get a move on before I be forced to give an unpleasant order."

Steve's face became grim. He eyed Pheron and Darius, who warily nodded, and then strode into the Antechamber. The rest followed.

"Fire Thrower!" Flinn exclaimed, from his seat behind the king's desk. "So good of ye to join us!"

Steve quickly glanced around the room. Occupying two of the plush arm chairs circling the hearth were Mikal and Lissa, who were guarded by three of the pirates. No other guards were in attendance.

"I like this room," Flinn was saying. "It would seem that only my power be allowed to work in here. None of my crew be able to use theirs. Plus, I have to assume that ye and yer lady can also use yers?"

Steve ignited a hand in response.

"I knew it. Now, ye can see we have yer boy king and his girl. Surrender the stone and we will leave. That is the only trade I be making today, mate. I do suggest ye take it."

Steve glanced over at his wife as a thought occurred. "Honey? Do you remember what Thaden did to us in Verdayn?"

"Don' be pullin' no tricks," the pirate captain warned him, with a snarl. "I be tired of this game we be playin'. This wretched place be gettin' on my nerves. The sooner ye pass that stone over, the sooner we be sailin' away. Now, where is it? Who be holdin' it?"

Steve ignored the arrogant pirate captain and stared at

his wife. Sarah smiled. She gently pulled on the gold chain encircling her neck until the broken amulet appeared. She caught Steve's eyes and nodded.

"Be ready," Steve quietly whispered to Pheron.

"Ready fer what?" Flinn asked. "Ye better not be plannin' on…"

Steve nodded to Sarah, who tightened her hold on the amulet. Her eyes closed, and the Antechamber promptly winked out. They were now all outside the castle's west gate, standing in bright sunshine. Guards and civilians alike scrambled.

Steve ignited his hands and immediately blasted a jet of flames straight at Flinn, who managed to deflect it at the last possible moment. Flinn's eyes opened wide as he took in their surroundings. He didn't know what had happened, nor where they had been taken. Flinn caught sight of the open drawbridge and immediately whirled around to see the castle in the distance.

"Ye killed yer king," Flinn snarled. "Did ye think I was bluffin'?"

"I treated you the same way I would treat any other bully," Steve calmly answered. "You threatened Mikal and Lissa. You tried to use them as leverage, so they were taken away. Don't believe me? Look around!"

With disbelief written all over his features, Captain Flinn risked a quick glance around the surrounding area. Sure enough, Mikal and Lissa had both vanished.

"Can't find them, can you? What's the matter? Well, you'll also notice Sarah is gone, too. Do you know what that means? You've lost your leverage. Now, hand over your Alchos Stone and you might make it through this."

Inexplicably, the door banged open at the guard's watch house and pirates began streaming out. What surprised Steve the most, though, was the shocked look on Flinn's face. He was acting as though he didn't know his own crew were hiding nearby.

With a chorus of yells, they attacked Steve and his companions. Pheron and Darius immediately drew their weapons and met the pirates head on. Fighting back-to-back, both Lentarian soldiers were able to hold their own against their adversaries.

More pirates streamed out of the guard tower. How did they get here? And where were the castle guards? There were now at least five pirates for each of the Lentarians, including Breslin and Athos.

Steve blasted off jet after jet. Several of the pirates threw themselves into the depths of the murky moat after being hit squarely in the chest.

Flinn, for his part, was using his jhorun to drive the Lentarians backward, toward the moat. Then Flinn's gaze shifted over to Gareth, who was paying more attention to Deez than to the pirate leader, and unfortunately, it cost him.

The blast of air hit Gareth squarely in the back and lifted the young wizard off the ground. He started drawing invisible symbols in the air, and he vanished before hitting the water.

A smirk appeared on Flinn's face as he turned back to Steve.

"Did ye see that? So much for yer wizard. He chose to flee instead of ... hey! Oy! Get away from me! What do ye think ye be doin', ye daft bug? Go away!"

Steve forced the last of the other pirates into the moat. He glanced back at Flinn and noticed the pirate captain was now facing a new adversary.

Deez had singled out the one who attacked Gareth and, thanks to his new ability to think for himself, determined this biped was bad. The Hive would support his decision.

Flinn fired blast after blast of air toward the heavily armored ten-legged insect, yet the mighty bug continued to approach. Deez's ten legs and his ability to cling to surfaces made him immune as he came within attacking range.

"Blast it to hell and back again," Flinn darkly muttered, as he drew his cutlass. "Ye think ye can take me, ye ugly brute? Think again! It'll be a dark day for piracy when a mere bug can..."

Sarah suddenly popped into view. Steve couldn't tell who was more surprised, Flinn or his wife. She immediately vanished and reappeared a hundred feet away. Steve shot a blast of fire high into the air, and she materialized by his side a second or two later.

"Where'd all these other pirates come from?" she asked, bewildered. "There must be two dozen. I haven't seen that many even when their ship was beached near R'Tal."

"Tell me about it," Steve agreed. He fired off three successive blasts and pirates flung themselves out of the way. "I think this is Usol's doing."

"What do we do?" Sarah asked. She turned to look back at the castle. "I could go round up some more soldiers and bring them here."

Steve nodded. "Please. I don't know why they haven't showed up already…"

His voice trailed off as a small cloud of dark smoke appeared out of nowhere and slowly sharpened into a humanoid form, directly in front of him. It wore dark green robes, had a full head of jet-black hair, and a full beard. The eyes were completely white, devoid of iris or pupil. Steve swallowed nervously. He had met someone before with eyes like that, and he was fortunate enough to call them ally. Here was someone, Steve thought with dismay, who was definitely not a friend.

"Usol," Steve whispered.

The figure swung his head around until those glowing white eyes were focused on him.

"Fire Thrower. You have until I count to three to surrender the…"

A blast of hurricane-force wind suddenly flattened the nearby trees. The jet of air caught Steve squarely on the chest and pushed him, and Sarah, well out of harm's way. Sarah teleported them to safety, nearly a quarter mile away.

"What the hell happened?" Steve wanted to know. "Was that Flinn? He's getting stronger, and that's not something I like to admit."

Sarah shook her head and pointed—wordlessly—back to the drawbridge they had teleported from. Two figures were circling each other, one in robes of white, and the other in dark green. Clearly, words were being thrown back and forth as each of the Ancients were angrily gesturing at one another.

"Usol and Eion," Steve said, amazed. "There's an

argument you don't want to get messed up with."

Another blast of air, a weaker one, assaulted them. Steve groaned. Flinn.

"Where is he?" Steve asked, as he turned to look for the pirate captain. "I don't see him anywhere."

"Neither do I," Sarah admitted. "He must be concealing himself."

"Damn," Steve swore. "If he's using his stone, there's no way we'll be able to…"

"Wait!" Sarah interrupted. She turned to him and gestured at his pocket. "You have a stone, too. Maybe you'd be able to find him?"

Another blast of air slammed into them both, carrying debris that stung like insect bites. Steve wiped his face and was surprised to see a smear of blood. Sarah had her own trickle of blood coming from a small cut on her chin.

"He wants to play? Let's play."

Steve wrapped his fingers around the emerald tetrahedron in his pocket. Almost immediately, he felt his jhorun tingle like crazy, but there was something else, as though his awareness was expanding.

He was suddenly conscious of what all of his friends were doing. Darius and Pheron were holding their own against the battling pirates, but unable to gain the advantage. Breslin was facing off against three pirates while Athos was up against two, using a throwing weapon, some type of modified boomerang.

Steve trusted his friends to be able to look out for themselves and, instead, focused on locating Flinn, who wouldn't be far away. The canny leader of the pirates desperately wanted to get his hands on the emerald stone.

Just then, he felt his gaze being pulled toward Darius. There was a disturbance near his Lentarian friend, a collection of shimmering heat waves that were rapidly on the move. Was it Flinn? The pirate captain *had* to be using his stone to conceal himself, but they'd never been able to track him before.

Usol's stone, deep within Steve's pocket, must be allowing him to see another holder of the stones. How cool was that?

Steve's face darkened. Flinn was racing closer and closer to Darius, who had no idea his life was in danger.

"Oh, *hell* no," Steve muttered.

He ignited his hand and generated a fire whip, whirling it around his head before slamming the flaming tendril down between Darius and Flinn. Alarmed, Darius jumped out of harm's way.

Just like that, Flinn appeared, an angry scowl on his face. Flinn snarled at Steve and vanished again, this time to sneak up on the unsuspecting Gareth and Deez. Steve groaned.

"I still see you," Steve whispered, as he twirled his fire whip and crashed it into the ground a dozen feet from Gareth.

Deez reacted first, jumping in front of Gareth. Thinking they were under attack, the guur readied both pincers and prepared to lunge at Steve.

THREAT DETECTED?

Steve addressed the friendly guur. "Yes! The threat is concealed, but I can see him.

Flinn appeared again, this time facing Steve.

"Ye cannot possibly see me, Fire Thrower. Ye were lucky with yer blasted fire. That's the only explanation."

Steve grinned at the pirate. "Nope. I can see you just fine. Don't believe me? Keep sneaking around. Next time, I won't deliberately miss."

"Impossible," Flinn all but whispered.

A loud commotion sounded near the drawbridge.

Two winged dragons were locked in mortal combat, necks twined together, talons raked across scaled torsos, and wings pummeled each other. Repeatedly the two dragons twisted to break holds, rolled on the ground, and then snapped at each other to gain the advantage. No one, not even the pirates, dared venture too close.

Steve squinted at the battling wyverians. At least it was easy to tell the Ancients apart. One of the dragons was bright white, while the other was a dark green. And, Steve noticed, Usol had somehow managed to make his dragon form larger than Eion's. The smaller white dragon kept getting pinned by the larger green one. Thankfully, the Master of the Winds was a skilled fighter, and always managed to twist away before Usol could deliver a fatal bite.

Steve turned to look for Flinn when a bright flash of light blinded him. As the spots began to clear, a noise only found in his world suddenly sounded—the trumpeting elephants. He spun back toward the battling Ancients. He was looking at two of his world's largest land mammals, the African elephant. One had a slightly noticeable tint of green on its tusks, while the other appeared paler than normal.

Before he could wonder why the Ancients had switched forms, the answer became clear: each elephant was roughly the same size. Trumpeting loudly, the two massive land mammals crashed together. Eion's elephant wrapped its long trunk around Usol's head and executed a half turn, throwing Usol to the ground.

Eion trumpeted victoriously, but not before shimmering into another form. This time, a full-grown adult griffin, with snowy white wings, appeared where the elephant had been standing. Usol was already changing his form to match. A griffin with streaks of dark green feathers on its wings was squawking angrily as it rose to its feet.

The extreme fight continued. Screeching griffins, wrestling creegs, grappling anacondas, snarling lions, and countless other animals appeared and disappeared in the blink of an eye. After a while, Steve started to notice a pattern: Eion would change forms first because Usol did not fight fair.

Steve lost track of who was winning and who was losing, and even with their color markings, the shifting between forms had become so fast that Steve could no longer keep up. Resigned to letting the Ancients fight it out between themselves, Steve turned his attention back to the much smaller battle among the humans. And one guur, Steve mentally added. Where was Flinn?

A low rumbling answered his question.

Steve scowled as he looked up at the insanely powerful jet of wind that was circling above his head, a blast much stronger than Flinn's usual. Clearly, Usol must have boosted

Flinn's jhorun once again.

The howling wind uprooted trees, picked up small boulders, and everything else in its path. Swirling high above his head, Steve watched—mesmerized—as a veritable mountain of debris coalesced above his head. Then, abruptly, the wind vanished. All the debris plummeted straight down, directly toward him.

Steve, watching the rubble fall, sighed. "Here we go again."

This time, however, his jhorun knew what to expect, as did he. He was ready. Steve allowed his mind to go blank and concentrate on acquiring additional power.

As he had that thought, a blast of fire spiraled out of nowhere and slammed into the mound of broken trees that had fallen on him. Within moments, the mountainous pile of broken wood went up in flames. Steve watched from his out-of-body point of view as the fires grew steadily larger. Once the fire spread over all four corners of the pile, he sent out his jhorun.

It was more than enough to replenish his strength and to reform his human body, as he did before. However, without Sarah there to bring him some clothes, he would either have to track his wife down in his birthday suit or cover up with flames. Not seeing Sarah anywhere, Steve chose the latter.

Steve? Are you there? Are you well?

Pravara! Were you the one who lit the pile of junk on fire?

Aye.

Thank you.

Giving his jhorun strict orders to keep his body engulfed in flames, Steve stepped away from the pile. Flinn had to be in the area. He wouldn't wander far, since he still hadn't got his hands on…

The stone!

Steve's hands flew to his side. Horrified, he raced back to the burning pile. His clothes were undoubtedly destroyed. What about Usol's stone? Would it be unaffected by the flames?

"Crap. Crap. Crap! CRAP!"

He could only hope that he could find what was left of

his clothes. The last thing he wanted to admit to Sarah was that he had lost the emerald tetrahedron. What would she say?

Steve looked at his burning hand. He could still remember wrapping his hand around the stone as he watched Flinn move around in stealth. His fingers flexed. He could almost imagine he was holding the large emerald once more.

Just like that, he was holding Usol's stone. Steve let out a yelp and almost dropped it. He held the sparkling emerald up to his face and watched the flames reflected in its faceted surfaces.

Why in the world did the stone appear in his hand? For that matter, *how*? He knew Sarah wasn't able to teleport the Alchos Stones, so… wait. Hadn't his wife teleported the entire Antechamber, complete with furniture and burning hearths, to the outside? Usol's stone had been in his pocket, yet Sarah had been able to teleport it. Why couldn't she before?

The answer came to him as he stared into the depths of the powerful jewel: possession. Sarah was clearly unable to teleport Flinn's stone away from him, but since she wasn't trying to separate Steve from his, suddenly, it became possible. Was that why the Stone returned to him? Was he the owner of it now?

Steve risked a glance at his companions. For the first time, he noticed many of the pirates were gone. Was that Sarah's doing? Pheron and Darius were now fighting side-by-side with a full squadron of armored soldiers, who were keeping the pirates at bay. Gareth and Deez were standing in front of the tiny guardhouse. Was that where Sarah and Emily were hiding?

Steve nodded. Everyone appeared safe for the moment. He had time to test his theory with the stone. He dropped it onto the ground beside him. Then he held out a hand and imagined the stone was back in his possession.

The glittering emerald vanished from the ground and appeared in his outstretched hand. Steve grunted. That was good to know. It could only mean it couldn't be stolen from him. It had to be freely given.

A new thought occurred. Since Flinn had stolen the

Essence of the Sea, didn't that mean it could be summoned by its owner's hand at a moment's notice? Steve shook his head. He was willing to wager all the gold in Lentari's vaults that Flinn wasn't aware of that little tidbit. And, since Flinn still carried the stolen stone, the true owner was just as unaware.

Nearby shouts attracted his attention. Pheron and Darius were facing even fewer pirates now. Surprised, Steve checked the surrounding area and saw there were only a few of the feisty pirates left. And, right before his eyes, one of them vanished.

Steve grinned. Sarah! She had to be watching. She was clearly sending the kidnapped pirates to Limbo, where she could retrieve them at her leisure. If Flinn wasn't careful, he'd end up fighting this battle completely alone.

Two more of the pirates vanished, leaving only Flinn and two others. Captain Flinn thrust his hand inside his jacket pocket and promptly vanished, much to the dismay of his two remaining crew members. Steve held his tongue as he watched Flinn's concealed form head for the last of his crew.

"Pheron? Darius? Would you step aside for a second?"

"The pirate captain has disappeared!" Pheron exclaimed. "We need to…"

"…move aside," Steve interrupted. "Trust me, pal."

More curious than anything, Pheron stepped aside and gestured to his men to follow suit, which they did. Once the Lentarian soldiers were safely out of the way, Steve blasted a jet of fire from each hand, which landed on either side of the pirates, cutting off their escape.

"Give it up, Flinn," Steve called out. "I can see you standing there. This is your only warning. If you try to escape, then I will stop you, and I think you know how I'll do it. Don't make me hurt you guys. I really don't want to, but I will."

Flinn appeared, stunned. Steve held up his hand and revealed Usol's stone. The large emerald sparkled radiantly in the afternoon sun. Flinn glanced at the battling Ancients, no doubt hoping to catch Usol's attention, but the Earth Guardian was otherwise preoccupied with the Master of the Winds.

"You have the power to end this," Steve told the pirate.

"There's nowhere for you to go. You only have two men left."

Right on cue, the two men vanished, leaving Flinn standing by himself. After a moment, the pirate captain sighed heavily and sat down on the nearest rock. Moments later, he was holding the *Essence of the Sea*. Flinn gazed into the depths of the large sapphire for a few moments before he surprised everyone by tossing the large gemstone to Steve.

"Very well. Ye have won this battle, Fire Thrower. Ye said once before that ye only wanted the stone and ye would let us leave if I gave it to ye. Tell yer lady to return my crew. Grant us safe passage to the *Emberbrand*. I have decided no amount o' treasure be worth this aggravation. I want nothing more than to leave this accursed land once and for all."

Steve stared at the stones in each of his hands before he slowly nodded. "I seem to recall saying that. Pheron, I'm not in any position to grant that request, but I'm pretty sure Mikal will go for it. Could you bring him here?"

Pheron nodded. "At once. You men, secure the area."

After the tall soldier had left, Flinn eyed Steve and scowled.

"I cannot say this will be the last time our paths cross, Fire Thrower."

"Nor can I," Steve returned.

"I have given ye my stone. Return my crew."

Steve nodded and immediately looked for Sarah. He didn't have to look far. His wife materialized next to him. She silently eyed Flinn, but not before turning a speculative eye to him.

"What happened to you? Why are you allowing your whole body to burn?"

"Uhh, I'm kinda not wearing anything, and, since you're here, would you mind teleporting me some clothes? Long story. I'll tell you later."

A set of clothes materialized in her arms. She passed them to Steve, who hurried into the guard shack to change.

"Teleporter," Flinn suddenly called.

Sarah turned to face the pirate captain. "I'm here."

"Give me back my crew, lass," Flinn ordered. "What have ye done with them?"

"Don't worry, they're safe. Time seems to stand still there, so they won't remember a thing once they're returned. Speaking of which, why should I? Quite frankly, I'm tired of that Jino fellow trying to inflict harm on me or my husband. You're lucky. I was tempted to drop them all in a dragon's nest."

"Our fightin' be over, lass. Ye and yer husband have won. For now. Give me back my crew and we will leave."

Steve appeared by her side, properly outfitted once more. He looked at Flinn and then back at his wife.

"Should I release his men?"

Steve nodded. He held his hands out. There was a large jewel in each hand. Sarah met his eyes and gave him a questioning look.

"It's another part of the long story I gotta tell you later."

"Where's Eion and Usol?"

"Can't you hear them?" Steve asked. He pointed south. "The last I saw, the two of them had become colossal snakes and were wrestling each other. If I had to venture a guess, I'd say they were anacondas."

Sarah shuddered. "I *hate* snakes."

"I'm not too crazy about them either, my dear."

Sarah suddenly straightened and looked back at Flinn. She pointed at his belt.

"The hammer you stole from Breslin. Give it back."

Flinn looked down at the tool on his belt and shrugged. He pulled the hammer free, gazed admiringly at it for a few moments, and then tossed it away. Breslin nodded appreciatively as he slid the hammer back into the loop on his belt.

Pheron reappeared, followed immediately by two full squadrons of armed soldiers. Walking calmly in their midst were Mikal and Lissa. The guards parted, allowing Mikal to approach Steve. He gave Flinn a neutral stare before turning to his former bodyguard.

"Did I understand that right? Do we finally have closure to this whole ordeal?"

Steve nodded and turned to Flinn. "Tell him what you told me earlier."

"Release my men and grant us safe passage to the *Emberbrand*," Flinn requested. "I wish to return home."

"And the Alchos Stone in your possession?" Mikal carefully asked.

Steve held up the blue sapphire for Mikal to see.

"And you're certain this isn't a replica?" Mikal asked. "We have been fooled before."

Steve solemnly nodded. "Trust me, pal. Er, I mean, Your Majesty. This thing is the real deal. Both of these things have some serious power."

Mikal then looked at Sarah and smiled. "Very well. Please return his crew."

Sarah nodded. "Of course."

Nearly a dozen disoriented pirates appeared next to Flinn. Rusty took a quick look around, cursed, and hurried to Flinn's side. Following his example, the rest of the pirates rushed to Flinn's side, drawing their weapons.

Steve scowled. He watched Jino lock eyes with his wife and utter some type of threat. Both of his hands ignited and he prepared to blast the sorry pirate with every ounce of jhorun he had.

Flinn held up a hand. "Nay, Fire Thrower. I will deal with this. Jino, stand down. They have won. We be leavin'."

"Did we get the stone?" Jino asked. "And how did we get back to the castle? I thought we were…"

"How long have ye had 'im in yer clutches?" Flinn asked, as he turned to Sarah.

"It's been a while," Sarah admitted. "Quite frankly, I'm tired of his attitude. I swore to myself that if I had to deal with him again, then I was going to personally feed him to the dragons. I figured it would be safer. For him."

"Captain?" Jino hesitantly asked. "You cannot possibly abandon the mission now. We're so close! We cannot let the Fire Thrower win. Say the word and I'll…"

"You'll do such thing, mate," Flinn dangerously growled. The captain turned back to Mikal. "Will ye allow us to leave?"

"You are aware that if you do that, then there's a damn good chance he could come back, don't you?" Steve whispered in Mikal's ear.

"Aye, I am aware," Mikal whispered back. "And, he may very well try. However, we will be prepared." Mikal faced Flinn and nodded. "All of you, right now. Leave, before I change my mind."

One of the younger pirates turned to Rusty.

"Q, we can't leave without Pedr! He was lost out there! What if he was attacked by the dragons? Or what if he was…"

"Pedr?" Steve repeated. "Don't worry about Pedr. He's safe and sound back in the *Seven Kingdoms* right now."

The boy stared incredulously at Steve. "But how? It takes many days of sailing to cross the Endless Sea."

Steve pointed at Sarah. "Not if you're married to the world's strongest teleporter. She took him to a village by the name of … of … blast. I don't remember."

"Miron," Sarah supplied. "He's safe and sound in Miron."

"I seriously underestimated ye," Flinn confessed.

"Don't worry about it," Steve said, waving off Flinn's remarks.

"I be talkin' about *her*," Flinn clarified, as he pointed at Sarah. Then he sighed and turned to face the vast, open waters to the east. "Where be the *Emberbrand*? Mister Alquin, kindly get yer arse over here and find the ship."

"Your ship is right where you left it," Gareth announced, with a smirk. The teenager pointed southeast. "It's in that little inlet less than two leagues from here."

"Ye knew where the ship be, and ye didn' bother it?" Flinn asked, amazed. "How? Why?"

"That'd be me," Gareth happily announced. "I found the ship hiding nearby, and Mikal was the one who decided we shouldn't do anything, 'cause it'd let you know we had figured out where the ship was berthed."

"I will be glad to put some distance between us and this blasted place," Flinn grumbled.

Pryllan?

Aye. Kahvel has decreed that six of our best flyers will escort the ship across the sea.

Nice. Can I relay that to Mikal?

Go ahead.

* * *

Mikal nodded. "That's good news, indeed. To think, it's finally over."

Steve turned to look south.

"Not yet, it isn't. Come on. We have to get those two to stop fighting."

"How?" Sarah asked.

"I have an idea."

Steve, Sarah, Emily, Gareth, Deez, Mikal, Lissa, and two squadrons of armed guards headed toward the sound of fighting. This time, they could hear the roaring of what sounded like feral cats. Big ones. When they crested the ridge and the two Ancients came into view once more, Steve came to a stop and whistled.

Two sabre-tooth tigers were circling and snarling at one another. Steve made sure both Alchos Stones were safe in his pockets and then ignited both hands. After a brief pause as he decided what he should do to attract their attention, he blasted the largest fireball he could create straight up into the air.

It worked.

Both of the prehistoric felines stopped their circling and turned to watch their group approach. Then, one of the felines, the one with a light green tint to its stripes, snarled again and went back to circling its adversary. Steve blasted a second fireball up into the air and then held up Usol's stone.

"What are you doing?" Sarah hissed out.

"I'm giving this back to him."

"What?! Why?"

"Because it's his."

"But … but…"

Usol, in tiger form, had stopped again. He saw Steve approaching with the stone and immediately shifted into his human form. Eion did the same and, before anyone could say anything, jumped in front of Steve.

"And just what do you think you're doing? Have I not made it clear that we *don't* want to give Usol back that gem?"

"I know you disagree with me," Steve began, as he looked

into Eion's pupil-less white eyes, "but, by your own words, this game, this wager… it should've been over." Steve turned to Usol and tossed him the large emerald. "Here. This is yours. Take it and let this be over."

Usol caught the gem with one hand and gazed down at it.

"You have no idea what you've done," Eion furiously hissed.

Steve turned to the Air Guardian. "What are you so concerned about?"

"He'll get his powers back!" the Master of the Winds protested.

Steve swung an arm in an open arc. "Look around, Eion. Usol is already using his powers. And wouldn't you? If you were in his shoes, and you had your powers taken from you, would you not start using them again if the agreed upon time had elapsed? You said the terms of the wager would last for fifty of our millennia. Then you told me this wager was created over a hundred millennia ago. Frankly, I'm surprised he waited this long to start using his powers."

"He doesn't deserve his powers," Eion grumbled.

"Who are you to judge?" Steve asked. "If you don't like something he's doing, then simply confront him and try to work it out."

"You don't think we've tried?"

"Your only attempt to confront me was to strip my powers away," Usol snapped, speaking at last. "There was no, 'hey, there's a problem here, or hey, you shouldn't have done that.' You had no right to do what you did. But, putting that aside, the human is correct. Our wager expired, but did you acknowledge it? No."

Steve shifted his weight to his left leg and felt into his left pocket. He retrieved the *Essence of the Sea* and tossed it to Eion.

"Here. Give this back to Aeia. Nothing is worth losing a friend."

The Earth Guardian stared at the blue stone with surprise etched all over his human face.

"You had two of the stones," Usol said, directing his comment to Steve. "You could have been the strongest, most feared human ever."

Steve shook his head and pulled Sarah to his side. He clutched her hand tightly in his. "No, thanks. I have everything I need right here."

Usol gazed down at the emerald tetrahedron a few moments longer before he surprised everyone by tossing it back to Steve.

"Keep it. Apology accepted."

"Wh—what? You don't want it? After all that's happened?"

"I don't need it any more. You have fun with it."

"Why in the world would you give it to me?" Steve sputtered. "I thought you hated me!"

"You are the first human I have ever encountered who actually sided with me during my plight."

"I sided with you? How? When?"

"Do you not recall what you said?" Usol's voice suddenly changed to an exact recreation of Steve's. "*Something about this whole situation doesn't sit well with me. It's like... well, it's like the other three Ancients ganged up on him.*" The voice returned to normal. "As they would say on your world, does any of that ring a bell?"

"You've been to our world, too?" Steve incredulously asked.

Usol nodded. "Many times."

"Wait. I said that before we found the key. It was in the second temple, so that means... wait. That was you? You were the monk?"

For the first time, Usol cracked a smile. "That was me. Word reached my ears of a human who was beginning to rebel against my, and you'll forgive me for saying this, goodie-two-shoes brother, so I was curious. I wanted to see for myself what you were like. So, as for the stone, I think you'll find it useful. Farewell."

With that, Usol vanished. Steve turned to Eion and held up his hands, as though he was being held at gunpoint.

"I'm sorry, pal. I had to do what I felt was right."

"While I'm not certain how my sisters are going to take this news, I honestly can't say that I am too surprised."

"He was already using his powers," Steve pointed out.

"However, he clearly wanted the stone back. Probably to show you he had it. Once the jinx was lifted in your eyes, so to speak, his fight was over."

"You have made your point, Steve. Very well. I will be off."

"Where are you headed, if you don't mind me asking?"

Eion held up the large blue sapphire.

"I will search for Aeia and give her back her stone. I need to tell her I'm sorry."

"Good luck, pal."

Epilogue

Simply incredible," Kri'Entu said, probably for the fifth time in the last thirty minutes. "To think that you faced such extreme adversaries, all on your own, my son. I am so very proud of you."

"We both are," Ny'Callé corrected.

"Well, I wasn't exactly alone," Mikal corrected. He intertwined his fingers with Lissa's and pulled her close. "I would not have been able to survive without Lissa's guidance."

"And do not forget your former bodyguards," Lissa quietly reminded him. "Or the dwarves, or the dragons, or the shealk, or the griffins, or…"

"I get it, I get it," Mikal laughed. He turned to his parents. "Needless to say, I had a lot of help. We all came together."

"Sir Steve, Lady Sarah, you once more have our thanks for looking after our son," the king announced, as he glanced at his son's former bodyguards standing quietly in the Great Hall. "And, even though I'm sure you already have, please convey our utmost thanks to the wyverians for their support in this matter."

"We've already thanked everyone involved," Steve assured the king, "but, since you asked, we will pass along official thanks from Your Majesties."

"Invaders from across the Great Sea," the king mused. "I never would have imagined it."

Steve nodded. "I don't think anyone did."

"And who is this?" Ny'Callé asked, as she rose from her throne and approached Emily. "I do not recall meeting you before."

"Because you haven't," Sarah informed her. "Allow me. Emily, this is Ny'Callé. She is queen of Lentari. Your Majesty, allow me to present Dr. Emily Benz, of Phoenix, Arizona. Another new friend of ours needed medical aid, and Emily was able to give him that aid."

"She is from your world?" Kri'Entu asked.

Both Steve and Sarah nodded.

"She is," Mikal confirmed.

"Lady Emily, please step forth."

"Wait, what are they doing?" Emily nervously asked Sarah.

Sarah gave her a reassuring smile. "Oh, just go with it. I think they have something up their sleeves."

"Lady Emily," Kri'Entu formally began, "I understand you are a visitor to our fair kingdom, from none other than the Nohrin's home world. Is that so?"

"Um, er, yes, it is," Emily acknowledged.

"I also understand that you enjoy spending time here," the king continued.

"Your kingdom is marvelous," Emily said, performing a small curtsy. "Your people are so very lucky to live here."

"Then allow me to make you an honorary citizen of Lentari, Lady Emily. You are hereby encouraged to visit whenever you'd like."

The paleontologist's mouth dropped open. "Seriously?"

"And," Mikal continued, "since you've expressed a desire to live here, you are more than welcome to stay, if that is your choice."

The short blonde woman was all smiles.

"Oh, wow! I think I'll take you up on that! I just have to give notice back home and tie up a few loose ends. Oh! This is so exciting! Thank you! Thank you so much!"

"Saw that coming," Steve whispered.

"Everyone did," Sarah agreed.

"One final item to address," Kri'Entu stated, raising his voice. "Sir Steve, am I to understand you are now the owner of one of the fabled Alchos Stones?"

Steve shrugged. "It would appear so. It certainly caught me off guard."

"And where is the stone now?" the king asked.

"Safe and sound, back home," Steve assured them.

"For now," Sarah mumbled.

"What was that?" Kri'Entu asked, frowning.

Sarah smiled at the king. "Oh, it's nothing to worry about. Steve just has to be careful around the stone. He, er, has unfortunately learned of a few abilities the stone has, which has now transferred to him regardless of whether he's holding it."

"Would you care to enlighten us?" Kri'Entu asked, interested.

"Well, one of the last things Usol said to Steve before he departed was to have fun with the stone. I didn't think he meant that literally. The stone has the ability to allow the owner to shift forms."

The king's eyebrows shot up. "Indeed?"

"Oh, yeah," Steve grumbled.

"Is that a bad thing?" the queen asked.

"Apparently, the blasted thing has a sense of humor and is *highly* susceptible. Do you know that Sarah called me a horse's ass, and before I knew what was happening, that damn stone changed me to a donkey?"

"Right there in the middle of the mall," Sarah confirmed. She locked eyes with the queen. "Do you remember the mall?"

Ny'Callé nodded. "I do. Oh, no. What happened?"

"Well, my husband was in a bad mood, and was behaving poorly. So, I told him he was acting like an ass and poof! A small fuzzy donkey appeared, wearing his clothes. I laughed so hard, for so long, that I gave myself a headache."

"And that's not all," Steve sourly added. "Watch this." He held up a hand with his palm facing up. "If I so much as think about that damn stone, then I … see? It just appeared in my hand. I have to be so very careful now. And you? You're a snot. You don't have to be enjoying this so much."

"This has been the best three weeks of my life," Sarah confirmed. "Ever since we got back, and have had to deal with the repercussions of having that stone in our house, Steve has gone through hell. I've never laughed so much in my entire life!"

"I'll learn to control it," Steve vowed. "If Flinn could control his, then I should be able to control mine."

As the procession ended, and people started exiting the Great Hall, Steve hooked his arm through Emily's and pulled her close to Mikal.

"Are you going to tell her?" Steve asked his former charge.

"Tell me what?" Emily wanted to know.

"He hasn't told her yet?" Sarah asked, with mock outrage.

"*Who* hasn't told me *what?*" Emily asked, growing frustrated.

At a nod from Steve, Mikal approached and handed Emily a broken piece of stone.

"Here."

"What am I supposed to do with this?"

Steve grinned and shoved his hands into his pockets. "I don't know. What can you tell *us* about it?"

Emily shrugged and looked at the fragment of stone. She opened her mouth but then a strange look appeared on her face. Her eyes became vacant as she stared at the object in her hand.

"It's a piece of pottery, broken off a vase that was created three hundred twenty-four years ago. This one came from a location near the sea. The temple! This came from somewhere close to the second temple! Wait. It's a piece of pottery from the original Capily, but how on earth could I possibly know that?"

"Consider it a gift," Mikal explained. "I thought it might come in useful for you. But, it only will work here, in Lentari."

"What will?" Emily asked. Comprehension dawned and her eyes opened wide. "Omigod, are you giving me a jhorun?"

"Gave," Mikal corrected. "Welcome to Lentari, Lady Emily."

Author's Note

All righty then. The Pirates of Perz have been dealt with, Captain Flinn has been put in his place, and that's the last you'll see of him. Or is it? :) I can honestly say that I've enjoyed creating a character with power as strong as Steve's. Think Professor X and Magneto. They both have extreme power, but both have a respect for the other. That's Flinn and Steve. Have we seen the last of Flinn and his band of pirates? The answer is perhaps. For now. Will he put in an appearance in the future? It's entirely possible!

Now, it's back to Pomme Valley. *Case of the Highland House Haunting* has already been started and progressing nicely. Zack is back home, in PV, after solving his wife's murder in Arizona. However, it looks like he has another case that warrants his attention when strange things start happening at one of Pomme Valley's historic houses. And, it just so happens he has a vested interest in that house, so he and the dogs *have* to figure out what's going on!

As for Lentari, no, I'm not done with the series. Not by a long shot. But, I will say that after the next corgi case file, I'm going to be starting a brand new fantasy series which will focus heavily on dragon riders. New world, new magic, new rules, and new characters. As many of you know, I've always loved dragons, and writing with a sense of humor. Will that transfer over to this new series? You'd better believe it!

Now, a favor. Would you care to help me out? Did you enjoy the book? Please consider leaving a review wherever you picked up your copy. We authors love reviews! They're one of the few things that can help us become more easily discovered by more readers.

Finally, if you want to make sure you never miss another announcement, or would like to sign up for my newsletter (I won't ever share your contact info with anyone else), then head over to my blog at www.AuthorJMPoole.com and sign up.

Happy reading!

J.
August, 2019

Jeffrey M. Poole is a professional writer who writes in both the fantasy and mystery genres. His series are listed below. Jeffrey lives in picturesque Southern Oregon, with his wife, Giliane, and their Welsh Corgi, Kinsey. His interests include archery, astronomy, archaeology, scuba diving, collecting movies, collecting swords, and tinkering with any electronic gadget he can get his hands on.

In March, 2015, Jeffrey became a proud member of SFWA, the Science Fiction & Fantasy Writers of America! Jeffrey encourages readers to connect with him on Facebook (facebook.com/bakkianchronicles). Fans can also follow him online at: www.AuthorJMPoole.com.

Scan the QR code to get his free newsletter!

BOOKS BY JEFFREY POOLE

Epic Fantasy
BAKKIAN CHRONICLES
The Prophecy
Insurrection
Amulet of Aria
Disneyland Debacle (short story)
Winter Wonderland (short story)

TALES OF LENTARI
Lost City
Something Wyverian This Way Comes
A Portal for Your Thoughts
Thoughts for A Portal
Wizard in the Woods
Close Encounters of the Magical Kind
The Hunt for Red Oskorlisk (short story)
May the Fang Be With You (Pirates trilogy #1)
The Hammer is Strong with This One (Pirates #2)
These are Not the Stones You're Looking For (Pirates #3)
Blast from the Past